Lumen

THE WESLEYAN
EARLY CLASSICS OF
SCIENCE FICTION
SERIES

GENERAL EDITOR,
ARTHUR B. EVANS

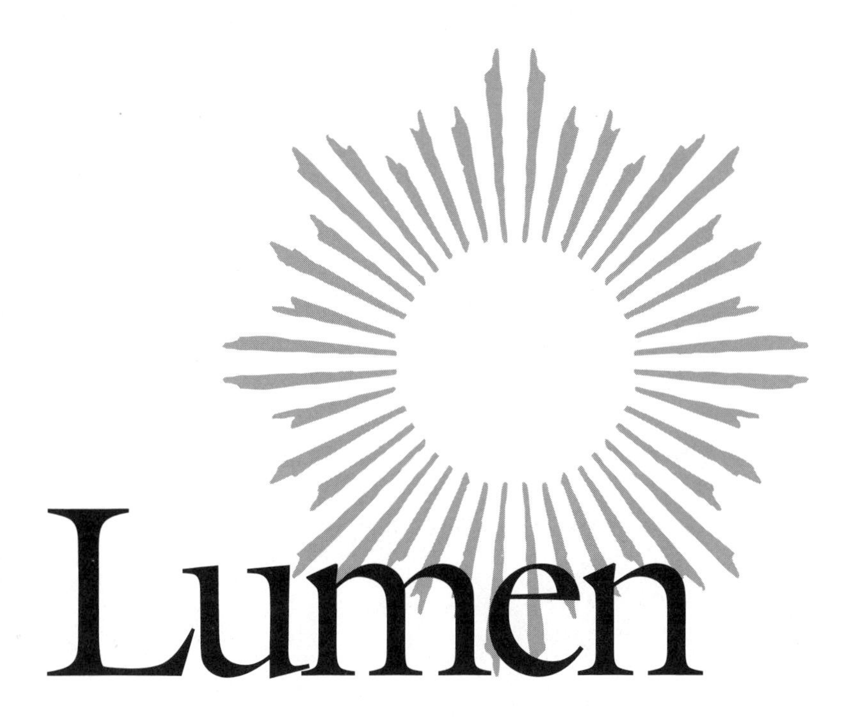

Lumen

Camille Flammarion

Translated and with an Introduction by

BRIAN STABLEFORD

Wesleyan University Press Middletown, Connecticut

Published by Wesleyan University Press,
Middletown, CT 06459
Translation, introduction, and notes

Set in Carter Cone Galliard by Keystone Typesetting, Inc.
Manufactured in the United States of America
ISBN 0-8195-6567-9 (cloth)
ISBN 0-8195-6568-7 (pbk.)

Cataloging data for this book is available
from the Library of Congress.

06 05 04 03 02 5 4 3 2 1

CONTENTS

ACKNOWLEDGMENTS

I should like to thank Bill Russell for the loan of some useful research materials and for his assistance in my attempts to solve some of the puzzles presented by the text, and Jane Stableford for her patience and assistance in proofreading the typescript.

INTRODUCTION

Nicolas Camille Flammarion was born on 25 February 1842 at Montigny-la-Roi in the Haut-Marne. His father had been a farmer, but a series of financial misfortunes reduced him to keeping a shop. Camille was apparently something of a child prodigy, forming an interest in astronomy at a very early age, being fascinated by his observation of a solar eclipse on 9 October 1847. He observed a second eclipse on 28 July 1851 and contrived to retain a certain childlike sense of wonder in his contemplation of the starry firmament for the rest of his life.

He began to record his astronomical and meteorological observations at the age of eleven and began to write voluminously in his teens—another habit that remained with him over time. In 1856, the family's continuing financial difficulties caused them to move to Paris, where Camille was apprenticed to an engraver. He continued his studies in amateur astronomy alongside assiduous attempts to increase his education generally, and by the time he was sixteen, he had produced an unpublished "Voyage extatique aux régions lunaires, correspondence d'un philosophe adolescent" [A Visionary Journey to the Regions of the Moon, Related by an Adolescent Philosopher][1] and a 500-page manuscript modestly entitled *Cosmologie Universelle* [Universal Cosmology], which eventually saw print in 1885 as *Le Monde avant le création de l'homme* [The World before the Creation of Humankind]. A physician called to treat Flammarion noticed the latter work and was sufficiently impressed to recommend the young man to Urbain Le Verrier (1811–77), who was then in charge of the Paris Observatoire.

Le Verrier accepted Flammarion as an assistant, putting him to work in the Bureau des Calculs. Flammarion did not find this routine work to his taste and was frustrated by the lack of opportunity to make his own observations. Consequently, when the publication of *La Pluralité des mondes habitées* [The Plurality of Habitable Worlds] in 1862 gave him hope that he might be able to make a living as a writer, he left. Advertised by its subtitle as a study of the conditions of habitability of the planets in the solar system from the viewpoints of astronomy, physiology, and natural philosophy, *La Pluralité des mondes habitées* was a very successful work—it went through thirteen more editions in the next thirty years—and Flammarion also became a frequent contributor to several periodicals; but he could not support himself adequately on his writing income and he obtained a position in the Bureau des Longitudes, which allowed him to make further use of his experience as a calculator.

Flammarion did not allow his duties at the bureau to impede his literary production. He may well have seen his next book, *Les Habitantes de l'autre monde; révélations d'outre-tombe* [The Inhabitants of the Other World: Revelations of the Afterlife] (2 vols., 1862–63), as a companion piece to its predecessor—he had met Allan Kardec, the French founder of "psychic research" while researching *La Pluralité des mondes habitées*—but he must soon have been apprised of the fact that reporting alleged revelations from beyond the grave channeled by a spiritualist medium (Mlle Huet) would not do his scientific career any good. His next book of the same kind, *Des Forces naturelles inconnues* [Unknown Natural Forces] (1865), was initially issued under the pseudonym Hermès, but he abandoned such subterfuges thereafter. He was always careful, however, to make it clear that his interest in psychic phenomena was that of an open-minded scientific researcher; he was not a follower of the spiritualist faith and refused to consider the texts he produced during his experiments in automatic writing as anything other than the product of his own imagination.

Flammarion followed up his first work of speculative science with *Les Mondes imaginaires et les mondes réels* [Real and Imaginary Worlds] (1864). The first part of the book was a revisitation of the various worlds in the solar system, supplemented with a speculative note about planets illuminated by double stars, but the second was a thoroughgoing historical and critical survey of mythological, philosophical, and literary speculations about the inhabitants of the planets and stars. His scientific work of this period included pieces for the *Annuaire de cosmos* [Cosmic Yearbook], and he began his own *Annuaire astronomique et météorologique* [Astronomical and Meteorological Yearbook], initially in *Le Magasin pittoresque* [The Illustrated Magazine].

Although he constructed a telescope of his own in 1866, Flammarion returned to the Observatoire in 1867 to take part in a project observing and mapping double stars. He also continued his meteorological observations, undertaking many balloon flights in order to observe atmospheric phenomena at closer range, resulting in his pioneering study, *L'Atmosphère* [The Atmosphere] (1871). He continued, in the meantime, to produce popular articles and books with increasing rapidity, taking in vulcanology and climatology as well as astronomy. He was a frequent contributor to such periodicals as *Le Cosmos* [The Cosmos], *L'Intransigéant* [The Intransigent], and *Le Siècle* [The Century].

Flammarion's greatest success as a popularizer of science came in 1880 when the publishing company in which his younger brother Ernest (1846–1936) had become a partner in 1875 issued his paradigmatic guidebook for amateur astronomers, *Astronomie populaire* [Popular Astronomy]. One admirer of his work, Monsieur Meret, was moved to make him a present of an estate in Juvisy-sur-Orge twenty miles south of Paris, to which Flammarion and his wife of eight years, Sylvie, moved in 1882. They constructed a new telescope there to facilitate his work. All these projects proved to be enduring: the Flammarion publishing firm still exists; *Astronomie populaire* was continually updated by other hands after Flammarion's death; and the Juvisy telescope is still operational. Flammarion also founded the journal *L'Astronomie* [Astronomy], which took over his *Annuaire astronomique et météorologique* and became the definitive periodical for amateur astronomers. In 1887 he combined forces with other interested parties to found the Societé Astronomique de France, another organization that persists to the present day. The Societé supervised the construction of the first telescope for use by the general public in the Latin Quarter of Paris.

Flammarion's most important endeavors in the popularization of science include his study *La Planète Mars et ses conditions d'habitabilité* [The Planet Mars and Its Habitability] (1892; second volume, 1909), which collated all observations of the planet made since 1636, including his own discovery (in 1876) of the seasonal changes affecting the dark regions — an observation as significant in its way as that of the "canali" publicized in 1877 by Schiaparelli.[2] Even before the outbreak of World War I in 1914, however, he had increasingly concentrated his efforts on his studies in psychical research, holding regular séances at Juvisy in parallel with his astronomical observations. The famous Italian medium Eusapia Palladino was one of many who performed there, but Flammarion also entertained such visiting scientists as the American astronomer Percival Lowell.[3]

After the war — which put an abrupt end to the continual reprinting of his early works — such new work as Flammarion published was almost all in the field of psychic research: the three volumes of *La Mort et son mystère* [Death and Its Mystery] appeared between 1920 and 1922, and *Les Maisons hantées, en marge de la mort et son mystère* [Haunted Houses: On the Margin of Death and Its Mystery] in 1923. Flammarion was deeply affected by the horrific casualties inflicted by the war — as was the English speculative writer Sir Arthur Conan Doyle, who became his friend after developing a similar interest in spiritualism — and his observations at Juvisy served as something of a refuge from the world after 1918. He died at his estate on 4 June 1925. His second wife, Gabrielle — whom he had married in 1919 — continued his work thereafter, assuming responsibility for further updates of the *Astronomie populaire*, which was by then his only work that retained substantial popular interest.

Although Camille Flammarion was not the first writer impelled by a fervent missionary zeal to make the revelations of science available to ordinary readers, the sheer extravagance of his production, in terms of ambition as well as quantity, made him the figurehead of a growing movement of amateur and popular science. His journeywork as a cataloguer of stars, on the other hand, was soon absorbed into the ever-growing database of astronomical knowledge; like many another assiduous collector of data who never happened upon a particular discovery of charismatic quality or talismanic significance, he would soon have faded into obscurity had not his name been so widely advertised by his popularizations.

Much of Flammarion's work for periodicals was hastily composed, and many of his books give the impression of being first drafts. Although he continually revised his most popular works as they went through consecutive editions, he almost invariably did so by inserting extra text rather than by rewriting existing chapters, further emphasizing an unfortunate tendency to repetition and only rarely contriving any stylistic improvement. He was never content to employ a useful metaphor or narrative device only once; certain key images and arguments recur throughout his work, appearing again and again with relatively little modification. These tendencies do, however, go with the territory; if Flammarion's career is compared with the heroic endeavors of such twentieth-century popularizers of science as Isaac Asimov and Arthur C. Clarke, one can easily find points of similarity in terms of method and idiosyncrasy as well as missionary enthusiasm.

Flammarion worked harder than any other man of his day to make the revelations of science accessible to ordinary readers, experimenting with every narrative device he could imagine in order to make his communications more effective. Although his reputation within the scientific community suffered, partly because of his success as a popularizer, partly because of his fondness for flights of wild fancy, and partly because of his unceasing attempts to apply the scientific method to studies of what would now be called the "paranormal," he did more to prepare the way for public acceptance of the cosmic perspectives of modern science than any other nineteenth-century writer. The scope of his imagination was inevitably restricted by the limitations of the scientific knowledge on which he drew (especially in biology), but no one matched his imaginative avidity or audacity.

In doing everything that he could to make people aware of a vast universe potentially filled with habitable worlds, whose life-forms must—by virtue of being adapted to different physical circumstances—be radically different from those found on Earth, Flammarion anticipated much of the substance of modern science fiction and helped lay the groundwork for its development. He was, however, writing at a time when the literary method of modern science fiction had not yet been perfected; the fact that his primary interest was in the didactic potential of his work directed him away from the story-forms that were to be developed by Jules Verne and H. G. Wells toward such hybrid formats as the philosophical dialogue and the dream-journey, and toward such artificial devices as crediting hypothetical intelligence and a voice to inanimate objects or symbolic figures. For this reason, most of Flammarion's adventures in speculative fiction seem to the modern reader to lie in an awkward gray area between fiction and nonfiction.

Although his early *voyage extatique* was his first experiment in romance, Flammarion first began to publish didactic fiction in popular magazines in the mid-1860s. *Lumen* is of particular interest to historians of science fiction not only because it comprises his first serious endeavor of this kind but also because it remained his boldest. It set out to dramatize the ideative content of two of his earliest works—*La Pluralité des mondes habitées* and *Dieu dans la nature* [God in Nature] (1867)—but changed direction in midstream to address that of a third: the translation he made in 1869 of Humphry Davy's *Consolations in Travel* (1830). *Lumen* provided a manifestly shaky start to the business of constructing didactic fictions, the various "récits" (actually dialogues) comprising it having been composed in three separate batches between 1866 and 1869,[4] but once the text finally hit its stride, it enabled Flammarion to produce a new and truly spectacular vision of the universe, which laid the groundwork for an entire tradition of modern visionary fantasy.

Lumen was first published in book form in the collection *Récits de l'infini* (1872; translated as *Stories of Infinity*, 1873), where it was supplemented by Flammarion's next two endeavors of the same kind: "Histoire d'une comète" (1869; translated as "The History of a Comet"), which views episodes in the history of Earth from the viewpoint of Halley's comet, and "Dans l'infini" (1872; translated as "In Infinity"), which describes the decoding of a cryptic communication from the spirit world. *Lumen* was first issued separately in 1887, although it also continued to feature in new editions of *Récits de l'infini*, which had attained its thirteenth edition by 1892. The final version of the French text—which incorporated some new material composed for the 1897 English translation—was a separate edition that was reprinted several times before 1914 (its final printing was advertised as the "seventieth thousand," presumably counting printings of the various editions of *Récits de l'infini* as well as separate editions).

The record of *Lumen*'s predecessors is comprehensively set out in the second part of *Les Mondes imaginaires et les mondes réels*. Thanks to this essay, we know the titles of almost all the relevant works that Flammarion had read before setting out to write *Lumen* in 1866 and can easily judge the extent of their impact on his imagination and influence on his method.

The first two chapters of this critical review are a survey of ideas contained in Oriental and Occidental mythologies, while the third covers the development of theological and mystical images of the universe in the first millennium of the Christian era. The fourth moves from Thomas Aquinas's *Summa Theologica* to the literary images of Dante, Ariosto, and Rabelais, by way of the speculations of Nicholas of Cusa.[5] Chapter 5 describes the Copernican revolution, and the significance of such supporters thereof as Giordano Bruno, Montaigne, and Galileo.[6] It includes a description of Johannes Kepler's *Somnium* (1634), a visionary fantasy that attempts to make the Copernican system accessible to the imagination by describing cosmic events as an observer on the moon would see them—and which digresses, in its final pages, to address the question of what lunar life might be like, given the necessity of its adaptation to extraordinarily long days and nights.[7]

The sixth and seventh chapters are devoted to imaginary voyages to the moon, including those of Francis Godwin and Cyrano de Bergerac, and such speculative essays as the 1640 supplement to John Wilkins's *Discovery of a World in the Moon* (1638) and Pierre Borel's *Discours nouveau prouvant le pluralité des mondes* (whose composition date Flammarion gives as 1647, although it was not published until 1657).[8] From Cyrano's bold, but unfortunately incomplete, *Histoire des états et empires du soleil* (1662) Flammarion moves on in the eighth chapter to more extravagant and wide-ranging cosmic voyages, including Athanasius Kircher's *Itinerarium Exstaticum* (1656),[9] but it is not until the ninth—entitled "Les grands voyages" that he reaches the crucial work that is now recognizable as the foundation stone of the tradition of the popularization of science, and which provided the model for *Lumen*: Bernard de Fontenelle's *Entretiens sur la pluralité des mondes* (1686; translated under various titles, the most accurate being *Conversations on the Plurality of Worlds*).

The first edition of *Entretiens sur la pluralité des mondes* consisted of five conversations, allegedly taking place on successive evenings between the first-person narrator and the Marquise de G***. Although a sixth evening was added in the second edition, its conversation served merely as a summary, and such revisions as were made as the book passed through many other editions before Fontenelle's death in 1757 were also mere tinkering, as much for the purpose of stylistic adjustment as to incorporate a handful of new discoveries. The work is conspicuously lighthearted and deftly witty; unlike previous works of natural philosophy employing the dialogue as a form of discourse—most notably Galileo's—it does not set up assertively opposed positions to dispute the truth, but establishes an innocent in search of both amusement and instruction, and an informant equally skilled in both.

The first conversation explains and justifies the Copernican model of the solar system. The second argues that the moon is a world not unlike Earth, perhaps inhabited. The third prevaricates ingeniously, first taking back the suggestion that the moon might be inhabited by arguing that as no clouds can be seen moving across the face of the moon, conditions on its surface must be very different from those supporting life on Earth, but then taking leave to wonder whether life-forms quite different from those on Earth might exist there, perhaps living beneath the surface.

From this specific case the narrator moves swiftly to the proposal that life in the universe might be infinitely various, and the fourth conversation elaborates this idea by wondering what life might be like on the other planets of the solar system. The fifth conversation introduces the notion that the stars are suns like ours, with their own families of planets, and wonders how various life might be beyond the solar system.

The fourth and fifth dialogues also go to some trouble to explain and elaborate the imaginative implications of René Descartes's theory of vortices,[10] which asserted that space is not really empty, because all aggregations of matter—from atoms to stars—are constantly revolving, establishing "whirlpools" around themselves by means of which they constantly interact with one another even though they may appear to observers to be separated by vast distances.

The content of Fontenelle's lighthearted conversations seems quite innocuous to the modern reader, and even Fontenelle's educated contemporaries—those, at any rate, who had read John Wilkins (whose *Discovery* had been translated into French in 1655)—could not have been overly surprised by the casual proposition that the moon is a world which human beings will be able to visit when the technology of flight is sufficiently improved. Fontenelle was, however, writing in a Catholic country, not long after Louis XIV's revocation of the Edict of Nantes,[11] which had withdrawn from Protestants the right to pursue their religion in their own way, forcing many of them to flee the ensuing persecution. In providing a direct challenge to the Church's cosmology, the conversations were trespassing on dangerous ground—and in making their key ideas more easily accessible to ordinary people, with plausible and commonsensical supporting arguments, they provided an active and powerful antidote to blind faith.

Fontenelle's previous works had included a dramatic comedy, *La comète* (1681), inspired by the comet of 1680—whose display had been far more impressive than the one put on in 1682 by Halley's comet—which had made much of the importance of comets in disproving the Aquinas-endorsed Aristotelian notion that the heavens consisted of a series of crystal spheres with the earth at their center. The *Entretiens* employs a similar lightness of tone and delicate wit to conceal its seriousness, but there could be no doubt that the narrator's protestation that the Marquise and his readers need not believe the ideas featured in the conversations is a protective device.

In the same year as the *Entretiens* Fontenelle produced the *Histoire des oracles* [History of Oracles], in which the myths and legends of the ancients were clinically analyzed as a record of the gradual development of a better understanding of nature, whose central progressive thread was the disposal of supernatural explanations and belief in magic. Although he carefully omitted any specific commentary on the prophecies and miracles that were key items of Christian faith, it was open to any reader to place them in the same sequence and subject them to the same skeptical scrutiny. It was, however, the *Entretiens* that became a huge best-seller, widely translated and continually reprinted. It helped secure Fontenelle's admission to the Académie Française, but he was not satisfied until he had also won admission to the Académie des Sciences, whose secretary he became in 1697. It was in that role that he produce a long series of *éloges* (eulogies) celebrating the work and achievements of every newly deceased member of the academy, collectively championing the notion that the scientific investigation of nature was not merely a solemn duty and a significant realm of heroic achievement but also a source of great delight.

Fontenelle continued to produce *éloges* until he died, a mere month short of his hundredth birthday. He was not only Camille Flammarion's great hero and chief inspiration but the principal influence on the subsequent development of science-based speculative thought and the methods used by its boldest pioneers. Like Flammarion, he is more or less forgotten today, but as in Flammarion's case that is because he achieved what he set out to do in making once-problematic ideas seem so obviously true that no further dispute was necessary or possible.

Flammarion's chapter on "les grands voyages" in the *Les Mondes imaginaires et les mondes réels* also includes descriptions of Gabriel Daniel's *Voyage du monde de Descartes* [Journey to Descartes's World] (1692) and Christian Huygens's *Cosmotheoros* [The Celestial World] (1698).[12] The subsequent chapter tracks the rich tradition of "voyages imaginaires" through the eighteenth century, including Jonathan Swift's *Gulliver's Travels* (1726), Ludvig Holberg's *Nils Klim* (1741), Voltaire's *Micromégas* (1752), and several less familiar works.[13]

The next chapter begins with the observation that while imaginative travelers' tales grew ever more numerous and extravagant in the eighteenth century, attempts to imagine what conditions on other worlds might actually be like became rather stagnant by virtue of the failure of observation to maintain a healthy flow of new data. Even so, Flammarion concedes that some valuable precedents were set by Emanuel Swedenborg, Imannuel Kant, and such flamboyant cosmic expeditions as *Voyages de Mylord Céton dans les sept planètes* [Journeys by Lord Ceton to the Seven Planets] (1765) by Marie-Anne de Roumier.[14]

Roumier's work, in particular, must be reckoned among the more important influences on Flammarion because of the extensive use it makes of the notion that the other worlds of the solar system are arenas into which souls embodied in the earth are routinely reincarnated, according to a definite scheme of moral propriety. Roumier's Mars is a "temple de la Gloire," where cadavers are heaped up in a kind of hell; its inhabitants include many great generals and conquerors, including Oliver Cromwell and Attila the Hun. The sun itself is the realm of truly great men: philosophers. One solar country accommodates a company ranging from Thales, Anaxagoras, and Pythagoras to Cassini, Descartes, and Newton; another's inhabitants range from Homer, Plato, and Sophocles to Pascal, Montesquieu, and La Rochefoucauld. Although the bodies of the violent retain their vulgar corporeality, the reincarnate philosophers are diaphanous; the thoughts in their heads and passions in their hearts can be clearly seen. The *Voyages de Mylord Céton* was one of many works reprinted in a thirty-six-volume series of *Voyages imaginaires* produced in Paris by Charles Garnier in 1787–89.[15]

The twelfth chapter of the second part of *Les Mondes imaginaires et les mondes réels*, which brings the story up to date by considering nineteenth-century works, is oddly slight, giving only brief mention to numerous works of fiction and nonfiction. The most elaborate consideration is given to Edgar Allan Poe's "Unparalleled Adventure of one Hans Pfaall" (1835).[16] Later editions of *Les mondes imaginaires et les mondes réels* added to the second part a thirteenth chapter that listed and annotated interplanetary voyages and speculative works touching on the subject of life on other worlds published after 1862. This includes thirty-one titles published between 1863 and 1876, but Flammarion gave up trying to keep track thereafter, and no further titles were added to the editions of the book published in the 1890s (by which time the number of such editions was in the mid-twenties). Rather perversely, however, he never went to the bother of revising any of the earlier chapters. Given the unsatisfactory nature of the chapter on the early nineteenth century, this omission is regrettable, all the more so because he subsequently became acquainted with a number of key works published before 1862.

Three such works, in particular, are relevant predecessors of *Lumen*: Nicolas Restif de la Bretonne's *Les Posthumes* [Posthumous Correspondence] (1802; but written in 1787–89), Humphry Davy's *Consolations in Travel; or, The Last Days of a Philosopher* (1830), and Edgar Allan Poe's *Eureka—An Essay on the Material and Spiritual Universe* (1848).[17] *Les Posthumes* is an epistolary piece in which the letters from a dead nobleman include an account of a cosmic voyage modeled on and perhaps satirizing Roumier's. It is possible that Flammarion never read it, but he certainly read *Consolations in Travel; or, The Last Days of a Philosopher*, which impressed him so profoundly that he was moved to translate it into French. His translation appeared in 1869, the year in which he resumed work on *Lumen* after a two-year gap, and it was obviously fresh in his mind when he wrote the remainder of the text.

Consolations in Travel consists of a series of six philosophical dialogues, whose hypothetical narrator is eventually given the name Philalethes ("love of truth"), although he remains unnamed in the first dialogue, which describes how he sat alone in the ruins of the Colosseum in Rome by the light of the full moon, ruminating on the transitory nature of human endeavor. These ruminations give rise to a vision in which a "superior intelligence," which he elects to call the Genius, carries him away on an educational voyage through time and space.

The narrator first reviews the history of humankind, observing the abrupt transition—a literal re-creation—of the species from brutal wildness to the birth of civilization and the subsequent intellectual, social, and technological progress of that civilization. The Genius then begins to explain the cosmic perspective into which the career of humankind needs to be set:

> Spiritual natures are eternal and indivisible, but their modes of being are as infinitely varied as the forms of matter. They have no relation to space, and, in their transitions, no dependence upon time, so that they can pass from one part of the universe to another by laws entirely independent of their motion. The quantity, or the number of spiritual essences, like the quantity or number of the atoms of the material world, are always the same; but their arrangements, like those of the materials which they are destined to guide or govern, are infinitely diversified; they are, in fact, parts more or less inferior of the infinite mind, and in the planetary systems, to one of which this globe you inhabit belongs, are in a state of probation, continually aiming at, and generally rising to a higher state of existence.[18]

The Genius tells the narrator that spiritual essences that were Socrates and Newton are "now in a higher and better state of planetary existence drinking intellectual light from a purer source" and conducts him to the planet Saturn, so that he might see its alien inhabitants:

> I saw moving on the surface below me immense masses, the forms of which I find it impossible to describe; they had systems for locomotion similar to those of the morse or sea-horse, but I saw with great surprise that they moved from place to place by

> six extremely thin membranes, which they used as wings. Their colours were varied and beautiful, but principally azure and rose-colour. I saw numerous convolutions of tubes, more analogous to the trunk of the elephant than anything else I can imagine, occupying what I supposed to be the upper parts of the body.[19]

The Genius explains that each of these trunklike tubes is "an organ of peculiar motion or sensation" and that their superior sensory apparatus and intelligence have allowed the Saturnians to discover far more about the universe and its laws than humankind ever could and to become far more virtuous. He reveals that the other planets in the solar system are inhabited by beings at various levels of intellectual and spiritual development and that the "higher natures" that exist elsewhere in the universe make use of "finer and more ethereal kinds of matter" in their organization. After death, therefore, men—among whom scientists are those most ready for rapid advancement—will make heavenly progress by slow and measured degrees, through a series of extraterrestrial incarnations: "The universe is everywhere full of life, but the modes of this life are infinitely diversified, and yet every form of it must be enjoyed and known by every spiritual nature before the consummation of all things."[20]

The narrator is permitted to glimpse one other mode of existence, when he observes cometary "globes . . . composed of different kinds of flame and of different colours" containing figures that remind him of human faces. Although they were once incarnate as men, these beings can no more remember their humanity than men can remember life in the womb. The only "sentiment or passion" that the spiritual essence or "monad" carries forward through all its successive metamorphoses is the love of knowledge, whose ultimate extrapolation is the love of God. If this love is misapplied to worldly ambition, the pursuit of oppressive power, the Genius explains, a spirit "sinks in the scale of existence . . . till its errors are corrected by painful discipline," but the narrator is not insulted by any vision of such subhuman modes of existence. The Genius concentrates on celebration of the progressive aspects of the posthuman situation, insisting that the cause of progress is not merely the highest good but the source of the greatest joy of which any imaginable being is capable.

Flammarion must have thought this vision wonderful, but he must also have regretted that the five dialogues following the first did not extrapolate it further, preferring instead to remain on Earth to debate matters of more immediate and intimate concern to the dying scientist. Although the first three parts of *Lumen* seem to be taking up where Fontenelle left off in his carefully structured and calculatedly casual representation of a universe filled with infinitely various forms of life, the fourth manifestly takes up where Davy left off in elaborating his cosmic scheme.

As in Fontenelle's *Entretiens*, the narrative voices in the dialogues constituting Flammarion's *Lumen* are not disputants but a willing teacher and his eager pupil; like the Latinate characters in Davy's *Consolations*, however, they are as much symbols as actual human beings. Although the teacher, Lumen, gives an elaborate account of his life on Earth, his name declares that he is also light itself: the light of the stars, as observed and analyzed by astronomers. His interrogator, Quaerens, is partly Flammarion and partly his imagined reader, but his name signifies "Seeker (of Knowledge)."

It has to be admitted that the first dialogue, which labors long and hard to establish its elementary ideas, is rather slow, stodgy, and repetitive. Flammarion—or perhaps his editor—seems to have been exceedingly doubtful as to the readiness and ability of his readers to follow the simplest corollaries of the limited velocity of light. The most interesting idea that the first dialogue raises—the principle that time and space are not absolute, but exist only relative to one another—is left stranded and never properly developed. This is bound to seem disappointing to the modern reader, who is sure to wonder what Flammarion thought of Albert Einstein's special theory of relativity when it was published in 1905,[21] and whether he cursed himself for not having expounded his own version of the idea more carefully and more boldly.

The second dialogue, whose central idea is that a viewpoint moving faster than light would be able to show events in reverse order,[22] suffers from the same faults, partly because Flammarion did not take the trouble to remove from the collected version material that originally served to recap the basic thesis for the benefit of new readers. It is only at the end of the second dialogue that the author picks up the pace and begins to broaden his imaginative horizons to take in wider vistas in both time and space; but once having done that, he fails to carry the extrapolations of the third dialogue very far forward. He might have cut the dialogue short when it had hardly got going because he simply ran out of steam, but it seems more probable that the editor of the periodical in which the serial version appeared aborted it—in which case Flammarion's decision to keep the first dialogue simple and to labor every point it made might have initially been wiser than it now seems.

The first three dialogues might be seen, collectively, as an extrapolation of a remark made by Fontenelle's narrator near the beginning of the *Entretiens*: "All philosophy," he tells the Marquise, "is based on two things only: curiosity and poor eyesight; if you had better eyesight you could see perfectly well whether or not these stars are solar systems, and if you were less curious, you wouldn't care. . . . The trouble is, we want to know more than we can see."[23] Better telescopes and brand new spectroscopes had improved the sight of the naked eye considerably by 1867, but Flammarion was eager to demonstrate what a *really* powerful eye might see, and it was for that reason that he gifted Lumen's spirit self with a power of vision that proved troublesome to explain and protect from criticism.

Although the slight gap between the first and second dialogues made no evident difference to Flammarion's outlook, he seems to have emerged as a changed man from the two-year interval between the third and fourth. Perhaps the marked change of attitude and tone merely reflects the fact that he now felt free to express himself more openly and say what he really thought about such matters as the human tendency to war and French prevarication over the principles of republicanism, but it might be that he really had undergone a change of heart. Were it not for the testimony of the notes, a modern reader might easily wonder whether the crucial gap had been 1869–71 rather than 1867–69, given that the Franco-Prussian

War would have provided ample excuse for the hardening of Flammarion's attitude to "great statesmen" and their warlike tendencies. It seems more likely, however, that he spent two frustrating years casting about for an editor willing to allow him to put forth his ideas as boldly as he wanted to—and that once having found one, he conceived an ardent ambition to make the most of the opportunity.

The crucial point in Lumen's discourse arrives when he explains that the form of the human body results from its adaptation to a specific set of physical circumstances rather than divine design and that sentient beings elsewhere in the universe are likely to be very different, by virtue of being adapted to a wide variety of environments. Fontenelle had made a similar point, but the arguments backing up his insistence that the life-forms on other worlds must be different from men had been conscientiously playful, giving a higher priority to the likelihood of divine versatility than the necessity of adaptation; his examples are calculated to amuse, and none too specific. Lumen, on the other hand, also insists that physical forms are the products of slow and never-ending processes of evolution, and this steps up his argument by another gear.

It is at this point that Davy's example becomes more crucial than Fontenelle's. Flammarion's evolutionary theory is thoroughly Lamarckian,[24] and its extrapolation from an earthly to a cosmic scale easily assimilates Davy's insistence that evolution is moral as well as physical and that souls are subject to their own evolutionary process as they move through successive incarnations. In moving on to this larger stage, however, Flammarion is determined to keep hold of the key element of the earlier dialogues: the insistence that human curiosity is confounded and confused by "poor eyesight." He remains deeply preoccupied with the idea that our image of the universe is conditioned by the particular properties of our senses—and this is the notion that fuels his exploration of the multitudinous possibilities open to alien life.

The one significant respect in which Flammarion flatly refuses the influence of Fontenelle is that he considers Descartes's theory of vortices hopelessly outdated. Even so, he holds to its essentials; like Descartes and Fontenelle, Flammarion clings to the idea that the emptiness of space is an illusion of poor eyesight and that it is actually full of connections binding visible entities together. Today, alas, Flammarion's talk of "undulations" (*ondulations* in French) and his contention that light might have hundreds or thousands of analogous "vibrations" seems just as primitive as Fontenelle's talk of Cartesian vortices—and yet, even though modern physicists have pared the number of fundamental forces to four, they have retained the notion that "empty" space is a seething sea of potential particles, replete with hidden and seemingly unexpressed energies.

It is, perhaps, ironic that the most striking anticipations in *Lumen* have little to do with the testimony of light and that they rest on the discredited foundation of Lamarck's theory of evolution. The historian of science might dismiss them as mere folly, but to the historian of science fiction they are very important. Flammarion was the first writer to apply the theory of evolution to the wholesale construction of authentically alien beings, and in so doing he established one of the ideative foundation stones on which modern science fiction is built. Although he continued to take an interest in hypothetical aliens, especially Martians, he never again exercised this kind of invention on the scale that he did in the fourth and fifth parts of *Lumen*, and that is why *Lumen* remains a uniquely interesting work and an astonishing product of its era.

We have grown so used to the idea of alien beings since H. G. Wells found a melodramatic role for them to play in *The War of the Worlds* (1898) that it is hard to imagine a time when the idea was new and wonderfully exotic. Kepler and Fontenelle deserve the credit for coming up with the idea that the life-forms existing on other planets must be very different from those of Earth because they would need to be adapted to very different physical circumstances, but Flammarion was the first person to attempt to extrapolate that notion to its hypothetical limit and to fill that range with examples by the dozen.

Perhaps Flammarion decided subsequently that he had been far too ambitious in *Lumen*, keeping his imagination under a much tighter rein after 1869—and the modern reader can hardly help forming the impression that he could have been far more ambitious than he was — but the fact remains that the last two parts of *Lumen* represent an amazing feat of the imagination, which no one dared to emulate for more than a generation. Although the decay of spiritualism and its associated researches has robbed *Lumen* of a significant pillar of the ideative foundations that Flammarion constructed to make the account plausible, modern readers can still recognize that the fourth and fifth dialogues constitute a remarkable triumph of pioneering imaginative exploration.

Perhaps *Lumen* would be considered even more original had it not been for the fact that its ambition to produce a coherent vision of the new book of destiny that had been opened by the astronomical discoveries of the early nineteenth century had been anticipated by Edgar Allan Poe. Flammarion had not had the opportunity to read Charles Baudelaire's 1864 translation of Poe's *Eureka* when he wrote *Les Mondes imaginaires et les mondes réels* in 1862 and probably had not yet got around to it when he wrote *Lumen* in 1866–69, but he certainly discovered sometime thereafter the extent to which he had been anticipated. He must have been pleased to discover that the most adventurous element of *Lumen* — the attempt to imagine and map the potential range of alien life-forms — had not been part of Poe's project.

In other works, Poe had anticipated many of the other strategies that Flammarion was to try out in the service of the popularization of science, and he had certainly deployed them to far better literary effect — but the real triumph of *Eureka* was that it construed certain aspects of the testimony of light more ingeniously and more accurately than *Lumen*, although the extent of its cleverness did not become obvious until the 1920s. Although it is the least-read of Poe's prose works, *Eureka* provides a magnificent example of the role that the creative imagination has to play in the interpretation of scientific data, and the extent to which the science-fictional imagination can assist the serious business of thought-experimentation. What it does not do, however, is to populate the universe it imagines in the way that the fourth and fifth dialogues of *Lumen* fill the universe with wondrously exotic life.

Poe was the first writer fully to grasp some of the key implications of nineteenth-century astronomy, particularly the realization that the stars were mortal—in consequence of which, whether it was infinite in space or not, the universe could not be infinite in time. Gravity, he therefore presumed, would determine the ultimate fate of the universe. *Eureka* imagines moons falling upon planets and planets into suns,

> and the general result of this precipitation must be the gathering of the myriad now-existing stars of the firmament into an almost infinitely less number of almost infinitely superior spheres. . . . But all this will be merely a climactic magnificence foreboding the great end. . . . While undergoing consolidation, the clusters themselves, with a speed prodigiously accumulative, have been rushing towards their own general centre, and now, with a thousandfold electric velocity, commensurate only with their material grandeur and with the spiritual passion of their appetite for oneness, the majestic remnants of the tribe of stars flash, at length, into a common embrace.[25]

Having attained this climax, Poe reaches further still, suggesting that this achievement of unity surely ought to be followed by a new expansive Creation, part of an eternal sequence that he characterizes as the pulsation of the "Heart Divine"—which is, by some essential analogy, also the beating of our own hearts. Poe probably means to imply more than the obvious analogy here; he was influenced considerably by Blaise Pascal,[26] whose famous dictum that "the heart has its reasons which reason knows not" refers to a kind of apprehension identical to the "intuition" that Poe cited as his guide in the speculative adventures of *Eureka*. Flammarion was eventually to borrow all of this, but he did not produce his own version until he wrote the second part of *La Fin du monde* [The End of the World].

Had it been more widely read, *Eureka* might have made as great an impact on the evolution of speculative fiction as Flammarion's work did, but there is no doubt that *Lumen* had the more profound impact on the development of European scientific romance. It is certainly arguable that other French writers who were heavily influenced by *Lumen* and its derivatives had little further influence outside their own country, but it is arguable too that this was unfortunate and that the evolution of American science fiction might have benefited had the Wellsian image of the alien as a monstrous competitor in a cosmic struggle for existence in which only the fittest would survive been more adequately supplemented by a Flammarionesque image of the alien as a precious element in the infinite variety of life in the cosmos. Despite the overarching example of Wells, British scientific romance did benefit to some extent from that kind of example in the first half of the twentieth century, and was the better for it.

Flammarion continued to experiment with the formats he had tested in *Lumen* and "Histoire d'une comète" throughout his career. He wrote only one more or less orthodox novel, the bildungsroman *Stella* (1897), which draws extensively on Flammarion's own experiences although its eponymous protagonist is female. His most successful works of speculative fiction after *Lumen* were, however, *Stella*'s predecessors, *Uranie* (1889) and *La Fin du monde* (1894). *Uranie* was surprisingly successful in the short term (although it was not reprinted as frequently as *Lumen*) and its best-seller status caused three different translations to be done in the United States within a matter of months. Although advertised as a novel, it is actually a portmanteau piece reminiscent of *Récits de l'infini* in more ways than one, comprising three pieces that must have been written separately and may have been published previously in periodicals.

The first part of *Uranie* is a *voyage extatique* in which the seventeen-year-old Flammarion, in his first year with Le Verrier at the Observatoire, is visited by the muse of astronomy, Uranie ("Urania" in English, although one of the three translations leaves the name in the French form). She takes him on a celestial voyage to view life on many other worlds, including a planet of the multiple star Gamma Andromedae, where androgynous dragonfly-like "humans" live in a symbiotic relationship with mobile plants. The catalogue of aliens included here is a straightforward extension of the one offered in the fourth dialogue of *Lumen*, and the entire piece is effectively a supplement to that dialogue.

The second part is also an appendix to *Lumen*, but to the pseudo-biographical elements of the first three dialogues rather than the substance of the fourth. It describes the life and early afterlife of a friend of Flammarion's, here called George Spero. The third is another *voyage extatique* in which Flammarion makes an unaccompanied dream-journey to Mars, which he explores with the aid of two human-seeming Martians, who lecture him extensively on the follies and moral weaknesses of humankind—especially war.

After awakening on Earth, Flammarion is visited by Spero's spirit just as the narrator of *Lumen* had been visited; Spero reveals that he was one of Flammarion's guides on Mars, having been reincarnate there as a female, but explains that Flammarion had been deluded into seeing the Martians as humans rather than as the six-limbed winged beings they really are. Uranie then reappears to restate and amplify some of the points made in the first dialogue of *Lumen*, summarizing them in a series of aphorisms.

La Fin du monde (1894) was less successful than *Uranie*, although it is considerably bolder in imaginative terms. It too is a portmanteau work, whose first part, "Au Vingtième siècle: les théories," had appeared separately as a serial in the previous year. This first part begins as a cautionary tale about the panic that might be expected to follow news that the earth is about to be struck by a comet—a possibility that Flammarion had popularized in a number of magazine articles. The story veers away from the sensational, however, when it is revealed that the close encounter will inflict only light casualties, and a conference of savants meets to discuss alternative ways in which the world might end. The eventual glancing contact is spectacular, but the world survives.

The second part of the story, "Dans millions d'années," consists of an ambitious future history of life on Earth, a counterpart to the past history contained in *Le Monde avant le création de l'homme* and dramatized in the second dialogue of *Lumen*. The concluding section displays the influence of *Eureka* as clearly as the fourth part of *Lumen* had shown the influence of Davy:

> Mankind had passed by transmigration through the worlds to a new life with God, and freed from the burdens of matter, soared with endless progress in eternal light.
>
> The immense gaseous nebula, which absorbed all former worlds, thus transformed into vapor, began to turn upon itself. And in the zones of condensation of its primordial star-mist, new worlds were born, as heretofore the earth was.
>
> So a new universe began, whose genesis some future Moses and Laplace would tell, a new creation, extraterrestrial, superhuman, inexhaustible.[27]

Stella attempts to take up where *Uranie* had left off, but it failed to please the same audience, presumably because its mildly satirical depiction of contemporary French society left something to be desired. Having been wooed away from the fashionable haut monde (where she mingled with such characters as M. Aimelafille [girl-lover] and M. Piėdevache [bovine charity]) by reading a book entitled *L'Affranchissement de la pensée par l'astronomie* [The Liberation of Thought by Astronomy] and subsequent dialogues with Flammarionesque savants, Stella d'Ossian falls in love with the young astronomer Raphaël Dargilan. Her nearest relatives, the Comte and Comtesse de Noirmoutier ("moutier" is a colloquial term for monastery, so the name's nearest English equivalent would probably be "Blackfriars") do not approve, but she marries him anyway. Shortly afterward Stella and Raphaël are caught up in a bizarre electrical storm that leaves them both dead, but Stella contrives to get a posthumous massage back to Earth to reassure those left behind that she and Raphaël are deliriously happy, having made sufficient progress in their earthly incarnation to be worthy of reincarnation on Mars.

Flammarion continued to produce shorter works in which factual material was dramatized by fictional devices until his production finally began to falter in the last years of his life. A few hybrid works produced in parallel to the books cited above can be found in *Dans le ciel et sur la terre* [In the Sky and on the Earth] (1886) and *Clairs de lune* [Moonlights] (1894). The last and best of several derivatives of *Lumen* is the longest item in *Rêves étoilés* [Starry Dreams]

(1914), the *voyage extatique* "Voyage dans le ciel," which can be found in English in E. E. Fournier d'Albe's translation of the collection, *Dreams of an Astronomer* (1923). A similar item from *Rêves étoilés* that was omitted from Fournier d'Albe's translation had appeared in English as "A Celestial Love" in the December 1896 issue of *The Arena*.[28]

Flammarion's last collection consisting entirely of fiction — *Rêves étoilés* is a mixture of fiction and nonfiction leaning more toward the latter — was *Contes philosophiques* [Philosophical Tales] (1911), whose six items include "Conversation avec un Marsien," a discourse on the folly of war in which the narrator dreams of meeting an inhabitant of Mars, and "Dialogue entre deux Académiciens et deux insects stercoraires," in which two dung beetles offer a view appropriately contrasted to that of two academicians on the subject of the conditions necessary to allow life to flourish on other worlds. The only sense in which these last revisitations carry the relevant arguments further than *Lumen* is that they are here expressed with a subtler and more playful irony.

Such work as this was perceived, even in Flammarion's own day, as essentially second-rate, but there is a certain injustice in that judgment and in the way that his name has been gradually erased from twentieth-century reference books. By 1945 the commentary on his career contained in the encyclopedic *Nouveau Petit Larousse* had been reduced to two seemingly dismissive words — *séduisant vulgarisateur* (seductive popularizer) — but it is a description that he would surely have worn with pride, and rightly so.

The writer who absorbed the imagery of *Lumen* and its successors most fully, and redeployed that imagery most productively, was the Belgian writer Joseph-Henri Boëx (1856–1940), who signed himself J. H. Rosny aîné (i.e., the elder; he and his younger brother Justin had shared the pseudonym J. H. Rosny between 1893 and 1907, and divided it in two when they went their separate ways). In the novella "Les Xipéhuz" (1887)[29] prehistoric men encounter inorganic aliens (whose name is untranslatable), which have clearly been drawn from a Flammarionesque catalogue. Although Boëx's

"La Mort de la terre" [The Death of the Earth] (1910) owes more to *La Fin du monde* than *Lumen* and his *Les Navigateurs de l'infini* [Navigators of Infinity] (1925) seems to owe its direct inspiration to the final part of *Uranie*, they both assume the same kind of evolutionary schema.

Both Boëx brothers served, under the chairmanship of Joris-Karl Huysmans, on the jury that awarded the first Prix Goncourt, so it is not entirely surprising that the prize was won by a book of a kind that would have stood no chance of winning the same competition at a later date: the striking visionary fantasy *Force ennemie* [Hostile Force] (1903) by John-Antoine Nau (Eugène Torquet).[30] *Force ennemie* employs Flammarion's notion of serial reincarnation in a far less optimistic fashion, afflicting a contemporary human with a kind of demonic possession by a soul whose present incarnation on another world is a perpetual torment. The most extravagant extrapolation of the notion of interplanetary reincarnation can be found in the two "planetary romances" that comprise the "Martian epic" of Octave Joncquel and Théo Varlet, *Les Titans du ciel* [The Titans of the Sky] (1921) and *L'Agonie de la terre* [The Death-throes of the Earth] (1922).[31] Although the prefatory material to these melodramas acknowledges a debt to H. G. Wells's *War of the Worlds*, the aftermath of the interplanetary war described therein is a further crisis caused by the fact that the souls of the Martian casualties seek reincarnation on Earth, as they believe is their due.

To trace the imaginative legacy of *Lumen* outside France would be a highly speculative process, but the kinship with it of two important British scientific romances is worthy of comment even if no direct influence can be proved. The cosmic vision contained in William Hope Hodgson's *The House on the Borderland* (1905) is Flammarionesque while it deals with the fate of the earth and the dying sun, but in the same way that the eponymous house is an allegory of the human mind, the whole universe is transformed by Hodgson's narrator's dream into an allegory of all that the mind must endure and contemplate. As with so many sons of clergymen who were converted to freethought by the discoveries of nineteenth-century science, Hodgson took a gloomy view of the tacit moral order of the Christless universe, and his cosmic vision is far less optimistic than Flammarion's. A similar element of gloom is present in the twentieth-century work that has most in common with *Lumen* and might be regarded as a definitive updating of it: Olaf Stapledon's *Star Maker* (1937).

Whether Stapledon ever read *Lumen* or not, *Star Maker* sets out to do a very similar job in presenting an image of the universe revealed by early twentieth-century telescopes, and imagining the many kinds of life that might be contained within it. Like Flammarion's cosmic schema, Stapledon's is a product of design, which has a progressive process built into it at the most fundamental level; and like Flammarion's vision, Stapledon's is haunted by the idea that humankind's role in the cosmic plan is cursed by the self-destructive tendencies exhibited by a predilection for war. Although Stapledon cannot in the end consider the designer of his schema anything more than an incomplete artist, who still has a great deal to learn about the craft of creation, he nonetheless concedes that progress *is* being made, and hopes that it might one day be made more rapidly.

Camille Flammarion—not to mention Lumen, George Spero, and Stella d'Ossian—would surely have approved wholeheartedly of the "two lights for guidance" offered to the reader in the final paragraph of Stapledon's novel:

"The first, our little glowing atom of community, with all that it signifies. The second, the cold light of the stars, symbol of the hypercosmical reality, with its crystal ecstasy."[32]

NOTES ON THE TRANSLATION

Récits de l'infini was first translated into English for the Roberts Brothers edition of 1874, which was probably pirated. The revised text of *Lumen* was newly translated into English for the separate edition published by Heinemann in the United Kingdom and Dodd Mead in the United States. That translation, signed "A. A. M. and R. M.," claims to be authorized and to contain "portions of the last chapter written specially for the English Edition." I have made such extensive use of this translation that the following text is effectively an edited version of it. Most of the changes I have made consist of reorganization of the syntax to make the text more readable and modernization of the language wherever it seemed appropriate. I have, however, compared the edited text carefully with both the first and second versions of the French text; I have amended it wherever I thought a closer correspondence to the original could be contrived and have tried to ensure that my revisions have not distorted the meaning of the original. The same comparison has enabled me to annotate the various metamorphoses of the text.

In all the French editions, the subdivisions of *Lumen* are referred to as "premier récit," "deuxième récit," and so on, but A. A. M. and R. M. chose to call them "conversations" (their affinities with Fontenelle are so obvious that one wonders why Flammarion did not), and I have done likewise. Although the Heinemann / Dodd Mead translation leaves the subtitles of the various parts in the original Latin, I have translated them into English.

The Heinemann / Dodd Mead text is embellished by numerous marginal glosses based on, but not restricted to, a series of glosses that first appeared in the headers on the recto pages of the first edition of *Récits de l'infini* and were reproduced on the contents page as subdivisions of each section; they are rather arbitrary as well as idiosyncratic and inconsistent—their variation between editions is only partly due to changes in the pattern of pagination. These glosses do not seem to me to be necessary or helpful even in the French editions, and they are positively annoying in A. A. M. and R. M.'s version, so I have made no provision to accommodate them.

In all previous editions the participants in the dialogues are identified at the beginning of each speech with a capitalized name—QUAERENS or LUMEN—which is followed by a dash in the French versions but not in the English ones. Although fairly commonplace in nineteenth-century French texts, this device is bound to seem unfamiliar and intrusive to the modern reader, so I have taken the alternative course of placing the seeker's prompts in italics and leaving Lumen's discourses in plain text.

THE FIRST CONVERSATION

The Resurrection of the Past

I

You promised, dear Lumen, to describe to me that most supreme of moments which immediately succeeds death, and to tell me how—according to natural law, odd as it may seem—you relived your past life and penetrated a long-standing mystery.

Yes, my old friend, the time has come to honor my promise. I hope that the lifelong sympathy that has existed between our souls will help you to understand the phenomenon that seems so strange to you. There are many concepts that a mortal mind finds hard to grasp. Death, which has delivered me from the weak and easily tired bodily senses, has not yet touched you with its liberating hand. You still belong to the living world. In spite of your isolation in this retreat, among the regal towers of the Faubourg St. Jacques, you are part of the life of the earth, occupied with its petty distinctions. So you must not be surprised if, in the course of my explanation, I ask you to isolate yourself even more remotely from the things that surround you, in order to give me the most intense attention of which your mind is capable.

I have ears only for you, O Lumen, and no purpose but to understand you. So speak freely, without digression. Acquaint me with those impressions I have yet to experience, which follow the cessation of life.

Where to you want me to begin my story?

If you can remember the moment when my trembling hand closed your eyes, I wish you would begin there.

Oh, the separation of the thinking principle from the nervous system leaves no memory. It is as if the impressions made upon the brain that constitute memory are entirely effaced, to be renewed thereafter in another form. The first sensation of identity felt after death resembles that which is felt during life on awakening from sleep in the morning, while still confused by nocturnal visions. The mind, hesitating between the past and the future, tries simultaneously to recover itself and to retain the evanescent dreams whose events and images are still present to it. At times when the mind is thus absorbed in the recollection of a delightful dream, the eyelids close, and the visions reappear while we remain half asleep. Our thinking faculty is similarly divided at death, between a reality that it does not yet comprehend and a dream whose disappearance is not yet complete. Impressions of the utmost diversity are mingled together, confusing the mind. If regret for the world left behind creeps into a mind overwhelmed by perishable emotions, a sense of indefinable sadness weighs upon the imagination, darkening and hindering clarity of vision.

Did you feel these sensations immediately after death?

After death? But it is not death. What you call death—the separation of the body from the soul—is not, strictly speaking, a material process, like the chemical separation of elements from a compound. One is no more conscious of this final separation, which seems to you so cruel, than a newborn baby is aware of birth. We are born into the heavenly life as unconsciously as we were born into the earthly life, except that the soul, no longer enveloped by its bodily shell, acquires a consciousness of its individuality and powers far more rapidly.

There is an essential variety in the faculties of perception possessed by different souls. There are those who, in earthly life, never lift their souls toward heaven and never feel a desire to penetrate the laws of creation; these, being still dominated by fleshly appetites, remain in a troubled and semiconscious state for a long time.

There are others whose aspirations have gladly flown upward toward the eternal heights; to these the moment of separation arrives with calmness and peace, because they know that progress is the law of being and that the life to come will be better than that which they have left behind.

These follow, step by step, the lethargy that reaches at last to the heart, and when—slowly and insensibly—the last pulsation ceases, the departed are already above the body whose fall into sleep they have been watching. Freeing themselves from the magnetic bond, they feel themselves swiftly borne by an unknown force toward the point of creation to which their sentiments, their aspirations, and their hopes have drawn them.

This conversation, my dear master, reminds me of the dialogues of Plato concerning the immortality of the soul. As Phaedrus asked his master Socrates, on the day he was forced to drink hemlock by the iniquitous judgment of the Athenians, I ask you, who have crossed the dread boundary: what is the essential difference between the soul and the body, given that the latter must die while the former cannot?

I shall not follow the example of Socrates by giving a metaphysical answer to this question. Nor shall I reply dogmatically, as the theologians do. Instead, I will give you a scientific answer—because you, like me, accept that only the results of the positive method[1] are of any value.

We discover in the human body three principles, different and yet completely unified: one, the body; two, the vital energy;[2] three, the soul. I name them thus in order that I may follow the method of reasoning a posteriori.[3]

The body is an association of molecules, which are themselves formed of groups of atoms. The atoms are inert, passive, immutable, and indestructible. They enter into the organism by means of respiration and alimentation. They renew the bodily tissues incessantly and are continually replaced by others. When they are cast out of the body, they go on to form other bodies. In a few months the human body is entirely renewed; neither in the blood, the flesh, the brain, nor the bones does an atom remain of those that constituted the body a few months before.

Atoms travel unceasingly from body to body, mainly by way of the noble medium of the atmosphere. A molecule of iron is the same whether it is incorporated in the blood that throbs in the temples of an illustrious man or part of a fragment of rusty metal. A molecule of oxygen is the same in the blush raised by a loving glance as when, in combination with hydrogen, it forms the flame of one of the thousand gas jets that illuminate Paris by night or falls from the clouds in a drop of water.

The bodies of the living are formed from the ashes of the dead, and if all the dead were to be resuscitated, the last comers might find the material for their bodies wanting, owing to their predecessors having appropriated all that was available. Moreover, during life many exchanges are made between enemies and friends, between men, animals and plants, which amaze the analyst who examines them with scientific eyes. That which you breathe, eat, and drink has been breathed, drunk, and eaten millions of times before.

Such is the human body: an assemblage of molecules of matter that are constantly being recycled.

The principle by which these molecules are grouped according to a certain form, so as to produce an organism, is the vital energy of life. The inert, passive atoms, incapable of self-determination, are ruled by a vital force that summons them, makes them come, takes hold of them, places and disperses them according to certain laws, and forms that marvelously organized body that the anatomist and the physiologist contemplate with wonder.

Atoms are indestructible; vital force is not. Atoms have no age; vital force is born, grows old, and dies. Why is a man of eighty older than a youth of twenty, given that the atoms that compose his body have only belonged to his frame for a few months, and that atoms themselves are neither old nor young? The constituent elements of his body, when analyzed, have no age. What is old in him? Only his vital energy, which is but one of the forms of the general energy of the universe, and which in his case has become exhausted.

Life is transmitted by generation, and sustains the body instinctively and automatically. It has a beginning and an end. It is an unconscious physical force, which organizes and maintains the body.

The soul, on the other hand, is an intellectual, thinking, immaterial being.

The world of ideas in which the soul lives is not the world of matter. It has no age; it does not grow old. Unlike the body, it is not changed in a few months. We feel that we preserve our identity over months, years, and decades: that our identity, our essential self, is always ours. If the soul did not exist, and the faculty of thinking were only a function of the brain, we should no longer be able to say that we possess a body, because it would be our body and our brain that possessed us. In that case, our consciousness would change continually; we would no longer have a feeling of identity, and we would no longer be responsible for the resolutions that passed through the brain many months before, secreted by its molecules.

The soul is not the vital force, for the latter is limited and transmitted by generation, has no consciousness of itself, is born, grows up, declines, and dies. All these states are opposed to that of the soul, which is immaterial, unlimited, not transmissible, and conscious.

The development of the vital force might be represented geometrically by a spindle, which swells out gradually toward the center and then decreases again to a point. When the soul reaches middle age, it does not become less and dwindle to its terminus, as a spindle does, but follows a parabolic curve directed into the infinite. Besides, the mode of existence of the soul is essentially different from that of the vital force. It is a spiritual mode.

The conceptions of the soul, such as the sentiments of justice and injustice, truth and falsehood, good and evil, as well as knowledge, mathematics, analysis, synthesis, contemplation, admiration, love, affection or hatred, esteem or contempt—in a word, the occupations of the soul, whatever they may be—are of an intellectual and moral order, which neither the atoms nor the physical forces can attain, but which have as real an existence as the physical order of things. The chemical or mechanical work of cerebral cells, however subtle they may be, can never produce an intellectual judgment such as, for example, the knowledge of the fact that four times four is sixteen or that the three angles of a triangle are equal to two right angles.

These three elements of the human being are reproduced in the universe at large:

1. The atoms comprising the material world, inert and passive.

2. The physical forces regulating the world, active and continually transformed.

3. God, the eternal and infinite spirit, intellectual organizer of the mathematical laws that the physical forces obey: the unknown being in whom reside the supreme principles of truth, beauty, and goodness.

The soul can be attached to the body only by means of the vital force. When life is extinct, the soul is naturally detached from the organism and ceases to have any immediate connection with time and space. The soul remains in that part of the universe where the earth happens to be at the moment of its separation from the body. You know that Earth is a planet like Venus and Jupiter. The earth continues to follow its orbit at a velocity of 12,700 kilometers per hour, so the soul, an hour after death, finds itself at that distance from its body, because of its immobility in space when no longer subject to the laws of matter. For this reason, we find ourselves in the heavens immediately after death—as we have actually been throughout our lives, although our weight bound us to the earth.

I ought to add, though, that the soul usually takes some time to disengage itself from the nervous organism and that it occasionally remains for many days, or even many months, magnetically connected with a body it is reluctant to forsake. It is, however, now possessed of special faculties by means of which it can transport itself from one point of space to another.

This is the first time that I have been able to understand death as a natural process and to comprehend the individual existence of the soul: its independence of the body and of life, its personality, its survival, and its manifest situation in the universe. This synthetic theory has, I hope, prepared me to understand and appreciate your revelation. You said that something singular happened to you on your entrance into the eternal life. At what moment did that event take place?

Well, my friend, let me continue my story. You will remember that my old clock had sounded the chimes of midnight, and the full moon shed its pale light on my deathbed, when my daughter, my grandson, and my friends withdrew to rest. You wished to remain with me, and you promised my daughter that you would not leave me until morning. I would thank you for your warm and tender devotion if we were not such true brothers.

We had been alone for about half an hour, while the moon was setting, when I took your hand and told you that life had already abandoned my extremities. You assured me that it was not so, but I was calmly observing my physiological state and I knew that I would cease breathing in a few minutes. You made as if to go to the room where my children were asleep, but I concentrated my powers by means of one final effort and stopped you. Returning to me with tears in your eyes, you said: "You're right; you've said your last farewells; there will be time enough to send for them in the morning." I felt that there was a contradiction in these words, but I did not say so. Do you remember that I asked you to open the window?

It was a beautiful night in October, more beautiful than those of which Ossian's Scottish bards used to sing.[4] Not far from the horizon, just level with my eyes, I could distinguish the Pleiades, veiled by mist, while Castor and Pollux floated triumphantly a little higher up. Higher still, forming a triangle with them, shone the beautiful star with golden rays that is named on maps of the zodiac as Capella.[5]

You see that my memory has not faded. When you had opened the window, the perfume of the roses sleeping beneath the wings of night came up to me and mingled with the silent radiance of the stars. I cannot tell you how sweet these last impressions of the earth were; language is inadequate to describe what I felt. In the hours of my greatest happiness and tenderest love I never felt such an intensity of joy, so glorious a serenity, such genuine bliss, as I experienced then in ecstatic enjoyment of the scented breath of the flowers and the soft gleam of distant stars . . .

When you bent over me, I returned to the external world, and with my hands clasped over my breast, my sight and my prayerful thoughts took flight together into space. Before my ears ceased to function I heard the last words that fell from my lips: "Adieu, my old friend! I feel that death is bearing me away to those unknown regions where, I trust, we shall one day meet again. When dawn's light effaces these stars, my mortal body alone will remain. Repeat my last wish to my daughter, that she should bring up her children in the contemplation of eternal goodness."

While you wept as you knelt by my bed, I said: "Recite the beautiful prayer of Jesus," and you began the Lord's Prayer with a tremulous voice . . .

". . . Forgive us our trespasses . . . as we forgive those . . . who trespass against us. . . ." Those were the last thoughts that entered into my soul by means of my senses. My sight grew dim as I stared at the star Capella, and I know nothing of what immediately followed that moment.

Years, days, and hours are constituted by the movements of the earth. In space, beyond the scope of these movements, terrestrial time no longer exists. Indeed, it is quite impossible to have any notion of time. I believe, however, that the event I am about to describe to you occurred on the very day of my death—for, as you will presently see, my body was not yet buried when this vision was offered to my soul.

Born in 1793, I was in my seventy-second year, so I was not a little surprised to find myself animated by a vivacity of spirit no less ardent than that of the best years of my adolescence. I had no body, and yet I was not incorporeal. I felt and saw that I was substantial, although the substance of which I was constituted bore no analogy to that of which terrestrial bodies are formed. I do not know how I traversed the celestial spaces, but I soon discovered that by means of some unknown force I was approaching a magnificent golden sun—whose splendor did not, however, dazzle me. I perceived that it was surrounded by a number of worlds, each consisting of one or several rings.

By means of the same unconscious force, I was driven toward one of these rings. I was a spectator of marvelous phenomena of light, for the starry spaces were crisscrossed everywhere by rainbow bridges. I lost sight of the golden sun and found myself in a sort of night colored with a thousand subtle hues.

My soul's sight was far more powerful than that of the eyes of the terrestrial organism I had left behind. To my surprise, this power appeared to be subject to my will. That sight of the soul is so marvelous that I cannot pause today to describe it. Suffice it to say that instead of merely seeing the stars in the sky, as you see them from Earth, I could clearly distinguish the worlds revolving around them. Bizarrely, when I wished that the central sun would go away, in order that I might examine these worlds without its hindrance, it disappeared from my sight and left me under the most favorable conditions for observing any one of them I wished.[6] Furthermore, when my attention was concentrated on one particular world, I could distinguish its continents and its seas, its clouds and its rivers, although they did not appear to become larger in the manner of objects seen through a telescope. I could see any particular thing that I fixed my gaze upon—such as a town or a tract of countryside—with perfect clarity and distinctness.

On arriving upon the ring-shaped world, I found myself clad in a form like that of its inhabitants, as if my soul had attracted to itself the constituent atoms of a new body. Living bodies on Earth are composed of molecules that do not touch one another and are constantly renewed by respiration, nutrition, and assimilation; here, the envelope of the soul is formed more rapidly. I felt myself more alive than the supernatural beings whose passions and sorrows Dante recorded. The ability to see a long way is certainly one of the essential faculties of this new world.

But my friend, if you will excuse what is perhaps a naïve question, is it not the case that the planets revolving around other stars must be confused with their primaries at such a distance? When you see our sun from afar, for instance, can you possibly distinguish Earth or any other planet from the star?

You have immediately seized upon the one geometrical objection that seems to contradict the preceding observation. Indeed, at a certain distance, the planets are absorbed into the radiance of their suns, and our terrestrial eyes could scarcely distinguish them. As you know, Earth is no longer visible from Saturn. But it is important to remember that this discrepancy arises as much from the imperfection of our sight as from the geometrical principle of decreasing surface area. Now, in the world on which I had just landed, the inhabitants are not incarnated in a gross form, as we are down here, but are free spirits endowed with supremely powerful faculties of perception. As I have told you, they can isolate the source of light from the object lighted, and they are also able to make out details that would be completely hidden from the eyes of Earth-dwellers at such a distance.

Are they enabled to do this by instruments superior to our telescopes?

Well, if this marvelous faculty is rendered less offensive by supposing that it is attained by means of some such instruments, you may adopt that theory. Imagine, if you will, a telescope equipped with a series of lenses and filters so arranged as to bring each of these distant worlds into view in succession, isolating them for separate study. But I should also tell you that these beings are endowed with a special sense in addition to ordinary sight, which enables them to regulate the powers of their marvelous optical apparatus. You must understand that this visionary power and optical construction are natural to their worlds, not supernatural. To assist in conceptualizing the faculties possessed by these extraterrestrial beings, consider for a moment the eyes of insects that have the ability to draw in, lengthen out, or flatten their eyes like the tubes of opera glasses so as to make the lenses magnify to different degrees, or those that can bring a multitude of fixed eyes to bear like the lenses of a microscope, in order to concentrate on something very tiny.

Because such things are outside my experience I cannot visualize them, but I concede the possibility. So, you are able to see the earth and can even distinguish the towns and villages on its surface?

Let me go on. I arrived on the aforementioned ring, which was as big as two hundred Earths like yours rolled into one, and found myself on a mountain crowned with arboreal palaces. It seemed to me that these fairy-tale castles were growing naturally, or were merely the result of a facile arrangement of branches and tall flowers. There was on the summit of the mountain a fairly populous town, where I noticed a group of old men, twenty or thirty in number, who were looking with the most fixed attention and anxious concern at a beautiful star in the southern constellation of Ara, the Altar, on the edge of the Milky Way. So absorbed were they in observing and examining this star, or one of the worlds belonging to its system, that they did not observe my arrival among them.

As for myself, on arriving in the world's atmosphere, I found myself reinvested in a material body in the same form as theirs. Even more to my surprise, I was astonished to hear them speaking of the earth—yes, of the earth—in that universal language of the spirits that all beings there comprehend, from the seraphim to the trees of the forest. Not only were they talking about the earth, but about France.

"What can be the meaning of these legal massacres?" they were saying. "Is it possible that brute force rules supreme there? Will civil war decimate that people, to the last of its defenders, and bathe the streets of that capital city, once so magnificent and so joyful, in rivers of blood?"

I, who had come from the earth with the swiftness of thought, having breathed only the day before in the bosom of a tranquil and peaceful capital, could not immediately understand the implication of this speech. I joined the group, fixing my eyes as they did upon the beautiful star, trying meanwhile to figure out what they were talking about. Presently, I perceived a pale blue sphere to the left of the star; that was the earth. You, my friend, are not ignorant of the fact that, in spite of the apparent paradox, the earth is really a star in the sky, as I reminded you only a moment ago. From afar, from one of the stars neighboring your solar system, that system appears to the spiritual sight I have described as a family of stars, composed of eight principal worlds arranged around the star that is their sun. Jupiter and Saturn catch the attention first because of their great size; then one notices Uranus and Neptune—and, at length, very near the sun-star, Mars and Earth. Venus is very difficult to make out, and Mercury is too close to the sun to be visible. Such is the appearance in the heavens of our planetary system.

My attention was fixed exclusively upon the little terrestrial sphere by the side of which I perceived the moon. I soon remarked the white snow of the North Pole, the yellow triangle of Africa, and the outlines of the ocean. While my attention was concentrated on our planet the sun-star was eclipsed from my sight. Then I was able to distinguish, in the middle of an azure expanse, a patch of brown. Pursuing my investigations, I discovered a city in the middle of this patch. I had no difficulty in recognizing that this continental patch was France and that the city was Paris. The first sign by which I recognized it was the silver ribbon of the Seine, which describes so many graceful convolutions to the west of the city.

The use of my new organs of sight enabled me to see the city in detail. On its eastern side I saw the nave and towers of Notre Dame in the form of a Latin cross. The boulevards wound around the north. To the south I could see the Luxembourg Gardens and the Observatory. The Panthéon's dome sat upon the Mount of Saint Geneviève like a gray hood. The grand avenue of the Champs-Élysées was a straight line running westward. Further out, I could distinguish the Bois de Boulogne, the environs of St. Cloud, Meudon Wood, Sèvres, Ville d'Avray, and Montretout. The whole scene was lit by splendid sunshine. Strange to tell, though, the hills were covered with snow, as if it were January, whereas I had left it in October while the countryside was perfectly green. I was fully convinced that I was looking at Paris, but because I could not understand the exclamations of my companions, I endeavored to ascertain more details.

My eyes were fixed most interestedly upon the neighborhood of the Observatory. That was my favorite district, and for forty years I had scarcely left it for more than a few months. Imagine my surprise, therefore, when I looked more closely at it only to find that the magnificent avenue of chestnuts between the Luxembourg and the Observatory was nowhere to be seen and that convent gardens were in its place. My artistic indignation was aroused against these affronts but was quickly superseded by even stranger sensations. I beheld a monastery in the middle of our beautiful orchard. The Boulevard St. Michel did not exist, nor did the Rue de Medici; instead, I saw a confused mass of little streets. I seemed to recognize the former Rue de l'Est and the Place St Michel, where an ancient fountain used to supply water to the people of the district, and I could make out a number of narrow lanes that existed in former times. The cupolas and the two lateral wings of the Observatory had disappeared.

By degrees, as I continued my observations of Paris, I discovered that many such details had been slightly altered. The Arc de Triomphe and all the magnificent avenues that met at the Étoile had disappeared. There was no Boulevard de Sébastopol, no Gare de l'Est—nor any other station, and no railway. The tower of St. Jacques was enclosed within a double row of old houses, and the Victory Column was reached by that route. The Bastille Column was also missing, for I should easily have recognized the figure upon it. An equestrian statue took the place of the Vendôme Column. The Rue Castiglione was an ancient green convent. The Rue de Rivoli had vanished. The Louvre was either unfinished or half demolished. Between the Court of Francis I and the Tuileries there were tumbledown hovels. There was no obelisk in the Place de la Concorde, but I saw a moving crowd there whose individual figures I was initially unable to distinguish. The Madeleine and the Rue Royale were invisible. Beyond the Île de St. Louis I saw a small island. There was nothing but an old wall instead of the outer boulevards, and the entire city was enclosed by fortifications. In brief, although I recognized the capital of France by means of several familiar buildings, it seemed to have been utterly transformed by some marvelous metamorphosis.

At first I fancied that instead of having just come from the earth I must have been many years in transit. Because the notion of time is essentially relative and there is nothing real or absolute in the measure of duration, I had lost all standards of measurement as soon as I had left the earth, so I told myself that years, or even centuries, might have passed without my perceiving them. I wondered whether the journey had only seemed short to me because of the great interest I had taken in my voyage through space—a commonplace notion used to illustrate the extent to which our experience of time is relative.

Not having any means of assuring myself of the facts of the case, I undoubtedly had grounds for concluding that I was separated by many centuries from the terrestrial life that was presently paraded before my eyes in Paris. I continued to imagine that I was seeing the twentieth or twenty-first century while I penetrated more deeply into the details of the living picture, examining all its features.

Gradually, I began to recognize the sites of the streets and public buildings that I had known in my early youth. The Hôtel de Ville appeared to be decorated with flags, and I could distinguish the square central dome of the Tuileries. One particular detail caught my attention, when I saw a summerhouse in an old convent garden, which set me atremble with joy. It was in that very spot that I had met, in my youth, the woman who loved me so deeply: my Sylvia,[7] so tender and so devoted, who gave up everything to join her destiny with mine. I saw the roof of the terrace where we loved to stroll in the evenings, studying the constellations. Oh, with what joy did I greet the promenades where we walked, always keeping in step, and the avenues where we took refuge from the prying eyes of strangers!

You can imagine how, as I looked at that summerhouse, that sight alone was sufficient to assure me, utterly and indubitably, that what lay before my eyes was not, as it was natural to suppose, the Paris of a time long after my death but actually a Paris that had disappeared: the Paris of old, at the beginning of this century or the end of the last!

In spite of everything, though, you can easily imagine that I could scarcely believe my eyes. It seemed so much more natural to think that Paris had grown old and had suffered these transformations since my departure from the earth—in an interval of time absolutely unknown to me—and so much easier to think that I beheld the city of the future.

I continued my observations carefully, in order to ascertain whether it really was the Paris of old, now partly demolished, that

I was looking at, or whether—by virtue of a phenomenon still more incredible—it was another Paris, another France, another world.

II

What an extraordinary situation for an analytical mind like yours, O Lumen! How did you manage to arrive at the true explanation?

While these reflections were passing through my mind, the old men on the mountain continued their conversation. Suddenly, I heard the most ancient—a venerable spirit whose Nestorian appearance[8] commanded both admiration and respect—cry out in a loud and mournful voice:

"Kneel, my brothers; let us beseech the universal God for forbearance. That world, that nation and that city continue to steep themselves in blood; another head—this time that of a king—is about to fall."

His companions appeared to understand him, for they knelt down on the mountain and lowered their white faces to the ground.

For my own part, I had not yet succeeded in distinguishing human beings in the streets and squares of Paris. So, being unable to follow the particular observation made by the old men, I remained standing and pursued my examination more minutely.

"Stranger," the old man said to me, "do you disapprove of the unanimous action of your brothers, since you do not add your prayer to theirs?"

"Senator," I replied, "I can neither approve nor disapprove of what I do not understand. Having only just arrived on this mountain, I do not know the cause of your righteous indignation."

I drew nearer to the old man then, and while his companions were rising to their feet and entering into conversation with one another, I asked him to tell me what he had seen.

He informed me that spirits of the level inhabiting that world are intuitively gifted with an inner perception of events in neighboring worlds and that they have a sort of magnetic attraction to the neighboring stars. These stars are between twelve and fifteen in number: they are the nearest; beyond that range perception becomes confused. Our sun is one of those neighboring stars. They have, in consequence, a vague but sensitive knowledge of the humanities inhabiting the various planets of our sun, and their relative intellectual and moral elevation.

Furthermore, whenever a great disturbance takes place among one of these humanities, either in the physical or the moral realm, they are subject to a sort of inner agitation, like that of a musical chord vibrating in resonance with another some distance away.

For a year — a year of that world being equal to ten of ours — they had felt themselves drawn by a special attraction toward the terrestrial planet, and they had observed with unusual interest and anxiety the march of events in that world. They had witnessed the end of a reign and the dawn of glorious liberty, the triumph of the rights of man and the assertion of the great principles of human dignity. Then they had seen the great cause of liberty placed in peril by those who should have been the first to defend it, and brute force substituted for reason and justice.

I realized that he was describing the great Revolution of 1789, and the fall of the old political order before the new. For some time they had been mournfully following the events of the Reign of Terror and the tyranny of that bloody era. They were afraid for the future of the earth and doubtful of the further progress of that humanity which, once emancipated, had so soon lost the treasure it had won.

I took care not to tell the senator that I had just arrived from Earth myself and that I had lived there seventy-two years. I do not know whether he was already aware of this, but I was so astonished by the vision before me that it completely absorbed my mind and I no longer thought of myself.

At last my sight was fully developed, and I perceived the spectacle in its every detail. I distinguished a scaffold in the middle of the Place de la Concorde, surrounded by a formidable array of military drums and cannon, and a motley crowd armed with pikes.

A cart, led by a red-clad man, bore the remains of Louis XVI in the direction of the Faubourg St. Honoré.

The fists of an intoxicated mob were raised to heaven.

Cavalrymen, sabers aloft, followed mournfully. Toward the Champs-Élysées there were ditches into which curiosity-seekers continually stumbled, but the agitation was concentrated in this area. It did not extend into the city center, which seemed dead and deserted; the Terror had delivered it into a kind of coma.

Because it was the year of my birth, I had no direct knowledge of the events of 1793, and it is difficult to express how it felt to be a witness of scenes I had only read about in history books. I have often debated the motions passed by the National Convention, but I must confess that the execution of men such as Lavoisier, the founder of chemistry; Bailly, the historian of astronomy; and André Chénier, the gentle poet, or the condemnation of Condorcet, the philosopher,[9] which could not be excused by reasons of state, aroused my indignation far more than the punishment of Louis XVI. To be allowed access to that vanished epoch struck me as an unparalleled opportunity, but you will appreciate that my interest was overwhelmed by a sentiment that was even more powerful:

How could it be that, at the end of the year 1864, events that I knew to have happened at the end of the previous century were taking place before my very eyes?

Indeed, it seems to me that a feeling of impossibility should have affected your contemplation profoundly. In the final analysis, visions are essentially illusory; we cannot admit their reality no matter how clearly we see them.

Yes, my friend, it was impossible. Now, can you imagine the state I was in, when I saw a paradox realized before my very eyes? A common saying declares that "one cannot believe one's eyes"; that was exactly my situation. It was impossible to deny what I saw, and impossible to admit it.

But was it not a product of your mind: a creation of your imagination or perhaps a recollection of some kind? Are you sure it was a reality, not some bizarre reflection drawn from your memory?

That was the first thought that came to mind, but it was so obvious that I had before my eyes the Paris of 1793, and the events of the 21st of January, that I could not doubt it for long. Besides, that explanation was forestalled by the fact that the old men of the mountain had preceded me in observing these phenomena. They had seen and analyzed them, and discussed them as actual facts without knowing anything of the history of our world, and were quite unaware of my knowledge of that history. Furthermore, we had before our eyes a present fact, not a fact long past.

But then, if the past can thus be merged with the present, if reality and vision can be allied in this way, if persons long since dead can be seen still acting on the stage of life, if the new structures and other metamorphoses of a city like Paris can disappear and give way to the city of yesteryear—in sum, if the present can vanish and the past be resurrected—what certainty can we have of anything? What becomes of observational science? What becomes of deduction and theory? On what solid foundations can we base our knowledge? If these things are true, ought we not henceforth to doubt everything, or believe everything?

Yes, my friend, these considerations and many others crossed my mind and tormented me; but they could not do away with the reality that I was observing. When I had assured myself that the events of 1793 were present before our eyes, I immediately thought that science, instead of fighting against that reality—for two truths can never be opposed to one another—ought to furnish me with an explanation of them. So I asked the question of physics and awaited its response.

What! Was it indeed a reality?

It was not only a reality, but perfectly comprehensible and capable of demonstration. You shall have an astronomical explanation.[10]

To begin with, I examined the position of the earth in the constellation of the Altar, as I have told you. I took the bearings of my position relative to the Pole Star and to the zodiac. I noticed that the constellations were not much different from those we see from Earth, and that except for a few particular stars their positions were evidently the same. Orion still reigned supreme in the region above the Equator; the Great Bear still pointed to the north as he pursued his circular course. On comparing the apparent movements, and coordinating them scientifically, I calculated that the point at which I saw the sun and its planets, including Earth, marked the seventeenth hour of right ascension—that is to say, about the 256th degree,[11] or very nearly; I had no instrument with which to make an exact measurement. I observed, in the second place, that it was on the forty-fourth degree from the South Pole.

I made these observations in order to ascertain the position of the star on which I found myself, and I was led to conclude that it was situated on the seventy-sixth degree of right ascension, and the forty-sixth degree of north declination.[12] In addition, I knew from the words of the old man that the star in whose system we were could not be far from our sun, since he considered it to be one of the neighboring stars. On combining these data, I had no difficulty in recalling the star that stands in the position I had determined. Only one star of the first magnitude answered to the description: Alpha Aurigae, or Capella. There could be no further doubt on that score.

Thus, I was definitely on a world in the solar system of that star. From that point our sun would appear to be an ordinary star in the constellation of the Altar, which is exactly opposite to Auriga when seen from Earth.

Next, I tried to remember the parallax of that star. I recalled that a friend of mine, a Russian astronomer, had made a calculation, subsequently confirmed, that its parallax was 0.046 of a second of arc.[13] My heart beat joyously when I realized that the mystery was solved.

Every geometrician knows that parallax can be translated mathematically into distance according to a fixed table of correspondences. In order to calculate the exact distance that separated Capella from Earth I had only to recall the distance that corresponded to 0.046 of a second.[14]

Expressed in millions of leagues, this number is 170,392,000, so the distance from the star where I was to the earth was 170,392,000,000,000 leagues.[15]

The principle was thus established and the problem three-quarters solved. Now, this is the main point of the argument, to which I call your attention especially, because you will find therein an explanation of the most marvelous realities.

Light, as you know, does not pass instantaneously from one place to another, but moves in successive waves. If you throw a stone into a pool of tranquil water, a series of undulations extends from the point at which the stone fell. Sound conducts itself through the air in this fashion when passing from one point to another, and light travels in space in the same way: it is transmitted in successive undulations.

The light of a star takes a certain time to reach the earth, and this time naturally depends on the distance that separates the star from the earth.

Sound travels at 340 meters per second. A cannon shot is heard immediately by those who are close by, a second later by persons who are at a distance of 340 meters, in three seconds by those who are a kilometer off, twelve seconds after the shot at four kilometers. It takes two minutes to reach those who are ten times further away, and those who live at a distance of a hundred kilometers hear this human thunder after five minutes.

Light travels with much greater swiftness, but it is not transmitted instantaneously, as the ancients supposed. It travels at the rate of 300,000 kilometers per second, and if it could travel in circles might go around the earth eight times in a second. It requires one second and a quarter to come from the moon to the earth, eight minutes and thirteen seconds to come from the sun, forty-two minutes from Jupiter, two hours from Uranus, and four hours from Neptune. Thus, we see the heavenly bodies not as they are at the moment we observe them, but as they were when the luminous ray that reaches us left them. If a volcano were to burst forth in eruption on one of the worlds I have named, we should not see the flames if it erupted on the moon until a second and a quarter had elapsed, if on Jupiter not until forty-two minutes had elapsed, if on Uranus not for two hours, and if on Neptune, we should not see the flames until four hours after the eruption.

The distances outside our planetary system are incomparably more vast, and the light takes much longer to reach us. Thus, a luminous ray coming from the star nearest to us, Alpha Centauri, takes more than four years to arrive; one from Sirius takes nearly ten years to cross the abyss that separates us from that sun.

Because the star Capella is the aforementioned distance from the earth, it is easy to calculate, at the rate of 300,000 kilometers per second, the time needed to cross it. The calculation gives a result of seventy-one years, eight months, and twenty-four days.[16] A luminous ray, therefore, that came from Capella would traverse space without interruption for seventy-one years, eight months, and twenty-four days before it became visible on Earth.

Similarly, a ray of light leaving Earth can only arrive at Capella after the same interval of time.

If the luminous ray that comes from that star takes nearly seventy-two years to reach us, it follows that we see the star as it was nearly seventy-two years ago?

You have understood perfectly. And it is precisely this fact that it is important to grasp firmly.

In other words, then, the ray of light is like a courier who brings dispatches from a distant country—and having been nearly seventy-two years on the way, his news is of events that occurred at the time of his departure seventy-two years before.

You have penetrated the mystery. Your illustration shows me that you have lifted the veil that shrouded it. To speak more accurately, the light represents a courier who brings not written news, but photographs—or, strictly speaking, the actual appearance of the country from which he came. We see this living picture just as it appeared, in all its aspects, at the moment when the luminous rays started out. Nothing is simpler, nothing more indubitable. When we examine the surface of a heavenly object with a telescope, we see not the actual surface as it is at the time of our observation, but the surface as it was when the light was emitted from it.

So, if a star whose light takes, say, ten years to reach us were annihilated today, we should continue to see it for ten years, because its last ray would not reach us until ten years had elapsed?

Precisely so. In brief, the rays of light that proceed from the stars do not reach us instantaneously but occupy a certain time in crossing the distance that separates us from them and shows us those stars not as they are now but as they were at the moment in which those rays set out to transmit the appearance of the stars to us.

Thus, there is a wondrous transformation of the past into the present. From the viewpoint of the star we observe, it is the past, which has already vanished; for the observer, it is the present, the actual. Strictly speaking, the past of the star *is*, scientifically speaking, the present of the observer. As the aspect of each world changes from year to year, almost from day to day, one can imagine these aspects emerging into space and advancing into the infinite, thus revealing their phases to the sight of far distant spectators. Each aspect or appearance is followed by another, and so on, in endless sequence. Thus, a series of undulations bears from afar the past histories of the worlds that the observer sees, revealing their various phases as they reach him in succession. The events that we see in the stars at present are already past, and what is actually happening there we cannot yet see.

Take aboard this fact, my friend, for it is important that you understand the precession of the waves of light and that you comprehend the essence of this undoubted truth: the appearance of things, borne to us by light, shows us those things not as they are at present, but as they were in that period of the past that preceded the interval of time needed for the light to traverse the distance separating us from those events.

We do not see any of the stars as they are, but as they were when the luminous rays that reach us left them. It is not the actual condition of the heavens that is visible, but their past history. There are distant stars that have been extinct for ten thousand years that we can still see because the rays of light set out from them before they were extinguished. Some of the double stars, whose nature and movements we labor carefully to reveal, ceased to exist long before astronomers began to make observations. If the visible heavens were to be annihilated today, we should still see stars tomorrow, next year, for a hundred years, a thousand years, and even for fifty or a hundred thousand years or more, with the sole exception of the nearest stars, which would disappear successively as the time needed for their luminous rays to reach us expired. Alpha Centauri would go out first, after four years, Sirius after ten, and so on.

Now, my friend, you can easily apply this scientific theory to the explanation of the strange facts of which I was a witness. If, from the earth, one sees the star Capella not as it is at the moment of observation, but as it was seventy-two years before, then by the same token, from Capella one would see the earth as it was seventy-two years earlier. Light requires the same time to traverse the same distance.

Master, I have listened attentively to your explanation. But does the earth shine at such a distance like a star? Surely it is not luminous?

It reflects the light of the sun into space; the greater the distance, the more our planet resembles a star. All the light radiated by the sun upon its surface is condensed into a disc that becomes smaller and smaller. Seen from the moon, our earth appears fourteen times more luminous than the full moon appears to us, because it is fourteen times larger. Seen from the planet Venus, the earth appears as bright as Jupiter appears to us. From the planet Mars, the earth is the morning and the evening star, presenting phases like those that Venus presents to us. Thus, although Earth is not luminous itself, it shines afar like the moon and the planets, by virtue of the light that it receives from the sun and reflects into space. Now, the events taking place on Neptune, if seen from the earth, would suffer a delay of four hours; the view of life on Earth could only reach Neptune in the same time. Nearly seventy-two years, therefore, separate Capella and the earth.

Although this view of things is new to me, I now understand perfectly how, since the light was nearly seventy-two years in traversing the abyss that separates the earth from Capella, you did not see the earth as it was on October 1864, on the date of your death, but as it appeared in January 1793. And I understand just as clearly that what you saw was neither a vision, nor a phenomenon of memory, nor a supernatural experience, but an actual, scientific, and incontestable fact—and that in actual fact, what had long passed away on the earth was only then present to an observer at that distance. But permit me to ask you a supplementary question. In coming from the earth to Capella, must you not have crossed that distance more rapidly than light itself?

Have I not answered that question already in telling you that I crossed that distance with the swiftness of thought? On the very day of my death I found myself in the vicinity of this star, which I had admired and loved throughout my earthly life.

Ah, Master, everything is now explained, and yet this vision is no less astounding. To be able to see the past in the present is a truly extraordinary phenomenon, no less surprising than the seeming impossibility of seeing the stars not as they are when one makes the observation, nor even as they were at the same moment, but only as they have been in different epochs, according to their distances and the time the light of each one has taken in coming to the earth!

The natural astonishment that you feel in contemplating this fact is merely a prelude, I daresay, to the things which you must grasp now. At first sight, it undoubtedly seems extraordinary that by removing oneself to a distance in space one can become a witness of events long past, reversing, so to speak, the flow of time. But this is no more strange than what I have yet to communicate, which will seem more fanciful still, if you wish to listen for a while longer to the story of the day that followed my death.

Go on, I beg of you. I am thirsty for more.

III

After having turned away from the bloody scenes of the Place de la Révolution, my gaze was drawn toward an edifice of an already antiquated style, situated in front of Notre Dame and taking the place of the square that presently extends in front of the cathedral. I saw a group of five people before the entrance to the cathedral, reclining in the sunshine on wooden benches, with their heads bare. When they got up and crossed the road, I perceived that one was my father, younger than I could remember him, another my mother, younger still, and a third a cousin of mine who died in the same year as my father, nearly forty years ago. I found it difficult at first to recognize these persons, for instead of facing them I was looking at them from high above their heads. I was not a little surprised by this unexpected encounter, but then I remembered that my parents had lived in the Place Notre Dame before my birth.

I cannot tell you how profoundly affected I was by this sight; it seemed that my perception failed, as if clouds were extended over Paris. I felt for a moment as though I had been carried away by a whirlwind—for, as you are aware, I had lost all sense of time.

When I began to see objects distinctly again, I noticed a troop of children running across the Place de Panthéon. They seemed to be school children coming out of class, for they had their portfolios and their books in their hands. They seemed to be going home, gamboling and gesticulating. Two of them attracted my particular attention because I saw that they were quarreling and just about to fight. Another little fellow was coming forward to separate them when he received a blow on the shoulder and was knocked down. At the same time, I saw a woman running toward him. It was my mother.

Never — no, never, in my seventy-two years of earthly existence, among all the adventures, astonishments, unexpected events, and strange occurrences with which it was crowded, never had I felt such a disturbance as that which overcame me when I recognized in that child — myself!

Yourself?

Myself! With the blond curls of a six-year-old, in my little collar embroidered by my mother's hands and my little pale blue blouse whose cuffs were always crumpled. There I was, exactly as you have seen me in the faded miniature that stood on my mantelpiece. My mother came to me and took me up in her arms, sharply reproving the other boys, then led me by the hand into the house, which was close to the Rue d'Ulm. Then, I saw that after passing through the house we reappeared together in the garden, in the midst of a numerous company.

Master, forgive me for criticizing, but I confess that it appears impossible to me that you could see yourself. You could not be two people, and since you were seventy-two years old, your infancy was long gone and utterly lost. You could not see something that no longer existed. At least, I cannot understand how you, as an old man, could see yourself as an infant.

What prevents you from admitting this fact on the same grounds as the preceding ones?

Because you cannot see yourself in duplicate, as an infant and an old man at the same time.

You have not thought it through, my friend. You have understood the general fact well enough, but you have not observed as yet that this particular is a logical corollary of it. You admit that the view I had of the earth was seventy-two years in arriving, do you not?

That events reached me only at that interval of time after they had taken place? In brief, that I saw the world of that epoch? You admit, likewise, that in seeing the streets of that time I also saw the children running through them? You admit all this?

Yes, certainly.

Well then, since I saw that troop of children, and I had been part of that troop, why should I not be able to see myself among them?

But you were no longer there among them!

Again, I repeat, this troop of children no longer exists—but I saw them as they were at the point of departure of the ray of light that reached me that day. Since I could distinguish the fifteen or eighteen children in the group, there was no reason why I should disappear from among them just because I myself was the distant spectator. Any other observer could see me in company with my comrades, so why should I be an exception? I saw them all, and I saw myself among them.

I had not grasped the full implications. It is, indeed, obvious that in seeing a troop of children of which you were one, you could not fail to see yourself as well as the others.

Now can you understand the state of surprise into which I was cast by the sight? That child was truly myself—flesh and bone, as the common expression has it—at the age of six. I saw myself as clearly as the company in the garden saw me. It was not a mirage, not a ghost, not a memory, not a picture: it was reality itself. It was definitely myself, my mind, my body. I was there, before my own eyes. Had my other senses only had the perfection of my sight, it seemed to me that I would have been able to touch and hear myself. I jumped about the garden and ran around the balustraded pond. Some time afterward, my grandfather took me on his knee and made me read from a big book.

No, I cannot describe how I felt! I must leave you to imagine it for yourself, if you have now convinced yourself adequately of the reality of the situation. Suffice it to say that I never had such a surprise in my life.

One reflection, especially, puzzled me. I said to myself: this child is really me; he is alive; he will grow up and ought to live for another sixty-six years. It is undoubtedly myself. And yet, on the other hand, here I am, having lived seventy-two years of terrestrial life. I, who now think and see these things, am still myself—and this child is also me. Am I then two beings, one there below on Earth and the other here in space: two complete persons, and yet quite distinct? Any observer, placed where I am, could see this child in the garden, as I see him, and at the same time see me here. I must be two—it is incontestable. My soul is in this child; it is here also. It is the same soul, my own soul; how can it animate two beings? What a strange thing! I cannot say that I delude myself, or that what I see is an optical illusion, because according to nature and the laws of science, I see at one and the same time a child and an old man: one there and one here; one innocent and joyous, the other pensive and agitated.

In truth, it is strange!

But true. Search through all creation and you will not find a paradox to match it.

Should I proceed with my story now? I watched myself grow up in the great city of Paris. I saw myself enter college in 1804 and do my first military service when the first consul was crowned emperor. One day, as I passed by the Carousel, I caught a glimpse of the authoritative and thoughtful face of Napoleon. I could not remember ever having seen him in my life, and it was interesting to see him pass thus across my field of view.

In 1810 I saw myself promoted to the Polytechnic. There I was talking about the course of study with François Arago,[17] my best friend. He was already on the staff of the institute, having replaced Monge at the school when the emperor objected to Binet on the grounds of his Jesuitism.[18] I saw myself, in like manner, all through the brilliant years of my youth, always planning expeditions for scientific exploration in the company of Arago and Humboldt[19]—travels that only the latter decided to undertake. Then I saw myself during the Hundred Days,[20] hurrying through the little wood of the old Luxembourg, then the Rue de l'Est and the avenue of the gardens in the Rue St. Jacques, to meet my beloved under the lilac trees.

All of our joyous private meetings and shared confidences, all the silences of our souls and the heady transports of our evening conversations, were presented to my astonished sight, no longer veiled by distance but before my very eyes.

I was present again at the battle against the Allies on the Hill of Montmartre, and saw their descent into the capital, and the fall of the statue in the Place Vendôme, when it was dragged through the streets with cries of joy. I saw the camp of the English and the Prussians in the Champs-Élysées, the destruction of the Louvre, the journey to Ghent, the entry of Louis XVIII. The flag of the island of Elba floated before my eyes, and later I sought out the far Atlantic isle where the eagle, his wings broken, was chained. The rotation of the earth soon brought before my eyes the emperor on St. Helena, lost in sad contemplation at the foot of a sycamore tree.[21]

The events of the passing years were revealed to me thus as I followed my own career: my marriage, my various enterprises, my acquaintances, my travels, my studies, and so on. At the same time, I witnessed the development of contemporary history. The restoration of Louis XVIII was followed by the brief reign of Charles X. I saw the barricades of the July Days of 1830,[22] and I saw the Column of the Bastille rise up not far from the throne of the Duc d'Orléans.

Passing rapidly over eighteen years, I perceived myself at the Luxembourg at the time when that magnificent avenue was opened: that avenue I loved so much, which is under the threat of a recent decree. I saw Arago again, this time at the Observatory, and I beheld the crowd outside the door of the new amphitheater. I recognized the Sorbonne of Cousin and Guizot.[23] Then I shuddered as I saw my mother's funeral pass. She was a stern woman, and perhaps a little too severe in her judgments, but I loved her dearly, as you know. The brief and singular Revolution of 1848 surprised me as much as it did when I first witnessed it. On the Place de la Bourse I saw Lamorcière, who was buried last year, and in the Champs-Élysées, Cavaignac, who has been dead for five or six years.[24] The second of December found me an observer in my solitary tower, and from there I witnessed many striking events that were unknown to me.

Did these events pass rapidly before you?

I had no perception of time, but the entire retrospective panorama appeared to me in a succession of scenes in less than a day, perhaps in a few hours.

Then I do not understand you at all! Forgive your old friend this interruption, which is a little rude. As I understood it, you saw the real events of your life, not merely images of them, but in view of the time necessary for the passage of light, these events appeared to you after they had happened. If, then, seventy-two terrestrial years had passed before your eyes, they should have taken seventy-two years to appear to you, not a few hours. If the year 1793 appeared to you only in 1864, the year 1864, in consequence, should not have appeared to you until 1936.

You have grounds for your new objection, and this proves to me that you have understood the theoretical considerations perfectly. I am grateful that you have raised the point, for I need to explain to you why it was not necessary to take seventy-two years to review my life—and how, in the grip of a force of which I had no consciousness, I concluded that review in less than a day.

Continuing to follow the course of my existence, I reached its later years, rendered memorable by the striking changes that had overtaken Paris. I saw our old friends, including you; my daughter and her charming children; my family and circle of acquaintances; and, last of all, I saw myself lying dead upon my bed, and was present at the final scene.

I had returned to the earth.

Drawn by the contemplation that absorbed my soul, I had quickly forgotten the mountain, the old men, and Capella. All of that had faded from my mind like a dream. I did not realize it right away, because the strange vision had captivated my attention. I cannot describe to you either the law or the power that allows souls to be transported with such rapidity from one place to another, but the truth of the matter is that I had returned to the earth, in less than a day, and had entered my room at the very moment of my burial.

Throughout this return voyage I had traveled faster than the rays of light, so the various phases of my life on Earth had unrolled themselves to my sight in successive stages as they occurred. When

I reached half way, I saw the rays of light arriving only thirty-six years behind time, showing me the earth not as it appeared seventy-two years ago, but thirty-six. When I had traveled three-quarters of the way I saw things as they had been eighteen years ago; halfway through that final quarter, as they were nine years previously, with the result that all the events of my life were condensed into less than a single day, because of the rapid rate at which my soul had traveled, which far surpassed the velocity of the rays of light.

That arrangement must have been a very strange experience!

Have any other objections arisen in your mind as you listened to me?

That was the most recent one — or, at least, the one that forced itself upon me so strongly as to obliterate all others.

I ought to point out that there is another — an astronomical one — that I shall hasten to dispel, for fear it might arise and cloud your mind. It concerns the earth's movement, not only in the course of its diurnal rotation, which would be sufficient in itself to prevent my seeing the phenomena in succession, but also its movement around the sun, which would have been greatly accelerated by the rapidity of my return to the earth, when seventy-two years passed before me in less than a day. It was surprising that I did not notice this at the time, but as I had only seen a comparatively small number of landscapes, panoramas, and facts, it is probable that while returning to our planet I had only fleeting glances, of a few seconds' duration, of each successive point of interest. Whatever the explanation may be, though, I can but give evidence that I have been witness to the rapid succession of events, throughout the century and my own life.

That difficulty had not escaped me; I had considered the matter and had come to the conclusion that you had moved around in space, in the same way that a balloon is spun around by the rotation of the globe. It is true that the inconceivable speed with which you would be whirled through space would be likely to make you dizzy; nevertheless, after hearing of your experience, the hypothesis forces itself upon me that spirits rush through space with the lightness and velocity of thought. Considering the intensity of your gaze as you approached certain parts of the earth, may it not be possible to infer that this very eagerness to see certain localities might be the reason for your being drawn to them — and, as it were, fixed above their point of vision?

As to this matter, I can affirm nothing because I know nothing, but I do not think that is the explanation. I did not see all the events of my life but only a few of the principal ones — which, successively unfolding, passed in review before me on the same visual ray. A magnetic attraction drew me imperiously, as if with a chain, to the earth — or, if you prefer, a force similar to that mysterious attraction of the stars, by reason of which stars of a lesser degree would inevitably fall upon those of the first magnitude were they not retained in their orbits by centrifugal force.

Having considered the effect of the concentration of thought upon a single point, and the ensuing attraction toward that point, I wonder whether the mainspring of the mechanism of dreams lies therein.

You are right, my friend. I can confirm this speculation, because I have made a special study of dreams, which extended over many years. When the soul, freed from the attentions, preoccupations, and encumbrance of the body, has a vision of an object that charms it, and toward which it is irresistibly drawn, everything disappears save for the object itself. That alone remains and becomes the center of a world of creations; the contemplative soul seizes and possesses it entirely, without reservation, and the entire universe is effaced from memory in order that its domination may become absolute. While I was drawn earthward I saw but one object, around which were grouped the ideas, the images, and the associations to which it had given birth.

Your rapid flight to Capella and your equally rapid return to Earth were governed by this psychological law, and you acted more freely than in a dream because your soul was not impeded by the machinery of your organism. In our former conversations you have often spoken about the force of the will. It must have been that force that enabled you to return and see yourself upon your deathbed before your mortal remains had been committed to the ground.

I did return, and I blessed my family for the sincerity of their grief. I soothed their grief and poured balm upon their wounded hearts, and I inspired my children with the belief that the body lying there was not my real self but merely the shell from which my soul had risen into an infinite celestial sphere far beyond their earthly ken.

I witnessed my own funeral procession. I took note of those who had called themselves my friends and who nevertheless, for some trifling reason, had begged to be excused from following my remains to their last resting place. I listened to the various comments of those following my bier, and although we are free in this region of peace from that thirst for praise that attaches to most of us while we are on Earth, I felt gratified nevertheless to know that I had left pleasant memories behind me.

When the stone of the vault, which separates the dead from the living, was rolled away, I bid a last farewell to my poor sleeping body, and as the sun set in its bed of purple and gold, I went out into the air until night had fallen, rapt in admiration of the beautiful scenes that unfolded in the heavens. The aurora borealis displayed itself above the North Pole in bands of glistening silver; shooting stars cascaded from Cassiopeia; and the full moon rose slowly in the east like a brand new world emerging from the waves. I saw scintillant Capella looking at me with a pure and bright expression, and I could distinguish the crowns surrounding it, like princes of a celestial divinity.

Then I forgot the earth, the moon, the planetary system, the sun, the comets, in favor of one intense and overpowering attraction toward a brilliantly shining star, and I felt myself carried toward it instinctively, far more rapidly than a lightning flash. After an interval, whose duration I cannot guess, I arrived upon the same ring and upon the same mountain from which I had first kept watch when I saw the old men occupied in following the history of the earth, seventy-one years and eight months ago. They were still absorbed in the contemplation of events happening in the city of Lyons on the 23rd of January 1793.

Capella had a mysterious attraction to me, I will readily avow, for—marvelous as it may seem—there are within creation certain invisible ties that do not break like mortal ties; there are means by which souls can communicate with one another in spite of the distance that separates them. On the evening of the second day, as the emerald moon enshrined itself in the third ring of gold—such is the sidereal measurement of time there—I found myself walking in a lonely avenue enameled with sweetly perfumed flowers. Imagine my delight when, while sauntering along as if in a dream, I saw my beautiful and beloved Sylvia coming toward me. She died while in her prime, and, in spite of an indefinable change, I recognized her features. Their expression had but deepened and become more spiritual, in happy accordance with her good and pure life.

I shall not pause to describe the joy of our meeting; this is not the time—perchance, someday, we may have the opportunity of discussing the different manifestations of affection in this world and the one beyond the grave. At present, I shall only say that we sought our native land on Earth, where we had passed so many happy and peaceful days together. We delighted in turning our gaze toward that luminous point, which our present constitution enabled us to perceive as a world: the one upon which we had lived in earthly form. We loved to marry the memory of the past to the reality of the present, and we sought to recall and review, in all the freshness of our new ecstatic sensations, the scenes of our youth. It was in this way that we revisited the happy years of our earthly love: the pavilion of the convent, the flower garden, the promenades in the delightful environs of Paris, and the solitary rambles that we took together, loving and beloved. To retrace these years we had only to travel together into space in the direction of the earth, where these light-borne scenes were photographed.

Now, my friend, by revealing these remarkable observations, I have fulfilled my promise to you. Look! Rosy dawn is breaking, and the morning star is already fading. I must return to the heavens. . . .

Just one more question, Lumen, before we close our conversation. If earthly scenes can be transmitted successively into space, can the present be kept perpetually before the eyes of distant spectators, limited only by the power of their spiritual sight?

Yes, my friend. Let us, for example, place our first observer on the moon. He would perceive terrestrial events a second and a quarter after they had happened. Let us place a second observer at four times the distance; he would be cognizant of them after five seconds. Double the distance, and a third would see them ten seconds after they had taken place. Again double the distance, and a fourth observer would have to wait twenty seconds before he could witness them; and so on, with ever-increasing delay, until at the sun's distance eight minutes and thirteen seconds must elapse before they could become visible.

Upon certain planets, as we have seen, hours must intervene between the action and the sight of it; still further off, days, months, and even years must elapse. On Alpha Centauri, earthly events are not visible until three years and six months after they have occurred.[25] There are stars so distant that light reaches them only after many centuries or thousands of years. Indeed, there are nebulae to which light takes millions of years to travel.

So it only requires a sufficiently piercing power of sight to witness historical and geological events that have long since passed. Could not one so gifted, in that case, see the Deluge, the Garden of Eden, Adam and . . .

I have told you, my old friend, that the rising of the sun in this hemisphere puts all spirits to flight, so I must go. Another conversation may be granted to us at some other time, when we can talk about matters that I have not been able to discuss today, opening new and further horizons. The stars are calling me and have already disappeared. Farewell, Seeker! Farewell!

THE SECOND CONVERSATION

The Reversal of Time

I

The revelations that were interrupted by the break of day, O Lumen, have left me hungry to hear more of this wonderful mystery. As a child to whom one shows a delicious fruit is eager to bite into it, then begs for more once he has tasted it, so my curiosity longs to renew its enjoyment of these paradoxes of nature. May I venture to ask a few questions about the matter, which have been suggested by friends to whom I have communicated the substance of your revelations, before inviting you to continue the story of your impressions of the regions beyond the earth?

I cannot agree to such an inquisition, my friend. However well disposed you might be to accept my communications, I believe that you have not fully understood my discourse and that all its details are not equally self-evident to you. My recital has been called "mystical" by those who have not quite understood that it is neither a romance nor a fantasy, but rather a scientific truth: a physical fact both demonstrable and demonstrated, as indisputable and as calculable as the fall of a meteorite or the motion of a cannonball.

The reason that you and your friends cannot adequately understand the reality of these facts is that they took place beyond this earth, in regions foreign to the scope of your impressions and inaccessible to your terrestrial senses. It is natural that you do not comprehend them—pardon my frankness, but in the spirit world one has to be frank; here, even thoughts are visible. You can comprehend only those things that you perceive, and as you persist in regarding your ideas of time and space as absolute, although they are only relative, you have closed your eyes to truths that are beyond the scope and imperceptible to the faculties of your terrestrial organism. So, my friend, I can do no more than continue the story of my extraterrestrial observations.

Never think, Lumen, that it is mere curiosity that urges me to draw you back from the bosom of the invisible world, where advanced souls partake of indescribable joys. I have a better understanding than you suppose of the magnitude of the problem and am inspired by studious avidity to delve further into it, in search of news even more dramatic and challenging than that you have already given me. On reflection, I have arrived at the conclusion that what we know is nothing and that of which we are ignorant is everything; I therefore welcome everything you tell me. I beg you to let me share your discoveries.

To tell the truth, my friend, you are either too ready to listen or not ready enough. In the latter case, you will not understand me; in the former, you will be too credulous and will not appreciate its true worth. However, I shall continue . . .

Beloved comrade of my earthly life . . .

The next matters that I shall relate to you are even more extraordinary than any that preceded them.

I am like Tantalus in the middle of his lake, or the spirits in the twenty-fourth canto of the Purgatorio,[1] *like the Hesperides holding out their hands for the fragrant fruit, like desirous Eve . . .*

Some time after my departure from the earth, while the eyes of my soul were still directed mournfully toward my native world, I found that on attentive examination I could perceive a triangular piece of darkly colored land.[2] It lay to the north of the Black Sea, on whose shores, toward the west, I could see a grievous number of my compatriots engaged in killing one another. I recalled to mind that relic of barbarism formerly called glorious, war, with which you are still beset and burdened. I remembered that in this corner of the

Crimea 800,000 men had fallen, in ignorance of the cause of their mutual massacre. Clouds were obscuring Europe.

At this time I was not on Capella but in empty space between that star and the earth, about half as far away from the sun as Vega.[3] Having left the earth some time before, I turned toward a group of stars that, seen from your planet, are to the left of Capella. In the meantime, my thoughts returned from time to time to the earth. Soon after making the aforementioned observations, my eyes being fixed on Paris, I was surprised to see it prey to an insurrection of the people.

Examining the scene more attentively, I discerned barricades on the boulevards near the Hôtel de Ville and along the streets, and the citizens firing at one another. The first idea that occurred to me was that a new revolution was taking place before my eyes and that Napoleon III was dethroned, but the occult sympathy of souls drew my sight to a barricade in the Faubourg St. Antoine, on which I saw lying prostrate the archbishop Denis August Affre,[4] with whom I had been slightly acquainted. His sightless eyes were turned toward the heavens, where I was, but he saw nothing. In his hand he held a green branch. I was, therefore, witnessing the events of 1848—the 25th of June, to be specific.

A few minutes, or perhaps a few hours, passed, during which my imagination and my reason took turns to seek an explanation of the curious experience of seeing 1848 after 1854!

When my sight was again attracted to the earth, I noticed that tricolor flags were being distributed in the main square of the city of Lyons. Attempting to distinguish the official who was making the distribution, I recognized the uniforms and remembered that after the accession of Louis Philippe, the young Duc d'Orléans had been sent to quell disturbances in the capital of the French manufacturing industry. It followed, therefore, that after 1854 and 1848 I now had events of 1831 before my eyes.

Presently, my glance turned to Paris on a public holiday. The king—a coarse-looking man with a rubicund face—was racing along in a magnificent chariot, just crossing the Pont Neuf. The weather was splendid. Lovely ladies posed like a bouquet of lilies on the white parapet of the bridge and brightly colored creatures could be seen floating above the city. I was evidently watching the entry of the Bourbons into Paris.[5] I should not have understood this latest strange sight had I not recollected that a number of balloons in the form of animals had been sent aloft on that occasion. From my exalted altitude they appeared to be wriggling across the roofs of the houses.

To see past events again was understandable enough, according to the physics of light, but to see things contrary to their actual sequence in time was too fantastic, and puzzled me more than I can say. Nevertheless, as I had these things before my eyes, I could not deny the fact, and I immediately cast about for some hypothesis to account for the singular phenomenon.

At first I supposed that it really was the earth that I saw, and that by a fiat of fate, the secret of which is known only to God, the history of France repeats itself and passes through the same phases over and over again: that events proceed in their course to a certain maximum, where they shine gloriously for a time and are then followed by a reaction to the original state of things, by virtue of an oscillation in human affairs like the variations is a magnetic needle or like the movements of the stars.[6] Perhaps, then, the personages whom I took for the Duc d'Orléans and Louis XVIII were other princes, who were repeating exactly what the former had done. This hypothesis appeared to be so very extraordinary, however, that I paused to consider a more plausible alternative.

Admitting the fact of the number of stars, with planets moving around them, is it not probable that a world exactly like the earth exists somewhere in the universe of space? The calculation of probabilities supplies an answer to this question. The greater the number of worlds, the greater will be the probability that the forces of nature have given birth to an organization like that of the earth. Now the real number of worlds surpasses all practicable or imaginable human calculation. If we could understand what "infinite" means, we might venture to say that the number is infinite. I concluded, therefore, that there is a very high probability in favor of the existence of many worlds exactly like the earth, on the surface of which the same history is accomplished and the same sequence of historical events takes place: worlds that are inhabited by identical species of vegetables and animals, and the same humanity, and where, I do not doubt, people and families like our own exist.[7]

In the second place, I asked myself whether another world analogous to the earth might not also be symmetrical to it. Then I entered in the geometry of the problem, and the metaphysical theory of images.[8] I arrived at the conclusion that it was possible for the world in question to be like the earth but in an inverse form. When you look at yourself in a mirror, you observe that the ring on your right hand has been transferred to the ring finger of your left, modifying its symbolic significance; if you wink your right eye, your reflection winks the left; when you reach out your right arm, your image reaches out the left. Is it impossible that in the infinity of the stars, a world exists that is exactly the converse of the terrestrial world? Surely, within an infinity of worlds, it is the nonexistence of such a world—of millions of them, even—that would be the real impossibility. Nature, of necessity, repeats herself, but still plays the same game of creation with all existing forms. I thought, therefore, that the world on which I saw these things was not the earth but a similar globe whose history was the exact opposite of yours.[9]

I have had that same idea myself. But was it not easy for you to test the hypothesis by examining its astronomical position to ascertain whether the earth or some other world was before your eyes?

That is precisely what I did, at once. The examination confirmed my opinion. The world on which I had just witnessed four events analogous to four terrestrial events but in reverse order did not appear to me to occupy its original position. The little constellation of the Altar no longer existed, and there was an irregular polygon of unknown stars in that part of the heavens where the earth appeared to be during the first episode of my experiences. I was thus convinced that it was not our earth that was before my eyes. I could no longer feel any doubt about it, and was satisfied that I now had for my field of exploration a world that was even more curious for the fact that it was not the earth—and that its history seemed to represent, in an inverse order, the scenes of our world's history.

Some events, it is true, did not appear to have corresponding ones on the earth, but in general the coincidence was very remarkable. I was all the more struck by this because the contempt I feel for the instigators of war had led me to hope that a folly so absurd and so infamous might not have existed in other worlds. On the contrary, however: the greater number of the events I witnessed were conflicts or preparations for conflict.

After a battle that appeared to me very much to resemble that of Waterloo I saw the battle of the Pyramids.[10] An image of Napoleon as emperor had become first consul, and I saw the Revolution succeed the Consulate. Some time after that, I observed the square in front of the Château of Versailles full of mourning coaches, and I recognized the botanist Jean-Jacques Rousseau[11] slowly walking along an open pathway from Ville d'Avray—philosophizing at that very moment, no doubt, upon the death of Louis XV. I was particularly struck by the festival galas at the beginning of Louis XV's reign—worthy successors of those of the Regency—during which the treasures of France glistened in precious stones on the fingers of a handful of adored courtesans. I saw Voltaire with his white cotton cap in his park at Ferney and, later on, Bossuet walking on the little terrace of his episcopal palace at Meaux.[12] That was not far from the little hill through which the railway is now cut, but I could not see the least trace of the railway line.

In this same succession of events I saw the highways covered with diligences[13] and large sailing ships on the seas. Steam engines, and all the factories that are nowadays moved by them, had disappeared. The telegraph did not exist, nor did any other application of electricity. Balloons, which I had seen more than once in my field of observation, were lost to sight; the last I saw was the shapeless globe sent up by the brothers Montgolfier at Annonay in the presence of the Estates-General.[14] The face of the earth was utterly changed. Paris, Lyons, Marseilles, Le Havre, and most especially Versailles, were unrecognizable; the first four had lost their immense activity; the last had gained an incomparable magnificence.[15]

I had formed a very imperfect idea of the splendor of the royal fêtes at Versailles. It was satisfying actually to be present at them, and it was not without interest that I recognized Louis XIV himself on the splendid western terrace, surrounded by a thousand nobles whose breasts were covered by decorations. It was evening; the last rays of gleaming sunshine were reflected from the royal facade, while gallant couples gravely descended the steps of the marble staircase and disappeared presently along the silent, shady avenues.

The preference of my sight was fixed on France—or at least toward that region of this unknown world that represented France to me—for absence makes the heart grow fonder, and when one is far from home one thinks of it all the more and returns with new interest to every such thought. Do not think that souls liberated from the body are scornful, indifferent, or devoid of memory—no, we are careful to preserve the faculty of remembrance; our hearts are not wholly absorbed in the life of the spirit. So it was, as you can imagine, with an instinctive feeling of delight that I saw the history of France unfolded again before me as if its phases were being accomplished in reverse order.

After the people had amalgamated into one nation, I saw the rule of a single sovereign established. After that came princely feudalism. Mazarin, Richelieu, Louis XIII, and Henry IV appeared to me at Saint-Germain.[16] The Bourbons and the Guises resumed their skirmishes for me.[17] I thought I could distinguish the night of St. Bartholomew.[18] I saw some particular events in the history of the provinces—for instance, one scene of the sorcery at Chaumont, which I had the opportunity to observe in front of the Church of St. Jean, and the massacre of the Protestants at Vassy.[19] The human comedy is too often a tragedy!

Suddenly I beheld in space the magnificent comet of 1577, in the form of a saber.[20] In grandiose array in the middle of a brilliantly decorated plain I recognized Francis I and Charles V of Spain saluting one another.[21] I perceived Louis XI on a terrace of the Bastille, attended by his two gloomy companions.[22] Later on, my gaze turned to a square in Rouen, where I observed flames and smoke, and in their midst I discerned the form of the Maid of Orleans.[23]

Convinced as I was that the world I was looking at was the exact counterpart of the earth, I divined beforehand the events that I was about to see. Thus, after having seen St. Louis dying before Tunis, I was present at the Eighth Crusade, and then at the Third, where I recognized Frederick Barbarossa by his beard.[24] Then, at the First Crusade, when Peter the Hermit and and Godfrey reminded me of Tasso, I was not at all surprised.[25]

I then witnessed, in succession, Hugh Capet leading a procession arrayed in his official cape, the Council of Tauriacum deciding that God's judgment would be pronounced at the battle of Fontanet, Charles the Bald ordering the massacre of a hundred thousand men and all the Merovingian nobility, Charlemagne crowned in Rome and his war against the Saxons and Lombards, Charles Martel hammering away at the Saracens, King Dagobert founding the Abbey of St. Denis—just as I had seen Alexander III laying the first stone of Notre Dame—Brunhilde dragged along the pavement by a horse, the Visigoths, the Vandals, the Ostrogoths, Clovis the Merovingian appearing in the land of the Salian Franks—in a word, the history of France from its very beginning, unrolling before me in an order inverse to the succession of events.[26]

This was what actually happened. Many historical questions that were very important but had hitherto been obscure to me were clarified. I ascertained, among other things, that the French were the original possessors of the right bank of the Rhine and that the Germans have no right to claim that river, still less to dispute the possession of the left bank.[27]

I can assure you that I took an immense interest in witnessing events of which I had previously had but the vaguest idea, derived from the oft-deceptive echoes of history, and in visiting landscapes that are now totally transformed. The vast and brilliant capital of modern civilization became old before me, shrinking to the size of an ordinary town, but was at the same time fortified with crenellated towers. I admired, by turns, the beautiful city of the fifteenth century, with its curious architectural styles, the celebrated tower of Nesle and the extensive Abbey of Saint-Germain-des-Prés.[28] In the gloomy court of the alchemist Nicolas Flamel, I recognized the place where the tower of St. Jacques now stands.[29] The round and pointed roofs had the singular effect of appearing to be mushrooms on the banks of a river. Then this feudal aspect disappeared, giving place to a solitary castle in the Seine valley surrounded by cottages. Finally, there was nothing but a fertile plain, where one could distinguish nothing but the huts of a few savages. Paris no longer existed, and the silent waters of the Seine flowed between fields of grass and willow trees.[30]

At the same time, I remarked that the seat of civilization was changed, and was now in the south. I will confess to you, my friend, that I never felt a greater delight than at the moment when I was permitted to see the Rome of the Caesars in all its splendor. It was the day of a triumph, and no doubt under the rule of the Syrian princes—for in the midst of magnificent surroundings, gorgeous chariots, the purple oriflammes of the Senate and of elegant women, and theater performers, I distinguished the emperor reclining luxuriously in a golden car, clothed in delicately colored silk covered with precious stones and gold and silver ornaments, which glittered in the golden sunlight. This could only have been Heliogabalus, the priest of the sun.[31] The Colosseum, the temple of Antoninus, the triumphal arches, and Trajan's column were standing; Rome was in all its ancient beauty and grandeur, that last majestic phase, which was no more than scenery in a theater to those crowned buffoons.

A little later I was present at the eruption of Vesuvius that overwhelmed Herculaneum and Pompeii. I saw Rome in flames, just for a moment, and although I was not able to distinguish Nero on his terrace I have no doubt that I beheld the conflagration of 64 A.D. and the signal for the persecution of the Christians.

A few hours later, my attention still being occupied in examining the extensive gardens by the Tiber, I had just seen the emperor near a terraced rose garden when, in consequence of the rotation of the earth on its axis, Judea was presented to my anxious gaze, which immediately distinguished Jerusalem and the mount of Golgotha.

Jesus was climbing the hill, accompanied by a few women, escorted by a troop of soldiers and followed by the Jewish populace. That spectacle is one that I shall never forget. It assumed a totally different aspect to me than it did to those who were living at the time and who took part in it, for the glorious future of the Christian Church — and its past too — was deployed for me as the crown of the Divine sacrifice. . . . I cannot dwell on it; you will understand what diverse emotions that supreme sight stirred in my soul . . .

A little later, returning to Rome, I recognized Julius Caesar prostrate in death, with Antony beside him, holding what seemed to me to be a scroll of papyrus in his left hand. The conspirators were hastening down to the Tiber's banks. With a perfectly natural curiosity I retraced the life of Julius Caesar and found him with Vercingetorix in the heart of Gaul — and I may state that none of the suppositions regarding the situation of Alesia are correct.[32] In fact, the fortress was situated on . . .

Master, pardon me for interrupting you, but I must take the opportunity to ask you a particular question regarding the dictator. Since you have seen Julius Caesar, pray tell me whether his appearance resembled that rendered by the Emperor Napoleon III, who actually reigned in Gaul, in his great work on the life of that famous general?

I should be delighted to enlighten you on this matter, my old friend, if it were possible for me to do so — but if you reflect for a moment, you will see that the laws of perspective forbid it.

Of perspective? You mean politics . . .

No, perspective, although these two matters strongly resemble one another — for in seeing great men from the height of heaven I do not see them as they appear to the vulgar. From the heavens we see men from above, not face to face — which is to say, in geometric terms, that when they are standing up, we have only a horizontal projection of them. You may remember that you once remarked to me, as we passed over the Vendôme Column in a balloon, that Napoleon seen from that height was not above the level of other men.[33] It was exactly the same with Caesar. In the other world, material measures disappear; only intellectual measures remain.

To continue, however, I retraced history from Julius Caesar to the

Consuls, and then to the kings of Latium in order to witness the rape of the Sabine women—which I was actually pleased to observe, as an example of ancient manners.[34] History has embellished many things, and I discovered that most events as represented to us are quite different from the actual facts. I saw King Candaules in Lydia, in the bathroom scene that you will remember,[35] then the invasion of Egypt by the Ethiopians, the oligarchical republic of Corinth, the eighth Olympiad in Greece, and Isaiah the prophet in Judea. I saw the building of the pyramids by troops of obedient slaves under chiefs mounted on dromedaries.

The great dynasties of Bactria and India appeared before me, and China showed the marvelous skill in the arts that she possessed even before the birth of the Western World. I had an opportunity to search for the Atlantis of Plato and saw that the opinions of Bailly on that continent are not without foundation.[36] In Gaul I could now distinguish nothing but vast forests and swamps; even the Druids had disappeared, and the savage inhabitants strongly resembled those we now find in Oceania. It was truly the Stone Age, as unearthed for us by modern archaeologists.

Even further on, I saw that the number of men diminished by degrees, and the domination of nature seemed to belong to a race of the great apes, to the cave bears, to lions, hyenas, and the rhinoceros. The time finally came when it was impossible to distinguish a single human being on the surface of the earth. Not the least vestige of that race could be seen: everything was gone. Earthquakes, volcanoes, deluges prevailed over the surface of the planet, and the presence of human life in the midst of such chaos was no longer possible.

I will confess, dear Lumen, that I have waited impatiently for the moment when you would arrive at the Garden of Eden, in order to learn how the creation of the human race on the earth was presented to you. I am surprised that you do not seem to have thought of making this important observation.

I relate to you only the things that I saw, my curious friend, and I am wary of substituting the dreams of my imagination for the evidence of my sight. I did not perceive the least trace of that Eden so poetically depicted in the primitive theogonies. After all, it would have been extraordinary if the resemblance between the world that I had before my eyes and the earth went as far as that — all the more so if the raison d'être of that terrestrial paradise really was to serve as the cradle of humanity — although I do not see why paradise should not have been, by the same token, the end-state of human society.

On the contrary: I think it would be more appropriate to suppose it to be at the end rather than the beginning, as the result of and recompense for rather than the misunderstood prelude to a life of suffering — but since you have not seen it, I shall not press the question.[37]

Finally, in concluding my observations of this singular world whose history was exactly the inverse of yours, I saw monstrous animals in combat on the shores of vast oceans. There were enormous serpents armed with formidable paws; crocodiles that flew in the air, sustained by wings whose span was greater than the length of their bodies; misshapen fishes with jaws wide enough to swallow an ox; birds of prey locked in terrible battles on desert islands. There were whole continents covered with forests, trees with enormous leaves entangled one with another: a vegetation both somber and severe, for the vegetable kingdom was devoid of both flowers and fruit. The mountains vomited forth clouds of flame and vapor; the rivers fell in cataracts; the ground opened in immense chasms in which hills, woods, streams, trees, and animals were engulfed.

Before long, however, it became impossible for me to see the surface of the globe. A universal sea appeared to cover it, and the vegetable kingdom, like the animal kingdom, was slowly effaced, giving place to a monotonous verdure interspersed with lightning and whitish smoke. Henceforth, it was a dying world. I was present at the last palpitations of its heart, intermittently revealed in the gloom by flashes of flame.

It seemed to me then that it rained everywhere over the whole surface, for the sun threw light on nothing but clouds and torrents of rain. The hemisphere opposite to the sun appeared less somber than before, and one could perceive a dull light gleaming through the tempests. This light increased in intensity and spread over the entire sphere. Great crevasses became red, like iron in the furnace — and just as iron in a hot furnace becomes bright red, then orange, then yellow, then in succession white and incandescent, so the world passed through all the progressive phases of heat. Its volume increased; its movements of rotation became slower.

The mysterious globe seemed like an immense sphere of molten metal enveloped in metallic vapors. Under the incessant action of this interior furnace and the elemental combats and combinations of this strange chemistry, it acquired enormous proportions, and the sphere of fire became a sphere of smoke. It went on developing without cessation and lost its personality. The sun, which at first had shed light on it, no longer surpassed it in brightness and increased so much in circumference itself that it became evident to me that the vaporous planet would soon lose its independent existence and be absorbed in the enlarged atmosphere of the sun.

It is a rare experience to witness the end of a world—and so, in my enthusiasm, I could not prevent myself crying out with a kind of vanity: "Behold the end of the world, O God! This, then, is the fate in store for all the inhabited worlds!"

"It is not the end," replied a voice within the hearing of my soul. "It is the beginning."

"How can it be the beginning?" I thought, immediately.

"The beginning of the earth itself," replied the same voice. "Thou hast seen the whole history of the earth over again, while withdrawing from it at a velocity greater than that of light."

This declaration did not surprise me as much as the first episode of my ultraterrestrial life because, accustomed as I was to the astonishing effects of the physics of light, I was now prepared for anything. I already had my doubts about the matter, because of certain details that I have withheld from you in order to avoid breaking the thread of my narrative, but that were nevertheless incomparably more extraordinary than the general succession of events.

But if it really was the earth, how did it come about that the astronomical calculations you made in order to recognize it in the constellation of the Altar indicated—as you have pointed out—that the world you were examining was not the earth?

That was because the constellation itself had changed in consequence of my voyage in space. The third magnitude stars Alpha, Gamma and Zeta and the fourth magnitude stars Beta, Delta, and Theta constitute that figure as seen from Earth, but my displacement toward the nebulous had reduced those stars to imperceptible points. It had placed other brilliant stars there, which were doubtless Alpha and Beta Aurigae, and Theta, Iota, and Eta—perhaps even Epsilon—of the same constellation: stars diametrically opposite to the aforementioned when seen from Earth but necessarily interposed there when I had passed them by. The celestial perspective had already changed, and it had become impossible, thus, to determine the position of our sun.

I had not thought of the inevitable change of perspective that would occur beyond Capella. So it really was the earth that you saw, and its history had therefore unraveled before you in reverse order. You saw ancient events taking place after modern events. By what new process had light thus enabled you to ascend the stream of time?

You have also informed me, Lumen, that you observed some curious particulars relating to the earth itself. I should like to ask you some questions about these matters. I shall listen with interest to the extraordinary account that should complete this tale, confident that my curiosity will be fully rewarded.

II

The first circumstance is connected with the battle of Waterloo.

No one remembers that catastrophe better than I. I received a musket ball in my shoulder there, near Mont Saint-Jean, and a saber cut on my right hand from one of Blücher's blackguards.[38]

Well, my old comrade, when taking part in this battle for a second time I found it quite different from what it had been in the past, as you may judge from what I shall relate to you.

When I had recognized the field of Waterloo, to the south of Brussels, I first distinguished a considerable number of dead bodies lying indiscriminately on the ground. Far away, through the mist, I perceived Napoleon walking backward, holding his horse by the bridle. The officers who accompanied him were also marching backward.

The cannon began to boom, and I saw the lurid gleam of their flashes from time to time. When my sight was sufficiently habituated to the scene, I perceived some soldiers coming to life out of the eternal light and standing up with an abrupt effort. Group by group, a considerable number of them were thus resuscitated. The dead horses revived with the dead cavalrymen, and the latter remounted.

As soon as two or three thousand men had returned to life, I saw them form unconsciously into lines of battle. The two armies took their positions facing one another and began to fight desperately, with a fury that one might have taken for hopelessness. As the combat intensified, on both sides the soldiers came to life more rapidly. French, English, Prussians, Germans, Hanoverians, Belgians, gray coats, blue uniforms, red, white, and green tunics: all rose from the field of the dead and fought. In the center of the French army I saw the emperor surrounded by a squared-up battalion—the Imperial Guard resuscitated!

Immense battalions issued forth from the two camps and engaged in a fierce onslaught; squadrons advanced from the left and the right; the pale manes of the white horses floated upon the wind. I remembered a strange picture by Raffet, and a spectral epigram by the German poet Sedlitz:[39]

The drum strangely sounds
Its powerful recall.
Reawakening in their graves,
The old soldiers perish.

And another:

It is the great parade,
Which at the midnight hour
In the Elysian fields
Dead Caesar inspects.[40]

It was really Waterloo, but a Waterloo of the afterlife, for the combatants were being raised from the dead. In this singular mirage, furthermore, they marched backward one against the other. Such a battle has a magical effect, and it impressed me all the more forcefully because I had seen the event before. It was strangely transformed into its counterpart. No less singular was the fact that the longer they fought, the more the number of combatants increased; each gap made in the serried ranks by the cannon was immediately filled up by a group of the resuscitated dead.

When the belligerents had spent the whole day tearing one another to pieces with cannon, grapeshot, and bullets, bayonets, sabres, and swords — when the great battle was over — not a single person had been killed. No one was even wounded. Even uniforms that had been torn and disordered before were now in good condition. The men were safe and sound, and the ranks in correct formation.

The two armies slowly withdrew from one another, as if the heat of the battle and all its fury had had no other object than the restoration to life, amid the combat, of the two hundred thousand corpses that had lain on the field a few hours before.

What an exemplary and desirable battle it was! Assuredly, it was the most singular of military episodes.

The moral aspect of it far surpassed the physical when I found that this battle resulted not in the defeat of Napoleon but in placing him upon the throne. Instead of losing the battle, it was the emperor who won it; instead of a prisoner, he became a sovereign. Waterloo was an 18th Brumaire![41]

Lumen, I can hardly begin to comprehend this new effect of the physics of light. If you have discovered the explanation, I beg you to give it to me.

I have already pointed you in the right direction by telling you that I was removed from the earth at a velocity greater than that of light.

Pray tell me how such a retrogression in space enables you to see events in an order inverse to that in which they took place.

The theory is perfectly simple. Suppose you set out from the earth with a velocity exactly equal to that of light. You would always have with you the aspect that the earth assumed at the moment you set out, since you would be receding from the globe with a swiftness precisely equal to that which bore the relevant appearance into space.[42] Thus, even if you voyaged for a thousand or a hundred thousand years, this image would always accompany you, like a still photograph whose original subject has grown old with the elapsing years.

I understood this already, from our first conversation.

Well, suppose now that you remove yourself from the earth with a velocity superior to that of light. What will happen?

You will rediscover, as rapidly as you advance into space, the rays that set out before you—which is to say, the successive images that, from second to second and instant to instant, take flight into the distance. If, for example, you set out in 1867 with a velocity equal to that of light, you would retain forever the visual image of the year 1867. If you went more rapidly, you would find before you the rays that had set out in former years and that bore upon them the images of those years.

In order to illustrate this point further, pray reflect on the many luminous rays that have set out from the earth in different epochs. Let us suppose the first to be at some instant of 1 January 1867. At the rate of 300,000 kilometers per second it has, at the moment at which I am speaking to you, already passed through sufficient space to reach a certain distance which I shall designate by the letter A.

Let us now suppose that a second ray set out from the earth a hundred years before, on 1 January 1767; it is a hundred years in advance of the first and is found at a much greater distance, which I will designate by the letter B.

A third ray, which I shall in like manner suppose to have set out on 1 January 1667 is further off still, by a distance equal to that which light would travel in a hundred years; I shall call the place this third ray has reached C. Then a fourth, a fifth, a sixth, and so on, launched 1 January 1467, 1367, 1267, etc., are posted at equal distances D, E, F, and so on, penetrating further and further into the infinite.

Here, then, we have a series of images distributed along the same line, from point to point in space. Now, the consciousness that goes forth, passing the points A, B, C, D, E, and F successively, can retrace the secular history of the earth in those epochs.

Master, what is the distance between these images?

The calculation is perfectly straightforward. The interval that separates them is, of necessity, that which light travels in a hundred years. At the rate of 75,000 leagues per second, it travels 4,500,000 leagues in a minute, 270,000,00 leagues in an hour, 6,480,800,000 leagues in a day, 2,366,820,000,000 in a year, allowing for leap years.[43] Consequently, the result would be that the interval between each two points of departure, at the distance of a century apart, would be 236,682,000,000,000 leagues.

Here then, as I say, we have a series of terrestrial images imprinted in space, at corresponding distances, one after another. Let us now suppose that between each of these centennial pictures we should find annual pictures, between each of which the distance is preserved in accordance with the time that light travels in a year, which I have just given you. Then, between each of the annual pictures we have those of every day, and as each day contains the pictures of each hour, each hour the images of its minutes, and each minute of its seconds, all in succession according to their respective distances, we shall have in a ray of light—or, rather, in a flash of light—composed of a series of distinct images in juxtaposition, an aerial register of the history of the earth.

When the spirit travels through this ethereal array of images with a swiftness greater than that of light, it sees the ancient pictures backward in succession. When it arrives at the distance at which the appearance of events that set out in 1767 is to be seen, it has already retraced a hundred years of terrestrial history. When it reaches the point at which the aspect of 1667 has arrived, it has retraced two centuries. When it attains to the image of 1567 it has seen, again, three centuries—and so on in succession.

I told you at the start that I directed my course toward a group of stars situated to the left of Capella. This group proved to lie at an incomparably greater distance than that star, although from the earth it appeared to be close beside it. This apparent proximity is entirely due to perspective. In order to give you an idea of the remoteness of this far-off universe,[44] I may tell you that it is no less vast in size than the Milky Way.

One might then ask to what distance the Milky Way would need to be transported to reduce it to the apparent size of this nebula. My learned friend Arago made this calculation—of which you must be aware, as he repeated it every year in his lecture course at the Observatory, which has been published since his death. It would be necessary to suppose the Milky Way to be transported to a distance equal to 334 times its own extent. Now, as light takes 15,000 years to traverse the Milky Way from one extreme to another, it follows that it cannot take less than 334 times 15,000 years—that is to say, 38,410,000 years—in coming therefrom.[45]

I have made my own ascent from the orbit of the earth to those remote regions, and if my spiritual sight had been more perfect I should have been able to distinguish the retrogression of history not merely for ten thousand or a hundred thousand years but for millions of years.

Can the mind cross the immeasurable spaces of the heavens in this way by its own power alone?

Not by its own power alone, but by making use of the forces of nature. Attraction is one of these forces. It is transmitted with a velocity incomparably superior to that of light, and the most rigorously exact astronomical calculations are obliged to consider that transmission as almost instantaneous.[46] I must add that if I have been able to perceive events at such distances, it is not by the apprehension of physical sight that I know them, but by a process incomparably more subtle, which belongs to the psychic order. As you know, the movements of the ether that constitute light do not achieve luminosity by themselves. It is not necessary to have an eye to perceive them, however; a soul vibrating under their influence perceives them as well, often incomparably better than an organic optical apparatus. This is the basis of psychic vision. Anyway, attraction crosses space—the 148,000,000 kilometers that separate the earth from the sun, for example—instantaneously, while light occupies 493 seconds in that same journey.

What length of time did your voyage to that remote universe occupy?

Have I not told you that time does not exist outside the movements of the earth? I might have employed a year or a hour in that examination; the duration would have been exactly the same in the infinite.[47]

I have thought it over, and the physical difficulties seem to me to be enormous. Will you permit me to submit to your consideration a strange thought that has just come into my head?

It is in order to hear your reactions that I am telling you this story.

I want to ask you whether the same inversion would take place in hearing as in sight. If you can see an event backward from its real occurrence, can you also hear a discourse backward, beginning at the end? This is an impertinent and perhaps silly question, but where does the paradox stop?

The paradox is only apparent. The physics of sound is essentially different from that of light. Sound only travels at the rate of 340 meters per second, and its effects have absolutely nothing in common with those of light. Nevertheless, it is evident that if we were to advance into the air with a velocity superior to that of sound, we should hear inversely the sounds that left the lips of a speaker. If, for example, someone were to recite an alexandrine,[48] an auditor moving with the aforesaid supersonic velocity, starting at the moment when he heard the last foot of the line, would hear successively the other eleven feet that had previously been uttered, and would thus hear the alexandrine backward.

As to the theory itself, it suggests a curious reflection, that nature might not have caused sound to travel at the rate of 340 meters per second, and that its velocity—which depends on the density and elasticity of air—might instead have been very much less. Why, for instance, might it not have been transmitted at the rate of only a few centimeters per second? Let us see what the result would be if this were the case. Men would not be able to speak to one another while walking together. Let two friends be conversing, and suppose one takes a step or two in advance—going on, say, by the distance of a meter. Now, if sound were to take many seconds to cross this meter, the consequence would be that, instead of hearing the phrases spoken in the right order by his friend, the foremost walker would hear in an inverse order the sounds conveying the earlier phrases. In that case we could not speak while walking, and three-fourths of mankind would not be able to hear one another.

These remarks, my friend, lead me to suggest to you, for your consideration in this connection, a subject well worth attention, which has hitherto received little notice: that of the adaptation of the human organism to its environment. The manner in which man sees, in which he hears, his sensations, his nervous system, his build, his weight, his density, his gait, his bodily functions — all his actions, in fact — are regulated and constituted by the condition of your planet. None of your acts is absolutely free and independent. Man is the obedient, though unconscious, creature of the organic forces of the earth.

Undoubtedly, the human soul, not being a function of the brain and existing independently of it, enjoys relative liberty — but this liberty is limited by its faculties, its powers, and its energies. It is determined, according to the causes that decide it, at the moment of the birth of every man. Could one know exactly the faculties of his soul and the circumstances that were to surround his life, one could write a man's life beforehand, in all its details.

The human organism is the produce of the planet. It is not by virtue of a divine fantasy, a miracle, or a direct creation that terrestrial man is constituted as he is. His form, his height, his weight, his senses and his whole organization are derivations of the conditions pertaining on your planet: the atmosphere that you breathe, the food that nourishes you, the gravity of the earth's surface, the density of terrestrial matter, etc., etc. The human body does not differ anatomically from those of the higher mammals, and if you go back to the origin of species, you will find gradual transformations established by unimpeachable evidence. The whole of terrestrial life, from mollusk to man, is the development of a single genealogical tree. The human form has its origin in the animal form. Man is the butterfly developed from the chrysalis of the paleontological ages.

It follows from this fact that on other worlds organic life must be different from what it is here, and that their humanities — which, like our own, are the result of the forces active on each planet — are absolutely different in form from terrestrial humanity. For example, on worlds where the humanities do not eat, the digestive apparatus and the intestines do not exist. On worlds that are very highly electric, the beings inhabiting them are gifted with an electric sense. On others, sight is adapted for the ultraviolet rays, and the eyes have no vision in common with yours; they do not see what you see, and they see what you cannot. The organs are adapted to the functions they have to fulfill.

We are not, then, the absolute type of creation? It seems that creation itself is a perpetual development of forces in action.

The soul itself is subject to a similar law. There is as much diversity in souls as in bodies. In order that the soul should exist as an independent, self-conscious being, and that it should preserve the recollection of its identity and be qualified for immortality, it is necessary that even in this life it must know that it really exists. Otherwise, it would be no more advanced the day after death than it was the day before and would fall as an insensible breath into a blind cosmos, neither more nor less than any other center of unconscious force.

Many people on the earth boast that they do not believe in anything but matter—without knowing what they are saying, since they do not know what matter is. These last-mentioned—and those, still more numerous, who do not think at all—are not immortal, since they have no consciousness of their existence. The spirits who experience the spiritual life as a reality are the only ones fitted for immortality.

Are there many of them?

Look, my friend, at the first light of morning, which summons me once again to return to the depths of space populated with things unknown on Earth: that rich mine in which spirits rediscover the wrecks of past existences, the secrets of many mysteries, the ruins of disintegrated worlds, and the genesis of worlds yet to come.

As to the rest, it would be superfluous to spin out this recital with useless details. My goal has been to make you see that in order to experience the spectacle of a world and system exactly opposite to yours, all that is needed is to recede from the earth with a velocity greater than that of light.

In such a flight of the soul toward the inaccessible horizons of the infinite, one retraces the luminous rays reflected by Earth and other planets for millions of years; and while observing the planets at that vast distance one can be present in vision at the events of their past histories. Thus one ascends the stream of time to its source. This faculty should illuminate the regions of eternity for you with a new clarity. If, as I hope, you will admit the scientific value of my exposition of these ultraterrestrial investigations, I look forward to unfolding their metaphysical consequences for you very soon.

THE THIRD CONVERSATION

Homo Homunculus

I have listened to you with interest, Lumen, but—I confess—without being entirely convinced that everything you have told me is a reality. Indeed, it is difficult to believe that it is possible to see with absolute certainty all the things of which you speak. When, for instance, there are clouds across your field of view, you cannot see clearly what passes on Earth. The same objection holds for the interiors of houses.

You are mistaken, my friend. The undulations of the ether pass through obstacles that you would think impenetrable.[1] Clouds are formed of molecules between which rays of light frequently pass. On the other hand, there are vistas and gaps here and there across which one can see only obliquely. Only in very rare cases is nothing at all distinguishable. Besides, light is not what it appears to be; it is a vibration of the ether, and there are other ways of seeing than by means of the retina and the optic nerve. The vibrations of ether are perceptible to senses other than those you possess. If this is your sole objection, therefore, I must say that is is far from being insurmountable.

You have a particular talent for the resolution of doubts. Perhaps this is one of the gifts granted to spiritual beings. I have been obliged to admit, successively, that you have been transported to Capella with a swiftness exceeding that of light; that you reached another world as a spirit; that your soul is liberated from the flesh; that your ultra-terrestrial perception is able to distinguish from that height all that passes here; that you can advance or recede in space according to your fancy; and, lastly, that clouds are no obstacles to your seeing the surface of the globe clearly. It must be admitted that there are some serious difficulties here.

You are much inclined to materialism, my old friend! Would you be very surprised if I undertook to prove to you that these difficulties are only apparent, and that all the objections opposed to them by your conception of phenomena are effects of ignorance? What would you think if I affirmed that no one has a single true notion of what takes place upon the earth and that human beings fail utterly to understand nature?

In the name of all the indisputable truths of modern science, I would dare to think that you were imposing on me.

God forbid! Listen to me, my friend. The marvelous discoveries of contemporary science ought to increase the range of your concepts. Human science has just discovered spectral analysis![2] By methodical examination of a mere ray of light shot from a faraway star you can discover what elements compose the star and fuel its brilliance. That knowledge, my brother, is of greater value than all the conquests of Alexander, Caesar, and Napoleon, all the discoveries of Ptolemy, Columbus, and Gutenberg, or all the books of Moses and Confucius. Just think: trillions of leagues span the abyss that separates us from Sirius, Arcturus, Vega, Capella, Castor, and Pollux, and yet it is now possible to analyze the constituent substances of those suns as accurately as you could if you were to take them in your hand and submit them to the crucible in your laboratory!

How, then, can you refuse to admit that by processes unknown to you the soul's sight could be sufficiently piercing to see a bright far-off world so clearly as to distinguish its smallest details? Does not the telegraph carry your thoughts from Europe to America in an inappreciable moment, through the ocean depths? Cannot two people converse in a low voice at a distance of thousands of leagues? And still you hesitate to admit the truth of my narrations because you do not altogether comprehend them? Can you explain how the telegraph message is transmitted? No, you cannot. Cease, then, to retain doubts that have not even the merit of being scientific.[3]

My objections, O learned master, have no other purpose than to elicit further enlightenment upon the subject. Far be it from me to deny the truth of all that you tell me; I only seek to form a rational and precise idea of it.

Be assured, my friend, that I take no offense at your objections. My only desire is to develop and increase the scope of your concepts. I can open your eyes right now to the utter inadequacy of your terrestrial faculties, and the fatal poverty of positivist science itself, by inviting you to consider that the causes of your sensory impressions are no more than modes of motion and that what is proudly termed "science" is only a severely limited organic perception.

The light that your eyes see and the sounds that your ears hear are different forms of motion that impress themselves upon you; odors, flavors, and so on are emanations which strike your olfactory nerves or touch your palate, causing vibratory motions to be transmitted to your brain. You can appreciate only a few such movements through the senses you possess, principally those of sight and hearing. Do you, in your simplicity, believe that you see and hear the natural world? Not at all. All that you do is to receive some of the movements acting upon your earthbound atom. Beyond the impressions you receive there are an infinitely greater number unperceived by you.

Pardon me, master, but this new aspect of nature is not clear enough for me to understand it. Would you . . .

This aspect is indeed new to you, but attentive consideration will enable you to grasp it. Sound is formed by vibrations in the air that strike upon the membrane of the tympanum and give you the impression of various tones. Human beings do not hear all sounds; when the vibrations are too slow—below forty per second—the sound is too low to be caught by your ear. When the vibrations are too rapid—above thirty-six thousand per second—the sound is too high to be received by your ear. Above and below these two limits, therefore, human beings do not perceive sounds; these vibrations exist, however, and are perceived by creatures of other kinds—certain insects, for example.

The same rules apply to light. The different aspects of light—the shades and colors of objects—are likewise due to the vibrations that strike the optic nerve and give you the impression of different degrees of light intensity. Human beings do not by any means see all that is visible. When the vibrations are too slow—under 458 trillion a second—light is too feeble and your eye sees nothing. When the vibrations are too rapid—over 727 trillion a second—light outruns your organic faculty of perception and is invisible to you.[4] Above and below these two limits the vibrations of ether still exist, and are perceived by other beings. You do not know, therefore, nor can you receive, any impressions other than those that can be made to vibrate upon the two chords of your organic lyre that are called the optic nerve and the auditory nerve.

Imagine for one instant the extent of all the sights and sounds that are imperceptible to you. All the undulatory movements that exist in the universe between the figures of thirty-six thousand and those represented by 458 trillion in the same unity of time can be neither heard nor seen by you, and remain utterly unknown to you.[5] Try to imagine that distance! Contemporary science is beginning to penetrate a little way into this invisible world; you know that it has recently analyzed the vibrations below 458 trillion—these are the caloric invisible rays[6]—and the vibrations above 727 trillion; the latter are the chemical rays,[7] equally invisible to the human eye. Scientific methods can enlarge the scope of the perceptions by only a little; you remain isolated in the midst of an infinitude.

Furthermore, there exists in nature an infinite number of other vibrations, which have no correspondence with your organization and therefore cannot be received by you; consequently, you remain utterly and forever ignorant of them.[8] If you had other strings to your lyre—ten, a hundred, a thousand—the harmony of nature could translate itself to you more completely, each of the myriad vibrations according to its kind. You would perceive a number of actualities that are certainly present around you whose existence you cannot even guess, and instead of two dominant notes you would be conscious of the great concert of harmonies that is all around you. Although you are so very ignorant, you are quite unconscious of it, because everyone around you is equally ignorant, and it is therefore impossible to compare your limited faculties with those of beings far more highly organized than the inhabitants of Earth.

The senses you do possess, however, suffice to indicate the existence of other senses, which are not only more powerful but of a totally different order. By means of the sense of touch, for example, you can feel the sensation of heat—so it is easy to imagine the existence of a special sense, analogous to that by which light reveals to you the appearance of exterior objects, that would render humankind capable of judging the form, substance, interior structure, and other qualities of an object by the action of the caloric waves radiating from it. The same reasoning would hold good for electricity. You might equally well imagine the existence of a sense that would endow the eye with the properties of a spectroscope and telescope combined into one, enabling it to see the chemical elements of which bodies are composed.

From a scientific point of view, therefore, you already have sufficient grounds for imagining modes of perception quite different from those that characterize human beings. These faculties exist in other worlds, and there are endless ways of perceiving the action of the forces of nature.

I must admit, master, that as you set out these possibilities a new and singular clarity enlightens my understanding, and your teachings seem to me to be a true interpretation of reality. I had already dreamed that such marvels might be possible, but I had not been able to explain them, enveloped as I still am in my terrestrial senses. One thing is certain: we must be lifted out of our earthbound limitations ere we are capable of comprehending, or even attempting to judge, the scope of the universe.

So, being endowed with only a few limited senses, we can only know the facts that are perceptible to them. The remainder is unknown to beings of our nature. Can it be that the unknown is infinitely greater than the known?

This "remainder" is immense; all that you know at present will seem as nothing by comparison. Not only do your senses not perceive physical movements—such as solar and terrestrial electricity, whose currents interact in the atmosphere; the magnetism of minerals and plants; the affinities of organisms; and so on—which are invisible to you, but they have even less perception of the movements of the moral world: its sympathies and antipathies, its presentiments, its spiritual attractions, and so on. I only speak the simple truth when I say that all that you know, and all that you could know, through the medium of your earthly senses is as nothing compared to that which is.

The truth is so profound that it might well be hypothesized that beings exist upon the earth essentially different from you, possessing neither eyes nor ears nor any of your other senses but endowed with other senses and capable of perceiving that which you cannot perceive—and who, while living in the same world as yourself, know that which you cannot know and form an idea of nature completely at variance with your own.[9]

All this is quite beyond my comprehension.

Moreover, my earthly friend, I can add most emphatically that the sensory impressions you receive, which constitute the bases of your science, are not perceptions of reality. No: light, lucidity, color, appearances, tones, noises, harmonies, sounds, perfumes—all the apparent qualities of entities—are nothing but forms. These forms enter into your mind by the avenues of the eye and the ear, or through the senses of smell and taste, and are represented to you by their appearances, not by the essence of the things themselves.[10] The real nature of things escapes your understanding entirely, and you are quite incapable of comprehending the universe.

Matter itself is not what you believe it to be. In absolute terms, one might say that nothing is really solid; your own body, a piece of iron or granite, is no more solid than the air you breathe. All these things are composed of atoms that do not touch one another and are perpetually in motion. The earth, an atom of the heavens, moves through space with a velocity of 643,000 leagues a day, but in proportion to their dimensions the atoms that constitute your body and circulate in your blood move much more rapidly. If your vision were sufficiently powerful to penetrate this stone, you would no longer see it thus, because your sight would pass through and beyond it. . . .

But I see by the disturbance of your brain and the rapid movement of the fluid that passes between its closely conjoined lobes that you no longer understand my revelations. I will not, therefore, pursue this subject, which I have mentioned merely in order to demonstrate how great would be the error of attaching any importance to difficulties born of your terrestrial senses and to assure you that neither you nor any other man of the earth could form even an approximate idea of the nature of the universe. Earthly man is a mere homunculus![11]

Ah, if you were only acquainted with the organisms that live on Mars or Uranus; if it had been granted to you to appreciate the senses that are in action on Venus or one of Saturn's rings; if, during centuries of travel, you had been permitted to glimpse the forms of life in the systems of the double stars, or the sensations of sight in the colored suns, or to glean the impressions of an electric sense of which you can know absolutely nothing in the clusters of multiple suns . . .

If a suitable comparison of this ultraterrestrial state had furnished you with the elements of a fresh knowledge, you would then have been able to comprehend that beings exist who can see, hear, feel—or, to be more accurate, understand—nature without eyes, ears, or a sense of smell; that an incredible number of senses exist in nature that are essentially different from yours; and that there is in creation an incalculable number of marvelous things that it is absolutely impossible for you to imagine.

In this general contemplation of the universe, my friend, one perceives the tie that unites the physical and spiritual worlds into a sodality; one sees from a higher ground the instinctive strength that raises certain souls, tried by the coarseness of matter but purified by sacrifice, toward the higher regions of spiritual light; and one understands how immense is the happiness reserved for those beings who, even while on Earth, have succeeded in gradually overcoming their lower nature.

To return to the transmission of light on Earth, does not light lose itself at last? Does the aspect of the earth remain eternally visible, rather than diminishing in proportion of the square of the distance and thus being finally annihilated?

The expression "at last" has no meaning, because there is no end in space. Light becomes attenuated, it is true, with distance; the senses become less vivid—but nothing is entirely lost. For example, a number perpetually reduced by halves never becomes equal to zero. The earth is not visible to all eyes at a particular distance; nevertheless, even though it may not be seen by all, it still exists, visible to spiritual sight alone. The image of a star, borne upon the wings of light, goes into the unfathomable depths of the mysterious abysses of space.

Vast regions exist in space that are without stars: regions decimated by time, whence worlds have been successively removed by the attractions of exterior suns. The image of a star in crossing these dark abysses would be in a position analogous to an image of a person or object that the photographer had forgotten and left in the camera. It is not impossible that such images encounter in these vast spaces dark stars—celestial mechanics testify to the existence of many such—in a condition of such sensitivity that they are capable of fixing the images of far-off worlds, perhaps because their surfaces are formed of iodine (as they might be, according to spectral analysis). By this means, the image of terrestrial events might be printed upon a dark globe; and if this globe turns upon itself, like other celestial bodies, it would present its longitudinal zones successively to the terrestrial image, and would thus take a sort of continuous photograph of successive events.[12] Furthermore, in ascending or descending a line of longitude, the track of the recorded images would no longer be a circle but a spiral, and after each rotation was completed the new images would not superimpose themselves on the old but would follow a new track above or below. The imagination could now suppose that this world is not spherical but cylindrical, and thus see in space an imperishable column around which would be engraved the great events of the world's history. . . .[13]

I have not seen any such realization myself; it is so short a time since I left the earth that I have barely done more than glance superficially at these celestial marvels. Before long, though, I shall seek to verify this hypothesis and see whether or not its reality forms a part of the infinite richness of the astral creations.

If the ray that leaves the earth is never obliterated, master, are our actions then eternal?

They certainly are. An act once accomplished can never be effaced, and no power can ever cause it to be as if it had never been. Say that a crime is committed in the heart of a desert country, that the criminal goes far away, remains unknown, and supposes that the deed that he has done is past and forever done with. He has washed his hands of it; he has repented; he believes his action obliterated—but, in reality, nothing is destroyed. At the moment when this act was accomplished, light seized it and carried it into space at lightning speed. It became incorporated into a ray of light; thus it will transmit itself eternally into the infinite. . . .

A good action done in secret, which the benefactor thinks concealed, is likewise taken into the possession of a ray of light; far from being forgotten, it will live forever.

Napoleon, in order to satisfy his personal ambition, was the willful cause of the deaths of five million men, whose ages averaged about thirty years—and who, according to the norms of life, had thirty-seven more years yet to live. By this calculation, therefore, he caused the destruction of 185,000,000 years of human life. His chastisement, his expiation, consists in being carried along by that ray of light that left the plain of Waterloo on 18 June 1815, to be moving perpetually in space with the speed of light itself: to have constantly in sight that critical scene where he saw the scaffolding of his vain ambition finally crumbling to pieces; to feel, without respite, the bitterness of despair; and to remain bound to this ray of light for the 185,000,000 years for whose destruction he was responsible. By acting thus, instead of fulfilling his mission more worthily, he has retarded for a similar length of time his progress in the spiritual life.[14]

If it were given to you to see that which goes on in the moral world as clearly as you now see that which passes in the physical one, you would recognize vibrations and transmissions of another nature, which imprint in the arcana of the spiritual world not merely actions but the most secret thoughts.

Lumen, your revelations are awful! Thus, our eternal destinies are intimately bound up with the fundamental construction of the universe. I have speculated often about the possibility of communication between worlds by means of light; many physicists have supposed that it will be possible to establish communication between the earth and the moon, and even the planets, by means of luminous signals. But suppose that one could send signals from the earth to a star by means of light; a hundred years, say, must come and go before the signal could reach its destination, and the reply could return only after the same interval of time had elapsed. Consequently, two centuries would elapse between the question and its answer. The terrestrial observer would have died long before his signal could have reached his sidereal observer, and the latter would doubtless have undergone a similar fate before his answer could have been received!

It would, indeed, be a conversation between the living and the dead.

Permit me one more question, master—one that is perhaps a little indiscreet, but a final one, for I see that Venus is paling and I fear that your voice will soon fade away. If actions are visible thus in the ethereal regions, can we therefore see, after our deaths, not merely our own actions but those of others—I mean, those that are of particular interest to us?

For instance, a pair of twin souls dwelling in perfect unity would desire to see again the delightful hours passed together on Earth; they might rush into space with a rapidity equal to that of light in order to have the same hours of joy always before their eyes. Then again, a husband might trace with interest the entire life of his companion; and should some unexpected situation have presented itself, he could at leisure examine the causes leading to it. He might even, if his disembodied companion resided in some neighboring region, call upon her to observe these retrospective incidents in association with himself. No denial could be admissible before such palpable evidence. Might not this power, exercised by these spirits, give rise to some strange revelations?

In the heavens, my friend, memories of this material kind have little value, and I am astonished that you still think them important.[15] What should have struck you particularly in all that we have said during our interviews is that by virtue of the physics of light we can see events after they have been accomplished—and, indeed, when they have entirely vanished from earthly ken.

Believe me, master, this truth will never be effaced from my memory. It is precisely this point that I find so exceedingly marvelous. Forget, I beg you, my last digression. To tell the truth, that which has most taxed and surpassed the bounds of my imagination since our first interview was the thought that the duration of the spirit's voyage may not only be zero, but negative or retrograde. The words "retrograde time" are a contradiction in terms—dare one believe it? You start out today for a star, and you arrive yesterday! What am I saying, yesterday? You arrive there seventy-two years ago, or a hundred years ago! The farther you travel, the sooner you will arrive! The terms of our language need to be remade for such extraordinary reckoning.

This is undeniable. Speaking in the terrestrial manner, there is no error in this mode of expression, since the earth was only in 1793, or whatever, for the world that we reached. You have, however, certain apparent paradoxes on your own little globe that assist the imagination of this one. For example, a telegram sent from Paris at noon arrives at Brest at twenty minutes before noon.[16] But the curious aspects of particular examples are not significant enough for you to dwell upon; what is important is the underlying revelation of which they are the metaphysical form and outward expression. Know that time is not an absolute reality but only a transitory measure caused by the movements of the earth in the solar system.

Regarded with the eyes of the soul rather than with those of the body, this picture of human life—not imaginary but real, such as it was, dissimulation being impossible—touches on one side the domain of theology, inasmuch as it explains in physical terms a mystery hitherto inexplicable; I mean the individual judgment of each of us after death. From the viewpoint of the whole, the present of a world is no longer a momentary actuality, which disappears as soon as it has appeared; a phase without consistency; a gateway through which the past is increasingly precipitating toward the future; a mathematical point plotted in space. On the contrary, it is an effective reality that flies away from this world with the swiftness of light, sinking forever into the infinite, thus remaining an *eternal* present.

The metaphysical reality of this vast problem is such that one can now conceive the omnipresence of the world throughout its duration. Events vanish from the place in which they were born, but they exist in space. This successive and ceaseless projection of all the facts enacted upon every world takes place in the bosom of the Infinite Being, whose ubiquity holds everything in eternal permanence.

All the events accomplished upon the earth's surface since its creation are visible in space at distances proportional to their remoteness in the past. The whole history of the globe, and the life of every one of its inhabitants, could thus be seen at a glance by an eye capable of embracing that space. Thus we understand, optically, that the eternal and omnipresent Spirit can see the entirety of the past at one and the same moment. That which is true of our earth is true of all the worlds in space. The entire history of the universe can thus be present at once to the universal ubiquity of the Creator.

I ought to add that God knows the entire past not only in consequence of this direct sight but also by the knowledge of everything in the present. If a naturalist like Cuvier[17] knows how to reconstruct, by means of a fragment of bone, any species of extinct animal, surely the Author of Nature knows by means of the present earth the earth that is past, the planetary system and sun of the past, and all the conditions of temperature, aggregations, and combinations by which the elements have produced the complex condition of things presently in existence.

By the same token, the future can be as completely present to God in its actual germs as the past is in its fruits. Each event is bound in an indissoluble manner with the past and the future. The future will be as inevitably the outcome of the present as the present is of the past. It is as logically deducible from it, and exists in it as exactly, as the past is inscribed therein for those who are able to decipher it.

I must emphasize, though, that the main point of this recital is to state and make you understand that the past life of all worlds, and of all beings, is always visible in space, thanks to the successive transmission of light across and through the vast regions of the infinite.

THE FOURTH CONVERSATION

Previous Lives

Two years have fled, O Lumen, since the day of our first mystical conversation. During this period, of which inhabitants of eternal space like you have been unconscious, but of which we dwellers on the earth have been very conscious, I have often devoted my thoughts to the great mysteries into which you have initiated me, and to the new horizons set out before my mind's eye. Since your departure from the earth you have doubtless made great advances, by means of your observations and studies, in progressively vaster fields of research. Doubtless, too, you have numberless marvels to relate to me now that my intelligence is better prepared to receive them. If I am worthy, and can comprehend them, please give me an account of the celestial voyages that have transported your spirit into the higher spheres, of the hitherto-unknown truths that they have imparted to you, of the grandeurs that they have exposed to you, and of the principles they have taught you in reference to the mysterious subject of the destiny of human and other beings.

I have prepared your mind, my dear old friend, to receive impressions stranger than any earthly spectacle has ever produced or could ever produce. It is nevertheless necessary that you keep your understanding free from all earthly prejudice. That which I am going to unfold will astonish you, but you must receive it attentively from the very beginning as an undeniable truth, not as a romance. This is the first condition that I demand from your studious ardor. When you understand — and you will understand, if you bring to the task a mathematical mind and an unprejudiced spirit — you will see that all the facts that constitute our ultraterrestrial existence are not only possible but real and in perfect harmony with our intellectual faculties, as already manifest upon the earth.

Be assured, Lumen, that I bring to you an open mind, cleared of all prejudice. I am eagerly expecting to hear revelations such as no human ear has ever heard before.

The events that will form the subject of this recital have not only the earth and its neighboring stars for their subject, but will extend over immense fields of sidereal astronomy and acquaint us with their marvels. Their enigmas will be solved, as former difficulties have been, by the study of light: a magic bridge thrown from one star to another, from the earth to the sun and from the earth to the stars; the universal movement that fills space, sustains worlds in their orbits, and constitutes the eternal life of nature. Take care, then, to keep ever in mind the fact of the successive transmission of light in space.[1]

I

Not long ago — although I can no longer express the interval in earthly terms — while in a melancholy region of Capella, I was contemplating the starry heavens at the commencement of a clear night. Occupied in the study of the star that is your sun, and the little blue planet near at hand which is your earth, I observed one of the scenes of my childhood: my young mother, sitting in the middle of a garden, holding my infant brother in her arms, and at her side a little girl of two summers — my sister — and a boy two years older, who was myself. I saw myself at an age when a human being is not yet conscious of his intellectual existence, although he bears upon his brow the germ of future promise.

While musing on this singular spectacle, which showed me my own self at the beginning of my earthly career, I felt my attention being drawn away from your planet by a superior power and directed toward another point in the heavens — which, even at that moment, seemed to be linked with the earth and my terrestrial career by some mysterious tie. I could not turn my gaze from this new point in the heavens, my eyes being, as it were, chained to the spot by some magnetic force that I was powerless to resist. Several times I endeavored to redirect my eyes and fix them upon the earth I love so dearly, but in vain; my gaze was always drawn back to the same unknown star.

This star, upon which my eyes sought instinctively to discern something, belongs to the constellation Virgo, whose form is slightly different as seen from Capella. Gamma Virginis is a double star — that is to say, an association of two suns, one of a silvery whiteness, the other a bright golden yellow, which revolve around one another once every 175 years — which can be seen from the earth with the naked eye. Around each of the suns that forms it there is a planetary system. My sight was fixed upon one of the planets belonging to the golden sun.

On that planet there are animals and vegetables as there are upon Earth; their forms bear a similarity to earthly ones, but there is an essential difference in their organic makeup. Their animal kingdom is analogous to yours: they have fishes in the sea, and quadrupeds in the air, in which men can fly without wings by reason of the extreme density of the atmosphere. The men of this planet possess almost the same form as those on Earth, but no hair grows upon their heads. They have three large, slender opposable thumbs instead of five fingers on their hands, and three talonlike toes instead of soles on their feet, the extremities of their arms and legs being as supple as India rubber. They have, nevertheless, two eyes, a nose, and a mouth, which make their faces resemble earthly faces. They do not have two ears set on either side of the head, but one only, in the shape of a cone, which is placed on the upper part of the skull like a little hat. They live in societies and wear clothing; thus, you see, they differ little in exterior appearances from the inhabitants of the earth.

Are there, then, in other worlds beings entirely different from us — but who are comparable to us in spite of their dissimilarities?

In general, the animal life of different worlds is separated by profound distinctions unimaginable by you. These forms are the result of fundamental conditions unique to each globe, and of the forces that regulate them. Matter, density, gravity, heat, light, electricity, atmosphere, and so on, differ in essential particulars from one world to another. Forms differ even within the same system; thus, the men of Saturn and Mercury do not in the least resemble those of Earth, and those who see them for the first time cannot recognize their heads, limbs, and sensory apparatus. By contrast, the forms of those in the planetary system of Gamma Virginis, toward which my attention was being persistently drawn, are nearly similar to those of the inhabitants of Earth, whom they also resemble morally and intellectually. Slightly inferior to ourselves, they belong to that scale in the order of souls that immediately precedes that of terrestrial humanity in the scheme of things.

But there is a wide divergence between individual human beings in all that pertains to intellect and morality alike. We in Europe differ greatly from the tribes of Abyssinia and the savages of the Pacific islands. What people do you take as a type of the highest degree of intelligence on the earth?

The Arabs. They are capable of producing their Keplers, their Newtons, their Galileos, their Archimedes, their Euclids, their d'Alemberts. Besides which, they sprang from those primitive hordes whose roots reach down to the bedrock of humanity. But it is not necessary to choose a people for a type. It is better to consider modern civilization as a whole. Nor is there so marked a difference as you appear to suppose between the brain capacity of a Negro and that of the Latin race. However, if you insist upon a comparison, I can assure you that the men of the planet of Gamma Virginis are nearly on a par with the Scandinavians.[2]

The most vital difference that exists between their world and the earth is the absence of sex. Neither plants, nor animals, nor human beings have sex. Generation is effectively spontaneous, the natural result of the union of certain physiological conditions in some of the fertile isles of the planet; humans are not formed in maternal wombs as they are on Earth. It would be useless to try to explain the process to you, whose earthly faculties prevent you from understanding the nature of a world so very different from your own.

A consequence of this organic system is that no form of marriage exists in this world and that the friendships between human beings are never mixed with the carnal desires — which are inevitably manifest on the earth between individuals of different sexes, even when the attraction is at its purest. You will probably remember that during the Protozoic period the inhabitants of Earth were all deaf, dumb and sexless. The division into sexes took place much later in the development of nature, among both animals and plants.[3]

Having been attracted toward this far-off planet, I examined its surface attentively with my spiritual sight. I was especially drawn, without knowing the cause, to a white city resembling from afar a region covered with snow — but it seemed improbable that it was snow, because it was unlikely that water could exist on that globe in the same chemical conditions as on Earth. On the outer fringe of this city an avenue led to a neighboring wood of yellow trees. I soon remarked three individuals who seemed to be slowly sauntering toward this wood. This little group comprised two friends engaged in close conversation and a third who was differentiated from the others both by the red garment he wore and the burden he bore — I thought he was probably their servant, their slave, or some domestic animal.

While studying the two principal personages intently, I observed the one on the right raise his face to the sky, as if someone had called to him from a balloon, and direct his gaze toward Capella — a star that was doubtless invisible to him, because it was daylight. Oh, my old friend, I shall never forget the sudden surprise this sight gave me! I can scarcely believe, even now, that I was not dreaming . . .

This person on the planet of Gamma Virginis, who was looking toward me without knowing it, was — dare I tell you? — well, it was *myself*!

What do you mean, yourself?

Myself, in person. I recognized myself immediately, and you can imagine my surprise.

I certainly can. I cannot understand this at all.

To be sure, the situation was so entirely novel that it cried out for explanation.

It was, in truth, myself—and I was not long in finding out not only that it was my former face and figure, but also that the person walking by my side was my dear Kathleen, an intimate friend and the companion of my studies upon that planet. My gaze followed them as far as the decorative wood, across picturesque valleys, beneath golden cupolas, under trees covered with large orange-tinted branches, and through hedges of elms with amber-colored leaves. A rippling brook babbled on the fine sand, and we seated ourselves on its bank. I recalled the sweet hours we had passed together, the happy years that glided by in that far-off land, the fraternal confidences and the impressions we shared in the midst of woodland scenes, silent plains, mist-covered hills, and little lakes that gladly reflected the heavens. With aspirations raised toward all that was great and sacred in nature we adored God in His works. With what joy did I see again this phase of my previous existence, and rivet anew the golden chain whose links had been broken by my life on Earth!

In truth, dear friend, it was my own self, who was then living on that plant of Gamma Virginis. I was really looking at myself. I could follow in sequence the events of my life and relive the happiest moments of that existence that is now so far remote. Had I had any doubt about my identity, moreover, the uncertainty would have died while I watched, for while I was pondering the matter I saw Berthor—my brother during that existence—come out of the wood. He approached us and joined in our conversation beside the murmurous brook.

Master, I still cannot understand how you could see yourself on that planet of Gamma Virginis. Were you gifted with ubiquity? Could you be in two places at once, like Francis of Assisi or Apollonius of Tyana?[4]

Not at all. On examining the astronomical co-ordinates of Gamma Virginis, however, and knowing its parallax as seen from Capella, I came to the conclusion that the light from that sun could not employ less than 172 years in traversing the distance separating it from Capella. I was, therefore, receiving the luminous ray that had left that world 172 years before. It so happens that at that epoch I was indeed living on the planet of which we speak, and that I was then in my twentieth year.

In verifying these periods and in comparing different planetary modes of representation, I found, in fact, that I was born on the world of Gamma Virginis in the year 45904—which corresponds to the year 1677 of the Christian era on Earth—and that I died, as a result of an accident, in the year 45913, which corresponds to the year 1767, each of that planet's years being equal to ten of yours. When I saw myself, as I have just told you, I appeared to be about twenty years of age by earthly reckoning, but within the local system of measurement I was only two years old. The age of fifteen—equivalent to 150 years on Earth—is often attained there, and is considered the natural limit of life.

The luminous ray—or, more precisely, the aspect or photograph of the world of Gamma Virginis—takes 172 years to traverse the immense space that separates it from Capella. Consequently, on finding myself in the vicinity of the latter star, I was receiving at that very moment the image that left the vicinity of Gamma Virginis 172 years previously. Although things had changed greatly—generations having followed generations, and my own death having taken place there, allowing time for me to be born again and to live seventy-two years upon the earth—light had taken all that time to cross the void separating Gamma Virginis from Capella, bringing me fresh impressions of events long past.

The duration of the passage of the light having been demonstrated, I have no objection to raise on that point, but I frankly admit that crediting an experience of such singularity taxes my imagination to the limit!

This is not a matter of imagination, my old friend. It is a reality, eternal and sacred, fixed in its appropriate place within the universal plan of creation. The light of every star, direct or reflected—in other words, the image of every sun and planet—is diffused in space according to a rate already known to you, and the luminous ray contains in itself all that is visible. As nothing can be lost, the history of each world is contained in the light that emanates from it incessantly, in successive waves, eternally traveling into space without any possibility of annihilation. True, the terrestrial eye cannot read it, but there are eyes immeasurably superior to your earthly ones.

I make use of the terms "sight" and "light" in these conversations in order that you may understand me. As I told you in a previous conversation, however, objectively speaking there is no such thing as "light," but merely vibrations in the ether. Neither is there any "sight," but only perceptions of the mind. Furthermore, even on the earth, when you examine the nature of a star with a telescope — or, better still, with a spectroscope — you know full well that what is before your eyes is not its actual state but its past state, transmitted to you by a ray of light that left it, say, ten thousand years ago. You know, too, that a certain number of stars whose physical and numerical properties your earthly astronomers are seeking to determine, have long ago ceased even to exist — may, indeed, have ceased to exist before the beginning of your world.

We know this. So you have seen, unfolded before your eyes, your existence previous to the last one, 172 years after it had elapsed.

Say, rather, one phase of that existence; but I would have been able to review my entire life by moving closer to that planet — and, indeed, still could — as I have already done with respect to my terrestrial existence.

So, through the medium of light, you have really seen your last two incarnations again?

Precisely; and what is more, I have seen them — and I continue to see them — simultaneously: side by side, as it were.

You can review them both at the same time?

The fact is easily explained. The light from the earth takes seventy-two years to reach Capella. The light from the planet of Gamma Virginis, being two and a half times as far away from Capella, takes two and a half times as long to travel. As I lived seventy-two years upon the earth, and a hundred years before that upon the other planet, these two periods reach me at precisely the same time on Capella. Thus, by simply looking at the two worlds at once, I have before me my two previous existences, which unfold exactly as they would if I were not there to observe them — without my being able, in either case, to alter any of the actions that I see myself upon the point of accomplishing, since those actions, although present and future to my actual observation, are in reality past.

A strange experience indeed! Very strange!

But what struck me most forcibly in this unexpected observation of two of my previous existences in two different worlds, as it was unfolded before me, was the bizarre resemblance these two lives bore to one another. I discovered that I had almost the same inclinations in the one as in the other, the same passions and the same faults. There was nothing criminal, or saintly, in either.

Furthermore — an extraordinary coincidence — I have witnessed scenes in the earlier life analogous to those I have seen on Earth. This is the explanation of the innate tastes that I brought into the terrestrial world for the poetry of the North: the poems of Ossian; the dreamy mountainous landscapes of Ireland; the aurora borealis; Scotland and Sweden; Norway with its fjords, and Spitzbergen with its desolate wastes; all of them attracted me. Ancient ruined towers; rocks and wild ravines; somber pines sighing in the northern wind; all these appealed to me on Earth and seemed to have some mysterious link to my deepest thoughts. When I saw Ireland for the first time, I felt as though I had lived there before. When I climbed the Rigi and the Finsteraarhorn for the first time and saw the superb sunrise over the snowy summits of the Alps, it seemed as though I had seen it all before. The specter of the Brocken[5] was not new to me, the reason being that I had inhabited similar regions in a former life on the planet of Gamma Virginis. A similar life, similar actions, similar circumstances, similar conditions: analogies everywhere! Almost all that I had seen, done, and thought on Earth, I had already seen, done, and thought a hundred years earlier, on that previous world.

I had always suspected it!

All in all, my terrestrial life taken as a whole was superior to the one preceding it. As no one can deny, each child born into the world brings with him different faculties, particular predispositions, innate dissimilarities, which can be explained to the philosophical mind — or accommodated to the viewpoint of eternal justice — only by the supposition of works previously accomplished by free souls. Although my terrestrial life was superior to the previous one—evincing, as it did, a more accurate and profound knowledge of the system of the world—I should admit that it lacked certain moral and physical qualities that my former existence possessed. On the other hand, I had faculties on that world denied to me on Earth.

For example, among the physical faculties lacking on Earth, that of flight is especially deserving of mention. I see that on the planet of Gamma Virginis I can fly as easily as walk, without any aeronautic apparatus or wings, simply by stretching my arms and legs as if I were swimming in water. On closely examining the mode of locomotion on that planet I clearly see that I have—or rather had—neither wings, balloon, nor any kind of mechanical appliance. At any given moment I can spring from the ground with a vigorous leap, spread out my arms, and swim in the air without fatigue. On other occasions, descending a steep mountain on foot, I spring out into space and float at will, moving slowly and obliquely with my feet pressed together, to any point I might desire, standing upright as soon as my feet touch the ground. Then again, when I wish to do so, I can fly slowly, in the manner of a dove describing an arc in returning to its dovecote. All this I distinctly see myself doing on that world.

Oh well! Not once, but a hundred or a thousand times, I have felt myself thus transported in my earthly dreams, softly, naturally, and without apparatus. How can such impossibilities so often present themselves to us in our dreams? They are inexplicable, for nothing analogous exists upon the earthly globe. Instinctively obeying this innate tendency, I have frequently soared into the atmosphere suspended from the car of a balloon, but the sensation is not the same; one does not feel oneself flying—on the contrary, one has the feeling of being stationary. Now I have the key to my dreams. During the slumber of my terrestrial senses, my soul enjoys reminiscences of its former existence.

But I, too, often feel and see myself flying in dreams without wings and machinery, simply by an effort of will, in exactly the way you describe. Is this, then, proof that I too have lived upon the planet of Gamma Virginis?

I do not know. If you had transcendent sight, or appropriate instruments, you might see that planet from your own and examine its surface — and if, perchance, you had existed there when the luminous rays departed that are now reaching the earth, you might perhaps rediscover yourself there. But your eyes are too feeble to permit such research. It does not follow that because you have been able to fly you must have lived on that particular world. There is a considerable number of worlds where flight is normal and all human beings possess that faculty. In fact, there are relatively few planets where living beings crawl as they do upon the earth.

The conclusion that follows from your experience is that your earthly life was not the first and that you had already lived on another world. Do you believe, then, in the plurality of the soul's existences?

Have you forgotten that you are speaking to a disembodied spirit? I ought to be well qualified to give such evidence, having had before me both my earthly life and my previous life on the planet of Gamma Virginis. Besides, I can recall many other existences.

Ah! That is precisely what I lack in order to possess a similar conviction. I can recall absolutely nothing that preceded my birth into this world.

You are still incarnate; you must wait for freedom before you can recall your spiritual life. The soul has full remembrance and full possession of itself only in the celestial life that is its normal state — that is to say, between incarnations. It then sees not only its life on the earth but all its previous lives.

How could a soul, enveloped in the gross materialities of the flesh and fixed there for a transitory term, recall its spiritual life? Would not such remembrance even prove hurtful? Would not the embodied soul's liberty of action be shackled were it able to see its life from beginning to end? Where would be the merit of striving if one's destiny could be foreseen? Souls incarnate upon the earth have not yet attained to a sufficiently elevated state of advancement for the memory of their previous existence to be of use to them.

The permanence of the impressions of the soul is not manifest in its passage through this world. The caterpillar does not remember its rudimentary existence in the egg. The sleeping chrysalis cannot recall the laborious days it spent crawling upon the leaves. The butterfly that flits from flower to flower has no memory of the time when its cocoon was dreaming while it hung suspended from its web, nor of the twilight when its larva trailed from plant to plant, nor of the night when it was buried like a nut in its shell. This does not alter the fact that the egg, the caterpillar, the chrysalis, and the butterfly are one and the same being.

In certain cases, even of terrestrial life, you have remarkable examples of forgetfulness, such as that of somnambulism—either natural or artificial—and also certain mental conditions that modern science studies. So it is not surprising that during one existence we should not remember our previous ones. Celestial life and planetary life represent two states liberated and distinct from one another.

Even so, master, if we had already lived before this life, something must remain with us; otherwise, these previous existences might as well never have been.

Do you call it nothing, then, to be born on the earth with innate tendencies? There is no such thing as intellectual heredity. Take two children of the same parentage, receiving exactly the same education, surrounded by the same care and having in every respect similar environments. Now examine each of them. Are they equal? In no way; equality of souls does not exist.[6] One is born with peaceful instincts and great intelligence; he will be good, learned, wise, perhaps illustrious among the thinkers of his age. The other one brings with him a domineering, perhaps envious or even brutal, instinct; his career defines and accentuates itself as each year passes, will lead him eventually to high rank in military life, and will give him the honor—little to be coveted, though still admired upon the earth—that attaches to the title of official assassin. Whether feebly or strongly pronounced, the dissimilarity of character—which depends neither upon family, nor race, nor education, nor material conditions—is manifest in every man. Reflect upon this at your leisure; you will arrive at the conviction that it is absolutely inexplicable and can be accounted for only by belief in an anterior existence of souls.

Have not most philosophers and theologians taught that the soul and the body are created at one and the same time?

And which, pray, is the precise moment of the soul's creation? Is it the moment of birth? Legislation, enlightened by anatomical physiology, knows that a child lives before being delivered from its uterine prison, so the destruction of an eight-month embryo is regarded as murder. At what period, do you suppose, does the soul appear in the fluid brain of the fetus or the embryo?

The ancients thought that the real spiritual quickening of the human being took place during the sixth week of gestation, but the modern belief is that it occurs at the moment of conception.[7]

Oh, bitter mockery! To accord with this view you would have the eternal designs of the Creator dependent for their execution upon the capricious desires and intermittent flames of two amorous hearts! You would dare to admit that our immortal being is created by the physical contact of two human beings! You would be disposed to believe that the Divine Mind that governs the world is influenced by intrigue, by passion and even by crime! Do you suppose that the number of souls depends on the number of flowers impregnated by the touch of sweet pollen dust borne to them on golden wings? Is not such a doctrine, such a supposition, an outrage to divine dignity and to the spiritual grandeur of the soul itself? And would it not, moreover, be a complete materialization of our intellectual faculties?

And yet . . .

Yes, it seems so to you because upon your planet no soul can incarnate itself otherwise than in a human embryo. That is the nature of life on Earth. But you must look through the veil. The soul is not an effect; the body serves only as its garment.[8]

I agree that it would indeed be odd if an event as important as the creation of an immortal soul could have a carnal cause and be the result of casual, more or less legitimate, unions. I also agree with you that organic causes cannot explain the different aptitudes with which human beings are born into the world. But I ask again: what would be the use of these various existences if, on beginning a new life, we retain no memory of those that precede it? Also, is it really desirable to have in prospect a journey without end through worlds without end: an eternal transmigration? There must surely be an end to it eventually; after many aeons of voyaging we must some day finish our existence and seek repose—so would it not be as well to do so after one existence only?

Poor human! You do not understand either time or space. Do you not know that outside the movement of the stars time no longer exists and that eternity is no longer measurable? Do you not know that "space" is nothing but a vain word in the infinite extent of the sidereal universe, no longer measurable? You ignore everything: all principles and causes escape you. As a mere atom upon a movable atom, you have no proper appreciation of the universe—and yet, despite ignorance so dense and comprehension so obscure, you would attempt to judge everything, to envelop everything, to grasp everything! It would be easier to put an ocean into a nutshell than it would be to make you, with your terrestrial brain, understand the law of destiny.

Can you not, by making proper use of the faculty of induction that has been granted to you, gather together the direct consequences of observation supported by reason? Observation, sustained by proof, shows conclusively that we are not equal on coming into this world; that the past is not unlike the future and that the eternity which lies before us also lies behind us; that nothing is created in nature and nothing annihilated; that nature includes all things existing and that God, spirit, law, number, are no more outside nature than matter, weight, and motion; that moral truth, justice, wisdom and virtue exist in the progress of the world as surely as its physical reality; that justice demands equity in its distribution of its destinies; that our destinies are not accomplished upon this earthly planet; that the empyrean heaven does not exist and that the earth is but a star in the sky; that other inhabited planets soar with ours in the vast expanse, opening out to the wings of the soul an inexhaustible field of vision; and that the infinite in the universe corresponds, in the material creation, with the eternity of our intelligence in the spiritual creation. Are not certainties such as these, followed by the inductions with which they inspire us, sufficient to liberate your mind from ancient prejudices and to open out to an enlightened judgment the proud panorama of the vague and profound desires of our souls?

I could illustrate this general sketch by examples and details that would surprise you even more, but let it suffice for me to add that there are in nature other forces than those you know, which differ both in essence and in mode of action from electricity, attraction, light, etc. Now, among these natural and unknown forces there is one in particular, the study of which will ultimately lead to remarkable discoveries elucidating the problems of the soul and life. It is the psychic force. This invisible fluidic force establishes a mysterious bond between living beings, unknown to them. In many cases you have already been able to recognize its existence. Take the case of two beings who are in love. It is impossible for them to live separately. Should circumstances lead to their being separated, the two lovers become absent-minded and their souls, as it were, leave their bodies and span the distance that prevents their reunion. The thoughts of one are shared by the other, and they live together in spite of their separation. Should any misfortune touch one, the other immediately becomes conscious of it; such separations have been known to end in death.

How many instances have been recorded by unimpeachable witnesses of the sudden apparition, just at the moment of death—even though many leagues might separate them—of a person to an intimate friend, a wife to a husband, a mother to a son, or vice versa? Even the severest critic cannot deny, nowadays, that such facts are proven by circumstance. Twin children living ten leagues apart, under very different conditions, are stricken at the same time with the same malady, or, if one is excessively fatigued, the other feels the same without any apparent or assignable cause. And so on. These abundant facts prove that bonds of sympathy exist between souls, and even between bodies, and they invite us to realize, yet again, that we are very far from understanding the forces active in nature.

I communicate these assertions to you, my friend, mainly to demonstrate not only that you may have a foretaste of truth before death, but also that earthly existence is not so entirely deprived of light as to prevent one's intelligence from recognizing the principal traits of the moral world. Besides, all these truths will be emphasized by my continuing narrative, when you learn that it is not only the existence immediately previous to my last that I have seen again, thanks to the slowness of light, but also planetary lives before that: so far, more than ten existences preceding the one in which we came to know one another on the earth.

II

Reflection and study have already inclined me, Lumen, to believe in the plurality of the incarnations of the soul — but that doctrine lacks logical, moral, and even physical proofs as numerous and as weighty as those in favor of the plurality of the inhabited worlds. I admit that until now I had grave doubts on the subject. Modern optics and marvelous calculation, which enable us, as it were, to touch the other worlds, show us their years, their seasons, and their days, and acquaint us with the variety of their natural surfaces. All these elements have enabled contemporary astronomy to establish the fact of human existence in other worlds on a strong and imperishable foundation. I repeat, though, that this is not so in the case of palingenesis[9] *— although I am strongly inclined toward the doctrine of the transmigration of souls in the actual heaven, since this is the only means by which we can obtain an idea of eternal life. My desire, however, needs to be sustained by a helpful light and inspired by a confidence I do not yet possess.*

It is precisely that light that is under consideration and will be brought out by this conversation. I admit that I have an advantage over you, since I speak of things I have seen, and I shall limit myself strictly to the exact interpretation of the events of which my spiritual life actually consists. But since you can see the possibility of the scientific explanation of my story, matters will become clearer as you listen and your knowledge will increase.

It is for this reason, above all, that I am always eager to hear you.

Light, as you have understood, is the means of giving to the disincarnate soul a direct vision of its planetary existences.

After having reviewed my earthly existence, I saw once more my previous life on one of the planets of Gamma Virginis, light bringing the former to me only after 72 years and the latter after 172 years. I can see myself at present from Capella as I was upon the earth 72 years ago, and as I was upon the planet of Gamma Virginis 172 years ago. Thus, two existences both past and successive are shown to me as present and simultaneous, by virtue of the physics of the light that transmits them.

About five hundred years ago, I lived on a world whose astronomical position as seen from the earth is precisely that of the left breast of Andromeda—although the inhabitants of that world certainly do not suspect that the denizens of a distant little planet have joined the stars by means of fictitious lines, tracing the figures of men, women, animals, and diverse objects, incorporating all the stars in more or less imaginary figures in order to give them names. It would greatly astonish some of these planetary people if they were told that on Earth, certain stars bear the names "Heart of the Scorpion" (what a heart!), "Head of the Dog," "Tail of the Great Bear," "Eye of the Bull," "Neck of the Dragon" and "Brow of the Goat."

You are aware that neither the constellations drawn upon the celestial globe nor the positions of the stars upon that globe are either real or absolute. They are the result of the position of the earth in space, and thus are simply figments of perspective. Go to the top of a mountain and make a plan of the respective positions of all the summits surrounding you in that circular panorama: its hills, valleys, villages, and lakes. A plan so constructed could serve only for the place in which it was drawn. Transport yourself ten miles away; the same summits are visible, but their respective positions in regard to one another are different, resulting from changes in perspective. The panorama of the Alps and the Oberland, as seen from Lucerne and Pilatus, does not in the least resemble those seen from the Fulkhorn and the Schynige Platte above Interlaken—yet these are exactly the same summits and lakes.

It is exactly the same with the stars. The same stars are seen from Delta Andromedae and from the earth, but not a single constellation is recognizable because all the celestial perspectives have changed. Stars of the first magnitude have become second or third, while others formerly of lesser magnitudes, having become nearer, shine with increased brilliance. Above all, the apparent position of each star relative to the others has changed completely because of the different relationship of that star and the earth.

So the appearance of the constellations, which have long been assumed to be ineradicably traced upon the vault of the heavens, is an artifact of perspective. On changing position, the perspective shifts, and the sky is no longer the same. But if so, ought we not to have a change of celestial perspective every six months, since during this interval the earth has greatly altered its position, moving to a distance of seventy-four million leagues from the place it formerly occupied?

This objection proves that you have fully understood the principle of the deformation of the constellations as one moves in any direction in space. It would be as you suppose, if the earth's orbit were sufficiently vast in dimension for its two opposed points to offer altered views of the celestial scenery.

Seventy-four million leagues . . .

Are as nothing in the order of celestial distances and can no more affect the perspectives of the stars than taking a single step in the turret of the Pantheon would change the apparent positions of the buildings of Paris to the eye of an observer.

Certain charts of the Middle Ages represent the zodiac as an arch in the empyrean, and place some of the constellations — such as Andromeda, Lyra, Cassiopeia, and Aquila — in the same region as the Seraphim, the Cherubim, and the Thrones. That must have been mere fancy, since constellations have no real existence, being simply appearances due to perspective.

Evidently. The ancient heaven of theology certainly has no legitimate situation today, and simple common sense shows that it does not exist. Two truths cannot oppose one another; of necessity, the spiritual heaven should accord with the physical heaven, and the object of my various discourses is the demonstration of this truth.

Upon the world of Delta Andromedae of which I speak, there is nothing resembling the constellation of Andromeda. Those stars, which appear linked when seen from the earth, and have served in the celestial landscape to distinguish the daughter of Cepheus and Cassiopeia, are in reality distributed in space at all sorts of distances and in every direction. One cannot find, there or elsewhere, the least vestigial trace of terrestrial mythology.

All its poetry is lost! I shall, however, feel a certain satisfaction in believing that for a part of my life I have rested on the bosom of An-

dromeda. It is a pleasant fancy. There is a mythological perfume in it, and a sensation of comfort. I should like to be transported there without fear of the monster, and without fearing for young Perseus mounted on the famous Pegasus, bearing the head of Medusa. But now, thanks to the scalpel of science, there is no longer an unveiled princess bound to a rock on the seashore, or a virgin holding an ear of golden corn, or Orion pursuing the Pleiades. Venus has vanished from our evening sky, and old Saturn has laid down his scythe in the night. Science has caused these ancient myths to vanish! I regret its progress.

Do you, then, prefer illusion to reality? Do you not know that truth is immeasurably more beautiful, grander, and infinitely more marvelous than error, however the latter may be embellished? What can be comparable, in all the mythologies past and present, to the rapt scientific contemplation of celestial grandeur and the sublime movements of nature? What impression can strike the soul more profoundly than the fact of the expanse crowded with worlds, and the immensity of the sidereal systems? What voice is more eloquent than the silence of a starlit night? What wild flight of imagination could conceive an image surpassing that of the interstellar voyage of light, stamping with the seal of eternity the transitory events of the life of every world? So throw off your old errors, my friend, and be honestly proud of the majesty of science. Listen to what follows. . . .

By reason of the time that light employs in coming from the system of Delta Andromedae to Capella, I have reviewed my last-but-one existence, which ended five hundred years ago, in the present year of 1869. That world is very peculiar, according to our standards. It has only one kingdom, that being the animal kingdom; the vegetable kingdom does not exist there. But that animal kingdom is very different from ours and superior in kind although it is endowed with five senses similar to those on the earth.

It is a world without sleep and without fixity. It is entirely enveloped in a rose-colored ocean, less dense than terrestrial water but denser than our atmosphere. It is a substance holding a middle rank as a fluid, between air and water. Terrestrial chemistry does not produce any similar substance, so it would be in vain to try to represent it to you. Carbolic acid gas,[10] which can be held invisible at the bottom of a glass and can be poured out like water, is the nearest analogy I can offer you. Its existence is due to a fixed quantity of heat and electricity held in permanence upon that globe.

You are aware that the composition of all things upon the earth—whether mineral, vegetable, or animal—is a solid, liquid, or gaseous state and that the sole cause of these different conditions is the heat radiated from the sun upon the earth's surface. The interior heat of the globe now has hardly any effect on its surface. Less solar heat would liquefy gases and solidify liquids; greater heat would melt solids and evaporate liquids. Different quantities of heat could produce liquid air—yes, liquid air—and gaseous marble. If, by any cause whatsoever, the planet Earth were one day to fly out of its orbit at a tangent and rush away into the glacial obscurity of space, you would see all the water on Earth become solid, and gases in their turn become liquid, then turn solid themselves. You would see! No, you could not see this by remaining upon the earth, but from the depths of space you might witness this curious spectacle should your globe ever indulge in the freakish behavior of escaping its orbit. And take further note that, if colossal cold should ever descend suddenly, all creatures would find themselves instantly frozen on the spot, and the globe would carry into space the singular panorama of the whole human race and every other animal immovably congealed for all eternity, in the various attitudes assumed by each individual and creature at the moment of the catastrophe.

Worlds exist that are in such a state; they are eccentric worlds, the life of whose inhabitants has been insensibly arrested by the rapid flight of their planet away from its sun, transforming them into millions of statues. Most of them are lying down, asleep, because this profound change of temperature has taken many days in its accomplishment. There they lie, pell-mell, in the millions: dead, or, to be more accurate, sunk in a complete lethargy. The cold preserves them. Three or four thousand years later, when the planet returns from its dark and frozen aphelion to its brilliant perihelion, the sun's fertilizing heat caresses its surface with welcoming and rapidly increasing rays, and when it has reached the level that constitutes the normal temperature of these beings, they will be resuscitated at the age they had reached when sleep overtook them. They will take up their affairs from the moment of interruption — a lengthy interruption! — without any consciousness of the fact that they have slept dreamlessly for so many ages. One might see some continuing a game or finishing a phrase whose first words were uttered four thousand years before. All this is perfectly straightforward, for we have seen that time does not really exist; this, albeit on a larger scale, is exactly what passes on the earth when infusoria[11] revive, taking a fresh lease of life from the rain after several years of apparent death.

We must now return to our world of Andromeda. The rose-colored and quasi-liquid atmosphere, which surrounds it as entirely as an ocean without islands, is the abode of living beings, who are perpetually floating in the depths of that ocean, which none have ever sounded. From their birth to their death they have not a moment's repose; incessant activity is the condition of their existence. Should they become stationary, they would perish. In order to breathe — that is to say, to enable this fluid element to penetrate their torsos — they are constrained to keep their tentacles in unceasing motion and their lungs (I use the word to facilitate understanding) constantly open.

The external form of this human race resembles that of the sirens of antiquity, but is less elegant, and their organism approaches that of the seal. Do you see the essential difference between their constitution and that of terrestrial man? It is that we on Earth breathe without being conscious of the action and obtain oxygen without exertion, not being compelled to experience any difficulty in converting venous to arterial blood by the absorption of oxygen; upon this other world, by contrast, this nourishment is obtained only by labor, at the cost of incessant effort.

So this world is inferior to ours in the scale of progress?

Without a doubt, since I inhabited it before coming to the earth. But do not think that the earth is much superior by reason of our being able to breathe while we are asleep. It is undoubtedly a great advantage to be furnished with a pneumatic mechanism that opens automatically every time our organism needs the least breath of air and that operates mechanically and incessantly night and day — but man does not live on air alone. His earthly organism requires nourishment with something more solid, and this solid matter does not come to him automatically, as air does. What is the result?

Look at the earth for a moment. Look at its sorrow, its desolation! What a world of misery and brutality! Multitudes bowed down with bent backs to the soil, which they dig with toil and pain so that they may obtain their daily bread! All those heads bent down toward the grossness of matter instead of being raised up to the contemplation of nature! All those efforts and labors, bringing weakness and disease in their wake! All that traffic to amass a little gold at the expense of others! Man taking advantage of his brethren! Castes, aristocracies, robbery and ruin, ambitions, thrones, wars . . . in a word, personal interests, always selfish, often sordid: the reign of matter over mind.

Such is the everyday state of the earth: a condition forced upon you by the nature of your bodies, compelling you to kill in order to live, and to prefer the possession of material goods — which cannot be carried beyond the grave — to the possession of intellectual gifts, which the soul can keep as a rich and inalienable possession.

You speak as though it were possible to live without eating.

What! Can you believe that the beings of every world in space are restricted by an operation as ridiculous as that? Happily, in many of those worlds, the spirit is not subject to such ignominy.

It is not as difficult as you might initially suppose to believe in the possibility of atmospheric nutriment. The maintenance of life in animals, including human beings, depends on two processes: respiration and nutrition. The object of the former occurs naturally in the atmosphere; that of the second is ingested in food. Nutrition produces blood; from the blood come the tissues, the muscles, the bones, the cartilages, the flesh, the brain, the nerves — in a word, the organic constituents of the body. The oxygen we breathe can be considered as a nutritive substance itself, inasmuch as it combines with the principal aliments absorbed by the stomach to complete the formation of the blood and the development of the tissues.[12]

Now, in order to imagine nutrition passing entirely into the domain of the atmosphere, it is necessary to observe that a completely adequate diet is made up of albumen, sugar, fat, and salt, and also to imagine that an atmospheric fluid might be formed of these substances—existing in a gaseous state—as well as oxygen and nitrogen. These aliments are found in the solids that you absorb; digestion is the process that separates them and causes them to be assimilated into the appropriate organs. When, for example, you eat a loaf of bread, you introduce into your stomach a quantity of starch—a substance insoluble in water, which is not found in the blood. Saliva and pancreatic juice transform the insoluble starch into soluble sugar. Bile, pancreatic juice, and intestinal secretions change the sugar into fat. Both sugar and fat are present in the blood, and it is by the processes of alimentation that substances are separated and assimilated by your body.

It may astonish you, my friend, that after living five years—according to your terrestrial reckoning—in the celestial world, I can still remember all these material terms and condescend to make use of them; but the memories that I have brought from the earth are still vivid, and as we are presently discussing a matter of organic physiology, I feel no shame in calling things by their names.

If, then, we suppose that instead of being combined or mixed in the constitution of bodies, solid or liquid, these aliments could be found in a gaseous state in the composition of the atmosphere, we can thus imagine nutritive atmospheres that dispense with the gross and ridiculous functions of digestion.

That which a human being is capable of imagining in the restricted sphere of his observation, nature has put into practice in more than one place in the universe. Moreover, I can assure you that when one has ceased to be accustomed to the material process of introducing nourishment into the digestive system, one cannot help being struck by its brutality. This was brought home to me a few days ago while observing one of the richest nations on your planet. I was struck by the suave and angelic beauty of a maiden reclining in a gondola floating gently on the blue waters of the Bosphorus toward Constantinople. This young Circassian was reclining on red velvet cushions embroidered with brilliant silks, whose heavy gold tassels trailed in the water; a young black slave playing some stringed instrument knelt before her. Her form was so childlike and graceful, her curved arm so elegant, her eyes so pure and innocent, her pensive brow so calm beneath the light of heaven, that I was captivated for an instant by a nostalgic admiration for this masterpiece of living nature. Well, while this pure vision of awakening youth, as sweet as a flower opening its petals to the sun, held me in a kind of temporary enchantment, the boat reached the landing stage. The maiden, leaning on a slave, seated herself on a couch near a well-spread table, around which others had already gathered, and began to eat.

Yes, for nearly an hour, she was *eating*! I could scarcely tolerate the earthly recollections recalled by this ridiculous spectacle. To see a being like that partaking of food through the mouth, and making her charming body the receptacle for I don't know what substances! What vulgarity! Masticating morsels of some kind of animal, which her pearly teeth did not disdain to chew, and further fragments of another animal, which her virginal lips opened without hesitation to receive and swallow! What a diet: a medley of ingredients drawn from cattle or deer, which had lived in the mire and afterward been slaughtered. Horror! I turned away sadly from this strange contrast, and directed my gaze to the system of Saturn, where humanity need not stoop to such necessities.

The floating beings belonging to the world of Delta Andromedae, where my antepenultimate existence was accomplished, are submitted to an even more degrading manner of sustaining life than are the inhabitants of Earth. They have not the advantage of finding three parts of their nutriment supplied by the air, as is the case on your world; they must work to obtain what might be called their oxygen. They are condemned to use their lungs constantly to prepare the nutritious air they need, without sleeping—and without ever feeling satisfied, for in spite of their incessant toil they cannot absorb more than a small quantity at a time. Thus they pass their entire lives, dying at last as victims of the struggle for existence.

Better never to have been born! But might not the same judgment be applied to the earth? What is the use of being born, to tire oneself out with endless work and worry; to turn the same daily treadmill for sixty or a hundred years; to sleep, to eat, to work, to speak, to run, to err, to agitate, to dream, ad infinitum? Of what use is it all? Would not one be just as far advanced if one were extinguished the day after birth — or, better still, if one did not take the trouble to come into the world? The world would not go on in any worse fashion — and even if it did, no one would be any the wiser. Of what use is Nature herself, one might ask, and why does the universe exist at all?[13]

That is the great mystery. And yet, all destinies must be accomplished. The world of Delta Andromedae is definitely an inferior one. To give you an idea of the poor mental caliber of its inhabitants I will cite two examples, selecting the subjects of religion and politics, as these are generally the best criteria of the value of a people. Now, in religion, instead of seeking God in nature and basing their judgment on science, and instead of aspiring to the truth, using their eyes to see and their reason to comprehend — in sum, instead of establishing the foundations of their philosophy upon knowledge as exact as possible of the order that governs the world — they are divided into sects, which are voluntarily blind. They believe they render homage to their pretended God by ceasing to reason and think they adore Him in maintaining that their anthill is unique in space, by reciting phrases and injuring other sects — even, alas, by tortures and burnings at the stake — and in authorizing massacres and wars. There are assertions in their doctrines that seem to be expressly designed to outrage common sense — and it is precisely these that constitute their fundamental articles of faith!

They are equally stupid in politics. The most intelligent and pure-minded do not understand one another, with the result that the republic seems to be a form of government incapable of realization there. Tracing the annals of their history as far back as possible, one sees a cowardly and indifferent people deliberately choosing to be led by an individual claiming to be their Basileus[14] rather than governing themselves. This chief deprives them of three-fourths of their resources, keeping for himself and his friends the atmosphere containing the greatest amount of the rose essence — which is to say that he keeps the best in the land for his own use. He gives each of his subjects a number, and from time to time sends them to fight against neighboring peoples who, like themselves, are subject to a Basileus. Marshaling them like shoals of herring, he directs them on either side toward the field of battle, which they call "the field of honor," where they proceed to destroy one another like furious fools, without knowing why—and without, for that matter, the power to comprehend, as they do not even speak the same language. And do you imagine that those who, most favored by chance, live to return feel any hatred against their Basileus? Nothing of the kind. The remnant of the army who live to see their homes again think nothing more natural than to celebrate their thanksgivings in company with the dignitaries of their sects, supplicating their God to pour blessings upon and grant long life to the worthy man whom they designate their paternal Basile.

It follows from these observations that the inhabitants of Delta Andromedae are greatly our inferiors, both physically and intellectually, for the state of affairs on the earth is far from parallel. To sum up, upon their globe there is only one living kingdom, and that a mobile one without repose or sleep, kept in perpetual agitation by reason of an inexorable fate. Such a world seems very bizarre to me.

What, then, would you say of the one I inhabited fifteen centuries ago? A world also containing only one kingdom—not a mobile one, but on the contrary, one as fixed as your vegetable kingdom is?

What! Animals and men held down by roots?

III

My existence prior to that upon the world of Delta Andromedae was spent on Venus, a planet near to Earth, where I can remember myself as a woman. Not that I have seen myself there directly, for light requires the same length of time to travel from Venus to Capella as it would from Earth to Capella, and I consequently see Venus only as it was seventy-two years ago and not as it was nine hundred years ago, which was the epoch of my existence upon that planet.

My fourth life previous to my terrestrial one was passed upon an immense annular planet belonging to the constellation Cygnus, situated in the Milky Way. Now, this strange world is inhabited solely by trees.

What you mean is that thus far there are only plants there, neither animals nor intelligent beings capable of speech having appeared as yet?

Not exactly. True, there are only plants there—but in this vast world of plants there are vegetable races more advanced than those existing upon the earth. There are plants that live as we do; they feel, think, reason and communicate.

But that is impossible! Pardon me—I should say extraordinary, incomprehensible, and entirely inconceivable.

These intelligent vegetable races really exist—so much so that I myself belonged to one of them. Fifteen centuries ago I was a tree possessed of reason.

But how? How can a plant reason without a brain and speak without a tongue?

Tell me, I beg of you: by what process do you think, by what transformation of motion does your soul translate its mute conceptions into audible language?

I am considering the question, master, but I cannot find the underlying explanation of this fact, however ordinary it may be.

We have no right to declare an unknown fact impossible when we ourselves are so ignorant of the laws regulating our own being. Because the brain is the physiological organ of intelligence placed at the service of human beings on the earth, do you therefore believe that there are similar brains and spinal cords on all the worlds in space? That would be too childish an error. The law of progress governs the vital system of every world. These vital systems differ according to the secret nature of the special forces peculiar to each. When a world has reached a sufficient degree of evolution to fit it for entry to the service of moral life, mind appears upon it, in a more or less developed state. Do not imagine that the Eternal Father immediately creates a human race on each globe. Not so. The highest step in the ladder of the animal kingdom receives the human transfiguration by force of circumstance and by means of natural law, which ennobles it as soon as progress has brought it to a state of relative superiority.

Do you know why you have a chest, a stomach, two legs, two arms, and a head furnished with visual, auditory and olfactory senses? It is because the quadrupeds, the mammals that preceded the appearance of humans on the earth, had them already. Monkeys, dogs, lions, bears, horses, oxen, tigers, cats, etc. — and before them the woolly rhinoceros, the cave hyena, the Irish elk, the mastodon, the opossum, etc.; and prior to these the pleiosaurus. the ichthyosaurus, the iguanodon, the pterodactyl, etc.; and, again, before these the fishes, the crustacea, the mollusca, etc. — have been the result of the vital forces in action upon the earth, dependent upon the state of the soil, of the atmosphere, of inorganic chemistry, of the quantity of heat, and of terrestrial gravity. The earthly animal kingdom has followed, from its origin, this continuous and progressive march toward the perfection of its typical forms of mammalia, freeing itself more and more from the grossness of its material.

A human being is more beautiful than a horse, a horse than a bear, a bear than a tortoise. A similar law governs the vegetable kingdom. Heavy, coarse vegetables without leaves or flowers began the evolutionary sequence. Then, as the ages advanced, their forms became purer and graceful leaves appeared, filling the woods with silent shadows. Flowers, in their turn, began to beautify the gardens of the earth and spread sweet perfumes in an erstwhile-insipid atmosphere.

To the eye of the geologist who visits his scrutiny upon these tertiary, secondary, and primordial strata, the parallel progression of the two kingdoms is visible to this day. There was a period on the earth when a few islands had only just emerged from the bosom of the warm waters into an atmosphere supercharged with vapor, when the only living things distinguishing this organic kingdom were long floating filaments held in suspension in the waves. Seaweeds and seawracks were the first forms of vegetation.

Now, nameless creatures live upon the rocks; then sponges swell out here, while a tree of coral elevates itself there. Later on, the medusae detach themselves and float like balls of jelly. Are they animals? Are they plants? Science does not answer; they are animal-plants, zoophytes. But life is not limited to these forms; there are creatures no less primitive and just as simple, of a different kind. These are the tubeworms: creatures without eyes, ears, blood, nerves, will; a vegetative species, yet endowed with the power of motion.

Later still, rudimentary organs of sight and locomotion appeared, and life became less elementary. Then fishes and amphibious creatures came into existence. The animal kingdom began to form itself. But what would the result have been had the first creature never quit its rock—if these primitive elements of terrestrial life had remained stationary at the point of their formation, and if, for whatever reason, the faculty of locomotion had never made a beginning?[15]

The consequence would have been that in place of the system of terrestrial vitality being manifest in two different directions—the world of plants and the world of animals—it would have continued manifesting itself solely in the former direction, with the result that there would have been only one kingdom instead of two, and creative progress would have operated in that kingdom as it operated in the animal kingdom. It would not have been arrested at the formation of sensitives—superior plants that are already gifted with a veritable nervous system—nor would it have stopped at the formation of flowers, whose organic functions are already bordering on ours. Continuing its ascension, it would have produced in the vegetable kingdom that which has been produced in the animal kingdom. As things are, many vegetables feel and act; there would have been vegetables thinking and making themselves understood. The earth would not have been deprived of a human species on that account—but humankind, instead of being gifted with locomotion, as it actually is, would have been fixed by the feet.

Such is the state of the annular world in which I lived fifteen centuries ago, in the heart of the Milky Way.

Truthfully, this world of human plants astonishes me even more than the previous one, and I find it difficult to form a picture of the life and manners of these singular beings.

Their mode of life is, indeed, very different from yours. They neither build cities nor make voyages; they have no need of any form of government; they are ignorant of that scourge of terrestrial humanity, war; and they have none of that national self-love called patriotism, which is one of your characteristics. Prudent, patient, and gifted with constancy, they have neither the mobility nor the fragility of the denizens of the earth. Life there attains an average of five or six centuries, and it is calm, sweet, uniform, devoid of revolutions. But do not think that these human plants have only a vegetable existence. On the contrary, their existence is very personal and very positive.

They are not divided into castes, regulated by birth and fortune according to the absurd customs of the earth, but into families, whose native value differs precisely according to kind. Their social history is unwritten, but nothing that happens among them can be lost, inasmuch as they have neither emigrations nor conquests and their records and traditions are handed down from one generation to another. Everyone knows the history of his or her own race — for they also have two sexes, like those of the earth, and unions take place there in an analogous manner, although they are purer, more disinterested and invariably affectionate. Nor are these unions always consanguineous; impregnation can be effected at a distance.

But how, after all, can they communicate their thoughts, if it is true that they think. And how, moreover, was it possible for you to recognize yourself upon this singular world?

The same reply will satisfy both parts of your question. I was looking at that ring in the constellation of Cygnus because I was drawn there by the persistence of some irresistible instinct. It surprised me to see only vegetable growths upon its surface, and I immediately remarked the odd manner of their grouping: here two and two, there three and three, farther off ten and ten, besides others in larger clusters. Some seemed to be, as it were, seated beside a spring; others appeared to be lying down, with little shoots springing up around them. I looked for the species familiar to me upon the earth, such as pines, oaks, poplars, and willows, but I could not find any of those botanical specimens.

In the end I fixed my eyes upon a plant shaped like a fig tree without either leaves or fruit but full of brilliant scarlet flowers. I suddenly saw this enormous tree stretch out a bough like an enormous arm, raise the extremity of this arm to its head, and pluck one of the magnificent flowers ornamenting its crown—and then, with an inclination of the head, present the same to another tree growing some little distance apart, which was of slender and graceful form, bearing sweet blue flowers. This one appeared to receive the red flower with a certain pleasure, for it extended a branch—or, one might say, a cordial hand—to its neighbor, which was apparently taken in an enduring clasp.

Under certain circumstances, as you know, a gesture is sufficient to make yourself known to another. In that way, the meaning of this tableau was communicated to me. That gesture of a fig tree in the Milky Way awoke a world of memories within me. This human plant was myself as I was fifteen centuries ago; and in the fig trees with the violet flowers that were grouped round me I recognized my children—for I recollected that the tint of the flowers borne by the offspring is the result of the admixture of the two colors distinguishing their parents.

These human plants see without eyes, hear without ears, and speak without a larynx. Have you not flowers upon the earth that can discriminate not only night from day, but also the different hours of the day, the height of the sun above the horizon, a clear sky from a cloudy one, and that also perceive diverse sounds with exquisite sensitivity—and, in fact, not only hear one another perfectly, but butterfly messengers too. These rudiments are developed to a veritable degree of civilization upon the world of which I speak, and these beings are as complete in their kind as you on the earth are in yours. Their intelligence, it is true, is less advanced than the average intellect of terrestrial humanity, but in their manners and mutual relations they show in every way a sweetness and refinement that might often serve as a model to the dwellers upon the earth.

How is it possible, master, that they see without eyes and hear without ears?

You will cease to be astonished, my old friend, if you will only consider that light and sound are nothing other than two modes of motion. In order to appreciate either of these two modes it is necessary and sufficient to be endowed with an apparatus in correspondence with them, which might be no more than a simple nerve. The eye and the ear are the apparatus for your terrestrial nature; in another natural organization the optic nerve and the auditory nerve form quite different organs. Besides which, light and sound are not the only two modes of motion in nature. I could even say that "light" and "sound" are the result of your manner of feeling rather than reality itself.

There are in nature not one but ten, twenty, a hundred, or a thousand different modes of motion. Upon the earth you are so formed as to be able to appreciate these two in particular, so that they constitute almost the whole of your life and its external relations. On other worlds there are other senses with which nature can be appreciated in its various aspects. Some of these senses take the place of your eyes and ears, while others are in touch with perceptions entirely foreign to those received by terrestrial organs.

When you spoke just now of the human plants in the world of Cygnus, it occurred to me to ask whether earthly plants possess souls?

Most certainly. Terrestrial plants are gifted with a soul just as animals and men are. Without a potential soul no organization could exist. The form of a plant is determined by its soul.[16] An acorn and the kernel of a peach are planted side by side in the same soil, the same situation, under the same conditions; why should the first produce an oak and the second a peach tree? Because an organic force inherent in the oak will construct its particular species of vegetable, and another organic force—another soul, inherent in the peach—will similarly draw to itself other elements necessary to its specific body, just as the human soul uses the means placed at its disposal by nature to construct its body. Except that the soul of the plant has no self-consciousness.

The souls in vegetables, animals, and men have already attained to that degree of personality and authority that enables them to bend at will, and to command and govern at pleasure, all the impersonal forces that exist in the bosom of immeasurable nature. For example, the human monad, being superior to the monad of salt, carbon, or oxygen, absorbs and incorporates them in its structure.[17] On the earth, our human soul in our terrestrial body governs, without being conscious of it, all the elementary souls forming the constituent parts of its body.

Matter is not a solid and measurable substance; it is an assemblage of centers of forces. Substance is unimportant; between one atom and another there is a vast distance on the atomic scale. At the head of the various centers of force that constitute and form the human body is the human soul, governing all the ganglionic souls that are subordinated to it.

I must frankly admit, most wise instructor, that I cannot get a firm grip on this theory.

Then I shall illustrate it for you with an example that will establish it for you as a matter of fact.

A matter of fact? Are you then a reincarnation of the Princess Scheherazade, and have you been fascinating me with a new tale from the Thousand and One Nights?[18]

THE FIFTH CONVERSATION

Imagination Is Bold; Nature Is Bolder

You know the splendid constellation of Orion, which reigns like a sovereign over your winter nights, and the curious multiple star Theta Orionis, which is to be found below the sword suspended from the Belt and shines in the middle of the famous nebula.[1]

The system of Theta Orionis is one of the most unusual to be found in the vast treasure house that contains such a rich variety of celestial jewels. It is composed of four principal suns disposed in a quadrilateral. Two of these suns, forming what I may call the base of the quadrilateral, are accompanied, one by a single sun and the other by two. It is, therefore, a system of seven suns, each of them encircled by inhabited planets.

I was on a planet orbiting one of the secondary suns, which revolved in its turn around one of the four principal suns. That rotated in its turn, in concert with the others, around an invisible center of gravity in the interior of the quadrilateral. A celestial mechanism explains these movements, but I shall not dwell on the matter.

I was, in consequence, lighted and warmed on my planet by seven suns at the same time, including one that was larger and brighter than the rest because it was nearer, a second very large and equally bright, a third of moderate size, and two that were like twins. It never happens that these different suns are all above the horizon at the same time; there are day suns and night suns—which is to say that there is no "night," as properly defined.

What? Are there other such double and multiple suns in the heavens?

Very many of them. The system of which I am speaking, and others, are known to the astronomers of the earth, whose catalogues count systems of double stars, multiple stars, and colored stars by the thousand. You can study them yourself with your telescope.

Now, on the planet of Orion of which I was just speaking, the inhabitants are neither vegetable nor animal. They could not be placed within any classification of terrestrial life—not even the most basic categories, which constitute the vegetable and animal kingdoms. In truth, I hardly know what comparison to make in order that I might give you an idea of their form. Have you ever seen in a botanic garden the gigantic tapering plant *Cereus giganteus*?[2]

I know the plant well. Its name comes from its resemblance to the wax tapers placed in three or more branched stands to light churches.

Well, the humans of Theta Orionis bear some likeness to that form, but they move slowly and maintain an upright position by means of a process of suction, analogous to that of the ampullae of certain plants.[3] The lower part of the vertical stem is slightly elongated where it rests on the ground, like a starfish, with little appendages that fix themselves to the soil by means of suction. These beings often move in troops, changing their latitude according to the season, but the most singular peculiarity of their organization is one that illustrates the principle of which I have spoken to you, of the union of elementary souls in the human body.

One day I visited this world and found myself in the midst of an Orionic landscape. I beheld a being standing there like a plant ten meters high, without leaves or flowers. It consisted, in fact, of a cylindrical stalk, the uppermost part of which separated into many branches, like those of a chandelier. The central stem, as well as those of the branches, measured about a third of a meter in diameter. The tops of the stalk and branches were crowned with a silver-fringed diadem.

Suddenly, I saw this being agitate its branches and then vanish.

The fact is that in this world, individuals—although quite healthy—literally fall to pieces in an instant. The molecules of which they are constituted fall in unison to the ground. The personal existence of the organism comes to an end; its molecules separate and are dispersed.

They disintegrate, and the atoms fly apart like truants from school.

Almost. I recollect that such disintegrations of the body often took place within the course of a life. Sometimes it was the result of opposition, sometimes of fatigue, and in other instances of a lack of organic accord between different parts. They exist in their entirety, actual and complete, then are abruptly reduced to the simplest elementary forms. The cerebral molecule, which really constitutes each individual, feels itself descending in consequence of the fall of its sister molecules in the long branches, and it arrives on the ground surface solitary and independent.

This kind of vanishing trick would, on occasion, be a very convenient process down here. To get out of an embarrassing situation—a conjugal scene in the Molière mode, for example, or a bad quarter of a hour of the kind described by Rabelais, or a tragic situation such as mounting the scaffold to be executed. One would merely have to let loose one's constituent atoms and . . . Goodbye, everyone![4]

You choose to regard the matter as a joke, but I assure you that it is an undoubted reality. It would exist on the earth as well as on the planet in Orion if the principle of authority were not so firmly fixed within you. There it is only in an elementary form; your body is formed of animated molecules. According to one of your most eminent physiologists, your spinal marrow is a series of centers, linked together independently and yet under control. The essential constituents of your blood, flesh, and bones are similar. They are provinces that are self-governed but subject to a superior authority.

The working of this superior authority is a condition of human life: a condition that is less exclusive among the inferior animals. Each ring of the worm called *Lumbricus* is a complete individual, so that a worm consists of a series of similar beings constituting a living co-operative society.[5] Cut into rings, the worm would be so many independent individuals. In the tapeworm, a solitary creature, the head is of greater importance than the rest of the body and possesses the faculty of reproducing the rest of the body after it has been cut off. The leech is a further example of united individuals; cut it into five or six rings and the operation gives you as many leeches. Thus, also, a cutting of a branch of a tree will grow. In like manner, a crab's claw or a lizard's tail will be regenerated. In reality, the vertebrate animals, including human beings, are essentially composite in structure. The spinal cord, and the gross expansion of its material that is the brain, consist of segments placed in juxtaposition, whose individual nervous systems each possess an elementary soul.[6]

The law of authority in action upon the earth has determined in the animal series a preponderant direction. You are composed of a multitude of entities grouped together, dominated by the formative attraction of your personal soul—which, from the center of your being, has formed your body from its embryo and has united about itself in a microcosm a whole world of beings that have no consciousness of their individuality.

On the planet of Orion, then, nature itself is an absolute republic?

A republic governed by law.

But when a being finds itself thus disintegrated, how can it reconstitute itself as a whole thereafter?

By willpower, often without the least effort, or even by casual desire. Although separated from the cerebral molecule, the corporeal molecules are still intimately connected with one another. At a given moment, they combine, each taking its place. The directing molecule draws the other from a distance as a magnet attracts iron filings.

I can easily picture this Lilliputian army, when summoned by a whistle, drawing to its center to organize a reunion: all the little soldiers climbing over one another, taking their places in a trice to reconstruct the human taper that you have described. One really should leave the earth, to behold such rare wonders!

You are still judging universal nature by the atom that you have before your eyes, and you are able to comprehend only the facts that lie within the sphere of your observations—but I assure you that the earth is not the type of the universe.

The world of Theta Orionis, with its seven circling suns, is peopled by an organic system like that I have just described to you. I lived there 2,400 years ago, and I can see myself there in accordance with the time that light occupied in coming from that point in space to Capella.

While there, I was acquainted with the spirit who was incarnated on the earth in the present century and published his studies under the name of Allan Kardec.[7] During our terrestrial life we did not recollect that we had known one another before, but we often felt attracted to one another by peculiar intellectual sympathies. Now that he, like myself, has returned to the world of spirits, he also remembers the singular republic of Orion and can see it. Yes, this is very curious, but it is perfectly true. You have no idea, on your poor planet, of the unimaginable diversity of worlds, which affects their geological as much as their physiological organizations.

These conversations may serve to throw light on your knowledge of this general truth, which is so important in the conception of the universe, but the greatest scientific service they can render you is to make you understand that light is the mode of transmission of universal history. With the powerful visual faculty that we enjoy here, we can distinguish the surfaces of distant worlds. The eye of the spirit is not like the bodily eye.

In terrestrial sight the rays diverge, so that a very small object placed quite near the eye fills the interval of the two rays, while at a greater distance a larger object is necessary to fill the same space, which is increased in proportion. In our eyes, by contrast, the visual rays enter in parallel lines, so that we see each object in its real proportions and in its normal size, its apparent size being quite unaffected by distance. We do not see the whole of large objects, but only sections of them proportionate to the openings of our special retinas—but these parts are seen by us with equal clarity at any distance, when there is no atmosphere to veil it.[8] A tree in a prairie on a celestial body as far away as Theta Orionis is from Capella is perfectly visible to us.

On the other hand, in accordance with the principle of the successive transmission of the rays of light, all the events in nature, and the history of all worlds, are depicted in space as a universal tableau: the most true and magnificent in all creation.[9]

As these conversations have shown you, I have traversed a great many celestial countries and have also studied creation without fixing myself in any one place. I hope in the course of the next century to be reincarnated on a world within the retinue of Sirius. The humankind there is more beautiful than that of the earth; birth is effected by means of an organic system less ridiculous and less brutal than that on Earth, but the most remarkable characteristic of life on that world is that its humans can perceive the physicochemical operations that maintain the body. From every molecule of the body proceeds a nerve that transmits to the brain the various impressions it receives, so that the soul has absolute knowledge of its body and rules over it as a sovereign.

There is an immense variety of worlds. On one of the planets in the system of Aldebaran, very curious in this respect, the vegetables are all composed of a substance that is analogous to asbestos[10] because silica and magnesia predominate in its constitution. The animals feed on this substance exclusively, so most of the beings inhabiting this world are incombustible.[11]

Upon the world of which I speak, night is illuminated by phosphorescent light. I have visited other worlds where night does not exist at all—where day and night do not succeed one another as upon the earth, because every portion of their spheres is continuously supplied with light by several suns that never leave them in darkness for an instant. Sleep is unnecessary there, for humans, animals, or plants.

On your planet sleep consumes a third of your life, its primary cause being the rotation of the earth on its axis, which produces day and night in succession in the various parts of the globe. On these worlds where it is always day, the inhabitants never sleep, and it would greatly surprise them to learn that there exists a humankind that passes a third of its life in a lethargy resembling death.

Not far from this lies a world where night is almost unknown, even though it does not possess a nocturnal sun, like the one in the quadrilateral of Orion, and has no satellites. The rocks of its mountains, being of a chemical composition that reminds one of the phosphates and sulphates of barytes,[12] store up the solar light received during the day, and during the night they radiate a gentle, calm, translucent light that illuminates the scenery with a tranquil nocturnal clarity. There, too, one sees curious trees bearing flowers that shine in the evening like fireflies; they resemble horse chestnuts, but the snowy flowers are luminous.

Phosphorus is an important constituent of the composition of this curious and remarkable world. Its atmosphere is constantly electrified. Its animals are luminous as well as its plants, and its humanity partakes of the same quality. The temperature is very high, and the inhabitants have had little need to invent clothing. It so happens that certain passions are manifested by the illumination of the body.

This is, on a larger scale, what takes place on a small scale in your terrestrial meadows, where one sees glowworms silently consumed in amorous flame on mild summer evenings. In the fireflies seen in northern France the male is winged and nonluminous; the female, on the other hand, is luminous but cannot fly. In Italy both sexes are winged, and both can become luminous. The humankind that I am describing to you has all the advantages of the latter type.

Certain forms of terrestrial life recur among many of the kinds of extraterrestrial humanity. Thus, we find in some cases the same thing that occurs on Earth in the ant world, where all the males die of exhaustion on the day of their aerial unions; and in the world of bees, where the procreators are sacrificed pitilessly; and among spiders, where they are devoured by their companions unless they can escape immediately. There are versions of the habits of a great number of insects, which never see their offspring and lay their eggs in surroundings in which the newly born will find their first food.[13]

The human body on this earth owes its form and its state of being to the atmospheric environment, and to the conditions of density, weight, and nutrition by means of which terrestrial evolution operates. The human being proceeds from the fusion of a microscopic masculine corpuscle with a minute feminine ovule. This fusion gives birth to a little cell that is transformed into the embryo, in which the heart, the head, the limbs, and the different organs gradually appear. The nervous system of this embryo may be compared to arrays of delicate threads proceeding from a central point that will become the brain. Under the influence of solar light and vibrations in the air, one of these nerves is developed at its extremity and forms the eye. This is undefined at first and almost blind in an elementary state, like the eyes of the trilobites and fishes of the Silurian period, but it develops into the admirable eyes of birds, mammals, and humans. The senses of smell and taste proceed from the nerves in the same way. These latter senses, with that of touch, are the most primitive, the earliest, and the most necessary to life. There are two senses that place human beings in communication with the outer world — sight and hearing — but the eye is the only organ that puts us in communication with the entire universe.

Millions of these little nerve threads proceed from the brain, extending throughout the body, without producing any other than the five senses — unless we except certain sensations of touch that are intimate and personal, and which have been described as a sixth sense, of which you shall hear more. Now, there is no reason why the process of formation and limitation that has taken place on our little planet should be duplicated elsewhere. In proof of this I must tell you that not long ago I visited two worlds on which human beings have two senses of which we have no conception on Earth.

One of these senses may be described as electrical. One of the little nerve threads of which I have just told you is developed into a multitude of ramifications that form a sort of cornet. Under the scalpel and the microscope these appear to be tubes placed in juxtaposition, the outer extremities of which receive the electrical fluid and transmit it to the brain, much as our optic nerves receive the waves of light and our auditory nerves receive the undulations of sound.

The beings provided with this sense perceive the electrical condition of bodies, material objects, plants and flowers, animals, the atmosphere and clouds. To these beings the electrical sense is a source of knowledge that is entirely forbidden to us. Their organic sensations are completely different from yours. Their eyes are not constructed like yours — they do not see what you see, but they see what you do not; they are conscious only of the ultraviolet rays — but their mode of existence differs from yours most particularly by virtue of their electric sense; the electrical constitution of their world is the cause of the existence and development of this sense.

On a second world I found another sense, of quite a different character, which seemed even more striking. This was the sense of orientation. Another of the nerve threads proceeding from the brain produced a sort of winged ear, very light, by means of which the living being directly perceives his bearings. It is conscious of the points of the compass and turns instinctively to the north, south, east, or west. The atmosphere is full of emanations that you never perceive, but this singular sense orientates its possessors infallibly. It also enables them to discover things concealed in the center of the sun, and gives them an insight into some of nature's secrets that are completely hidden from you.

Thus I seek to demonstrate to you that in the vast domains of creation an infinite variety exists, and that eternity will be inexhaustibly occupied in gathering and partaking of its flowers and its fruits.

There are worlds where old age is unknown, where lovers are consumed in a delirious fantasy, transported by the intoxication of the body and careless of the morrow. Members of the active sex never survive these nuptials; the passive, oviparous sex, having secured the perpetuity of the species, fall into their final sleep. These celestial worlds where one never grows old are not without their advantages.

Worlds exist in which the vital movements of respiration and assimilation, and the organic periods — day and night, the seasons, and the years—are all of extreme length. Although the nervous system of the inhabitants is highly developed, and thought is prodigiously active, life there appears to be endless in duration. Those who die of old age have lived more than a thousand years, but they are so rare that only a few have been preserved in the historical records of this humankind. War between nations has never been invented, because there is only one race, one people, one language.

The natural constitution of these organisms is remarkable. Diseases are almost unknown; there are no doctors. As a result of their great mental activity, the extension of life becomes a perspective without end, and eventually burdensome. Suicide is, therefore, almost universal; the custom has been habitual since very ancient times. The few old men who, from whatever motive, have not put an end to their lives are looked upon as exceptional and rather eccentric individuals; suicide is the norm.

But it is impossible for me to describe to you all the curiosities of the universe, my dear friend. Let it suffice that I have raised the veil enough to give you a glimpse of the incommensurable diversity that exists in the animate produce of the many and various systems that are disseminated through space. While accompanying me in spirit on this interstellar voyage, you have passed several hours away from the earth. It is good to isolate oneself periodically in this way, among the celestial solitudes. The soul obtains a fuller possession of itself, and in its solitary reflections it penetrates profoundly into the universal reality.

Terrestrial humanity, you understand, is the result of the particular forces of the earth, morally as well as physically. Human strength, physique, and weight all depend on these forces. Organic functions are determined by the planet. If your life is divided between work and rest, activity and sleep, it is because of the rotation of the globe and the cycle of day and night. In the luminous globes and those lighted alternately by many suns there is no sleep. If you need to eat and drink, it is because of the insufficiency of the atmosphere. The bodies of beings who do not eat are not made like yours, since they have no need of a stomach or intestines. The terrestrial eye enables you to see the universe in a certain way; the Saturnian eye sees in a different manner.

There are senses that perceive things other than those you perceive in nature. Every world is inhabited by an essentially different race, and sometimes the inhabitants are neither animal nor vegetable. There are men of all possible forms, dimensions, weights, colors, sensations, and every other variable character. The universe is infinite. Our terrestrial existence is only one phase of the infinite. An inexhaustible diversity enriches the marvelous field of the Eternal Sower.

The role of science is to study all that the terrestrial senses are capable of perceiving. The role of philosophy is to form a synthesis of all defined and determined ideas and facts, and to develop the scope of thought.[14]

What would you say if I told you not only about the physical diversity of humankind, but also its moral and intellectual diversity? Its varieties are many—far too many, in fact, for you to understand them thoroughly. I will give you just one noteworthy example.

In your terrestrial humanity, intellectual or moral worth counts for nothing in advancing a man, whatever the value of his ideas or the worth of his character might be, unless he possesses the means and determination to push himself forward. No one searches for hidden merit. A man must needs make his own way, and struggle against intrigue, cupidity, and ambition—a strife which is the very opposite of what it ought to be. In consequence, therefore, the noblest and most worthy people remain in obscurity while position, wealth, and social distinction are often showered on worthless intriguers.

Well, I recently visited a world belonging to one of the most luminous regions of the Milky Way, where a completely different moral order exists: where the constitution of the government is such that only those distinguished for their virtues are placed at the head of the state, and their function is to seek out and place in responsible positions men worthy of their trust. In that country, in brief, the search for the discovery of merit and intelligence is as eager as that for gold and diamonds in yours. All is done there for the benefit of humanity. They have invented no Academy, because they cannot conceive that a man of worth should be compelled to waste his time in ceremonial visits—only to find, probably, that a titled nonentity more skilled in the cajoling of votes has been preferred to himself—instead of being sought after. Thus, the system prevailing in other worlds is far more enlightened than that of yours.

Now, my dear terrestrial friend, you know what the earth is in the universe; you know something of what the heavens contain; and you also know what life is, and what death is.

We shall soon see the first light of morning, which puts spirits to flight and brings our conversations to an end, as the approach of your terrestrial day causes the brightness of Venus to fade away. But I should like to add to the preceding ideas a very interesting remark suggested by the same observations. If you set out from the earth at the moment that a flash of lightning bursts forth, and if you traveled for an hour or more with the light, you would see the lightning as long as you continued to look at it. This fact is established by the foregoing principles. But if, instead of traveling with the exact velocity of light, you were to travel with a slightly lesser velocity, take note of the observation you would make.

I will suppose that this voyage away from the earth, during which you look at the lightning, lasts a minute. I will suppose also that the lightning lasts a thousandth of a second. You will, therefore, continue to see the lightning for 60,000 times its own duration in our first supposition that the voyage's velocity is identical to that of light. Light has occupied 60,000 thousandths[15] of a second in going from the earth to the point where you are; your voyage and that of light have coincided.

Now, if instead of flying with precisely the same velocity as light, you had flown a little less rapidly, and if you had employed a thousandth part of a second more to arrive at the same point, instead of always seeing the same moment of the lightning, you would have seen, successively, the different moments which constituted the total duration of the lightning, equal to the thousandth part of a second. In this entire minute you would have had time to see, first, the beginning of the lightning flash and could then analyze the development of it — its successive phases — to the very end.

You may imagine what strange discoveries one could make in the secret nature of lightning, increased 60,000 times in the order of its duration. What frightful battles you would have time to discover in the flame! What pandemonium! What sinister atoms! What a world, hidden by its volatile nature from the imperfect eyes of mortals!

If your imagination were adequate to allow you to separate and count the atoms that constitute the body of a man, that body would disappear before you, for it consists of thousands of millions of atoms in motion; to the analytical eye it would be a nebula animated by the forces of gravitation. Did not Swedenborg imagine that the universe by which he was surrounded, seen as a whole, was in the form of an immense man?[16] That was anthropomorphism — but there are analogies everywhere. What we know most certainly is that things are not what they appear to be, either in space or in time — but let us return to the delayed flash of lightning.

When you travel with the velocity of light, you see constantly before you the scene that was in existence at the moment of your departure. If you were carried away for a year at that same rate, the same event would remain before you throughout that time. But if, in order to see more distinctly an event that would have taken only a few seconds — such as a landslide, an avalanche, or an earthquake — you were to delay, slackening a little in your pace compared to that of light, you would see the progress of the catastrophe from its first moment to its second, and so on consecutively, so that you might see the end only after an hour of observation. For you, the event would last an hour instead of a few seconds. You would see the rocks and stones suspended in midair, and could thus ascertain the mode of production of the phenomenon and its incidental delays.

Your terrestrial scientific knowledge already enables you to take instantaneous photographs of the successive aspects of rapid phenomena, such as lightning, meteors, the waves of the sea, volcanic eruptions, falling buildings, and to make them pass before you graduated in accordance with their effect upon the retina. Similarly, on the other hand, you can photograph the pollination of a flower through each stage of expansion to its completion of the fruit, or the development of a child from birth to maturity, and project these phases upon a screen, depicting in a few seconds the life of a man or a tree.[17]

I see in your thoughts that you are comparing this effect to that of a microscope that could magnify time. That is exactly what it is; we thus see time amplified. Such a device could not, strictly speaking, be called a microscope, but rather a chronoscope or a chronotelescope (to see time from afar).

The duration of a reign might, by the same process, be augmented according to the pleasure of the body politic. Thus, for example, Napoleon II reigned for only three hours, but one could see him reign for fifteen successive years by dispersing the 180 minutes of the three hours over a period of 180 months, in removing oneself from the earth with a velocity a little inferior to that of light. So, by setting out at the very moment when the chamber had proclaimed Napoleon II emperor, one would arrive at the last minute of his supposed reign only at the end of fifteen years. Every minute would have lasted a month, every second twelve hours.

The conclusion of this conversation is based entirely on this principle, my dear seeker after knowledge. I have endeavored to show you that the physical law of the successive transmission of light in space is one of the fundamental elements of the conditions of eternal life. According to this law, every event is imperishable and the past is always present. The image of the earth as it was six thousand years ago is actually present in space at the distance that light has crossed in that six thousand years. The worlds situated in that region see the earth of that epoch. We could see again our own immediate existence and our various anterior existences; all that we require to do so is to be at the appropriate distance from the worlds in which we had lived. There are stars that you see from the earth that no longer exist, because they became extinct after they had emitted the luminous ray that has only just reached you. In the same way, you might hear at a distance the voice of a man who might be dead before the moment at which you heard him, if perchance he had been struck by apoplexy immediately after he had uttered his last cry.

I am pleased that this last sketch has enabled me, at the same time, to trace for you a picture of the possibility of living forms unknown to the earth. Here, too, you see that the revelations of Urania[18] are grander and more profound than those of all her sisters. The earth is only an atom in the universe.

I must stop here, for not all of these numerous and diverse applications of the laws of light are apparent to you. On the earth — in this dark cavern, as Plato appropriately termed it[19] — you vegetate in ignorance of the gigantic forces active in the universe; but the day will come when physical science will discover in light the principle of every movement and the inner rationale of things.

Already, within the last few years, spectrum analysis has demonstrated that by the examination of a luminous ray from the sun or from a star you can discover the constituent substances of that sun and star. Already you can determine, across a distance of millions and millions of kilometers, the nature of celestial bodies from which a ray of light has come to you! And the study of light will afford even more splendid results, both in experimental science and in its application to the philosophy of the universe.

But the refraction of the earth's atmosphere is projecting the light shed by the distant sun beyond the horizon. The vibrations of daylight will no longer let me talk to you. Farewell, my good friend — or perhaps *au revoir*. Great things are going to happen around you. When the storm is over, I might perhaps return for one last visit to give you proof of my existence and show that I have not forgotten you.

Then, later, when your life upon this little planet is done, I shall come to you once again, and together we shall resume our real journey through the indescribable splendors of immensity.[20] Nor can you ever, in your wildest dreams, form even a faint idea of the stupendous surprises and inconceivable wonders awaiting you there.

NOTES

INTRODUCTION

1. This title is recorded in the entry on Flammarion in Pierre Versins's *Encyclopédie de l'Utopie, des voyages extraordinaires et de la science fiction*, where its date of composition is given as 1858.

2. Giovanni Schiaparelli (1835–1910) was the Italian astronomer who publicized observations of "canali" (channels) on Mars made by his colleague Pietro Secchi (1818–78). The word was mistranslated into English as "canals."

3. Percival Lowell (1855–1916), inspired by the discoveries of Secchi, Schiaparelli, and Flammarion, constructed a very detailed speculative account of the Martian surface and its hypothetical resident civilization; his first study of the planet was published shortly after Flammarion's in 1896.

4. The 1872 edition of *Récits de l'infini* appends a footnote to the title of *Lumen*'s "Premier Récit" claiming that it was written in 1865. Although this date seems perfectly plausible, given the internal references to Lumen's earthly incarnation having ended in October 1864, subsequent editions issued by the family firm amend the footnote to read "Écrit en 1866." All editions agree that the second and third parts were written in 1867 and the fourth in 1869. Some of the material contained in the fourth part is moved into the fifth part in later editions, which is why the footnote attached to the title of that part in the 1892 edition also reads "Écrit en 1869," although new text was added to it subsequently.

5. The Italian theologian, philosopher, and Dominican monk St. Thomas Aquinas (1225–74) argued in his *Summa contra Gentiles* (1259–64) that reason and faith were compatible and absorbed the Earth-centered Aristotelian cosmology into the doctrine of the Church, thus giving it an "official" status that caused considerable problems when the disciples of Nicolaus Copernicus (1473–1543) began to challenge it with demonstrations that the sun was the actual hub of the solar system and that the earth moved around it. Flammarion cites the ascent through the celestial spheres described by Dante Alighieri (1265–1321) in the *Paradiso* (1300) as an

exemplary version of the subsequent Christian cosmology and Nicholas of Cusa (1401–64), author of *De docta Ignorantia* (1440–50), as a significant anticipator of Copernicus and early popularizer of the plurality of worlds. The Italian poet Ludovico Ariosto (1474–1533) included a brief satirical lunar voyage in his *Orlando Furioso* (1516; published 1532). François Rabelais is complimented for the broad range of exotic life-forms described in *Pantagruel* (1533).

6. Flammarion acknowledges the crucial roles played by Giordano Bruno (1548–1600), Michel de Montaigne (1533–92), and Galileo Galilei (1564–1642) in helping to win acceptance for the Copernican thesis that Earth and its companion planets orbit the sun and the corollary notion that the stars are distant suns.

7. Johannes Kepler (1571–1630) removed residual mathematical objections to the Copernican system by demonstrating that the planetary orbits are elliptical rather than circular. His *Somnium* (1634) is a pioneering work in the popularization of science, cast as a dream-journey in which an observer taken to the moon by a "daemon" observes astronomical phenomena and witnesses the manner in which lunar life-forms have adapted their way of life to the moon's slow period of rotation.

8. Bishop Francis Godwin (1562–1633) was the author of the posthumously published satirical lunar voyage *The Man in the Moone* (1638), issued under the name of its central character, Domingo Gonsales. Gonsales reappears in the similarly posthumous *Histoire comique contenant les états et empires de la lune* (1657) by Savinien Cyrano de Bergerac (1619–55), whose more wide-ranging sequel, *Fragment d'histoire comique contenant les états et empires du soleil* is unfortunately incomplete. John Wilkins (1614–72) was a significant popularizer of science and propagandist for technological progress. His *The Discovery of a World in the Moone* (1638) popularized the idea that the moon is a world, and its third edition (1640) added a supplement suggesting, in all seriousness, that we might one day be able to travel to it. Pierre Borel's *Discours nouveau prouvant la pluralité des mondes* (1657) extrapolated Wilkins's arguments considerably.

9. This work by the German mystical philosopher Athanasius Kircher (1602–80) was the first comprehensive odyssey taking in all the then-known worlds of the solar system.

10. René Descartes (1590–1650) was one of the founders of modern scientific thought, the most significant in France.

11. The Edict of Nantes, licensing the religious practices of Calvinism

and allowing them to be taught, had been issued by Henri IV in 1598. Although the edict itself was not revoked until 1685, the freedoms granted to French Protestants were gradually reduced during Louis XIV's reign.

12. Gabriel Daniel (1649–1728) wrote his *Voyage du monde de Descartes* to popularize Descartes's ideas. Christian Huygens (1629–95) was the Dutch physicist and astronomer who promulgated the wave theory of light and developed the pendulum clock. *Cosmotheoros* (1698) was yet another posthumously published work speculating about the habitability of the planets; Flammarion is severely critical of its central thesis that the inhabitants of other planets must have bodies similar to those of humans.

13. Flammarion passes over the antiscientific *Gulliver's Travels* (1726) by Jonathan Swift (1667–1745) very rapidly but devotes much more attention to *Nicolai Klimii iter subterraneum* (1741) by Baron Ludvig Holberg (1684–1754) because he approves of its exoticism and the dominance of women on the planet Nazar. He also approves of the anonymous *Relation du monde de Mercure* (1750)—actually by the Chevalier de Béthune—which he deems very ingenious because of its detailed account of a society of winged, unsleeping Mercurians. The third work given detailed consideration, *Micromégas* (1752) by Voltaire (François-Marie Arouet, 1694–1778), is similarly praised for its employment of a gigantic Sirian as a hypothetical viewpoint from which the follies of humankind are very obvious.

14. The Swedish scientist-turned-mystic Emanuel Swedenborg (1688–1772) was enormously influential. His visionary writings include a series of Kircheresque dream-voyages, which extend beyond the solar system to the planets of other stars; these *Arcana coelestia* (recorded in 1749–56; published in 13 vols. in 1833–42) were quickly translated into French and English. Although they are essentially allegorical, Flammarion approves of the manner in which Swedenborg had drawn on his scientific imagination in formulating his images of extraterrestrial life, as well as their unprecedented range. The cosmological speculations of the German idealist philosopher Immanuel Kant (1724–1804) are contained in *Allgemeine Naturgeschichte und Theorie des Himmels* (1755); it includes a Kircheresque scheme in which the inhabitants of the planets are more morally advanced the further removed they are from the sun.

15. The full title of this series was *Voyages imaginaires, songes, visions et romans cabalistiques*; its contents are listed in Pierre Versins's *Encyclopédie de l'Utopie, des voyages extraordinaires et de la science-fiction*, pp. 944–46, and in the Lofficiers' *French Science Fiction, Fantasy, Horror and Pulp Fiction*,

pp. 745–47. Flammarion must have had access to the set—he includes references to many other works of lesser relevance contained within it, including *Relation du monde de Mercure*. The intriguing Marie-Anne Roumier (alias Madame Robert) had a second work included in the series, entitled *Les Ondins* (1768); she also published several naturalistic works of fiction.

16. Edgar Allan Poe (1809–49) had been dead for thirteen years when Flammarion wrote *Les Mondes imaginaires et les mondes réels*; but his works were still in the process of being translated into French by Charles Baudelaire (1821–67), whose translation of *Eureka* was issued in 1864. Flammarion was probably influenced by other Poe works, including "The Conversation of Eiros and Charmion" (1839), but the absence of any corrective updating of the final chapter of his critical review of cosmological spculative fiction makes it difficult to determine exactly when he read them.

17. Nicolas-Edme Restif de la Bretonne (1734–1806) was one of the great eccentrics of his era, famed for the licentiousness of his life and works, but his reputation has increased steadily as the originality of his political ideas has become better appreciated; his most famous work is the notable Utopian fantasy *La Découverte Australe par un homme volant* (1781). Humphry Davy (1778–1829) was one of the leading British scientists of his day; *Consolations in Travel; or, The Last Days of a Philosopher was* issued posthumously, in the year following the death anticipated in its pages. Poe's *Eureka* was also its author's last work, and it too must have been written in an ominous frame of mind.

18. Davy, *Consolations in Travel*, p. 41–42.

19. Ibid., pp. 44–45

20. Ibid., p. 49.

21. It is unlikely, but not impossible, that Albert Einstein (1879–1955) read *Lumen* before developing the special theory of relativity; the thought-experiment that led him to it is not dissimilar to the one Flammarion conducts, although he reached a far bolder and more remarkable conclusion.

22. Flammarion's description of events taking place in reverse sequence was almost certainly the inspiration of the first "reversed time" novel, *L'Horloge des siècles* (1902), by the writer and illustrator Albert Robida (1848–1926), one of the founding fathers of French scientific romance. More recent uses of the device include Philip K. Dick's *Counter-Clock World* (1967) and Martin Amis's *Time's Arrow* (1991).

23. The English version of this quote is taken from p. 11 of the most

recent translation of *Conversations on the Plurality of Worlds*, by H. A. Hargreaves (1990).

24. Jean-Baptiste, Chevalier de Lamarck (1744–1829), published his *Philosophie Zoologique* in 1809. Although modern Darwinians use the word "Lamarckism" to refer, narrowly and pejoratively, to the notion that characteristics acquired by an organism as a result of adaptive effort can be passed on to its offspring, that was only one element of Lamarck's evolutionary theory. Its central hypothesis was that the "vital force" animating living organisms is invariably subject to a progressive imperative. One remarkable — but unfortunately absurd — consequence of this worldview is that every existing organism is, or at least ought to be, engaged in a continuous and everlasting struggle to better itself within the evolutionary scheme. It is this notion that Humphry Davy appropriated to a cosmic perspective in *Consolations in Travel*, and it is Davy's extrapolation of Lamarckism to a cosmic scale to which *Lumen* adds further narrative flesh. In his later years Lamarck also attempted to become a pioneer of meteorological science; although he never constructed a worthwhile theory, he was an assiduous observer of atmospheric phenomena, and Flammarion's endeavors in that area were consciously carrying forward work that Lamarck had begun.

25. Poe, *Eureka*, in *Complete Works of Edgar Allan Poe*, 10:318–19.

26. This is one of the most famous of the aphorisms collected in the posthumously published *Pensées* of mathematician and philosopher Blaise Pascal (1623–62).

27. Flammarion, *La Fin du monde* (*Omega: The Last Days of the World*, trans. J. B. Walker), p. 286.

28. A description of "A Celestial Love" can be found on p. 249 of Everett F. Bleiler's *Science Fiction: The Early Years*. A French version, "Un amour dans les étoiles," appears in the original edition of *Rêves étoilés* but is omitted from Fournier d'Albe's translation of that collection, presumably because the translation in *The Arena* (by Frederick W. Jones) retained the copyright.

29. There are two English translations of this story; Damon Knight's version, "The Shapes," appeared in *100 Years of Science Fiction* (1969), while George Edgar Slusser's version is in *The Xipéhuz and the Death of the Earth* (1978); the second item in the latter collection is the only English version of the second title cited. A comprehensive description of Rosny's science fiction output can be found in J. P. Vernier, "The Science Fiction of J. H. Rosny the Elder," *Science-Fiction Studies* 2 ,no. 2 (July 1975).

30. Eugène Torquet (1860–1918) was a casualty of the First World War; *Force ennemie* was his only work of science fiction.

31. Little is known about Octave Joncquel, but Théodore-Louis-Etienne Varlet (1878–1938) was a notable writer of fiction and nonfiction who moved on from a peripheral association with the decadent movement to produce a number of science fiction novels. He complained bitterly that one of them, *La Grande panne* (1930), had been plagiarized by A. Rowley Hilliard in "Death from the Stars," which appeared in the October 1931 issue of *Wonder Stories*.

32. Stapledon, *Star Maker*, p. 333.

THE FIRST CONVERSATION

1. The notion of "the positive method" ("les méthodes positives" in the original) derives from the work of the French philosopher August Comte (1798–1857), who proposed that the development of human thought and society had passed through three stages: the theological, the metaphysical, and the positive, or scientific. Although "positivism" is nowadays used to signify a relatively crude and restrictive scientific methodology, Comte's view of science was not unduly narrow; I have translated "positive" as "scientific" wherever it seems appropriate.

2. The first edition has "la force vitale" here as well as later in the passage, but I have used "vital energy" wherever the phrase was changed to "l'énergie vitale" in later editions and "vital force" where it was not. The notion can be traced back to Aristotle's contention that the phenomenon of life cannot be fully explained in material terms, but that living organisms must be possessed of something nonmaterial that differentiates them from inanimate bodies. The most influential vitalist in late-nineteenth-century France, although he did not begin publishing until long after the appearance of *Lumen*, was Henri Bergson (1859–1941), who made extensive use of the notion of *élan vital*—usually translated as "life force"—in the theory of creative evolution that he developed along lines of argument pioneered in Lamarck's *Philosophie Zoologique*. Although Comtean positivists rejected the notion of *élan vital* as a metaphysical abomination, it was not until the 1920s, when the notion of genetic mutation provided a new account of the source of the variations upon which natural selection was supposed to act, that the redundancy of the notion finally became obvious. Bergson shared

Flammarion's strong interest in psychic research and may have been influenced by his ideas.

3. "A posteriori" is one of a pair of contrasting terms — the other being "a priori" — used to distinguish two sorts of proposition, or the proofs supporting them. An a priori proposition is one that can be proved true or false without reference to our experience of the world, solely by logical analysis. The a posteriori method is, by contrast, that which seeks to establish the truth or falsehood of a proposition by relating it to the world and judging whether experience sustains or refutes it.

4. Ossian, the son of Finn or Fingal, was the supposed author of two Scottish epic poems published — and largely fabricated — by James Macpherson (1736–96). In spite of widespread doubts about their authenticity, the Ossianic epics were widely praised throughout Europe and strongly influenced the German Romantic movement.

5. The French editions have "Capella ou la Chèvre" — "Capella or the She-Goat" but A. A. M. and R. M. wisely ignore the secondary description.

6. Flammarion inserts the following footnote: "Transcendent physiological anatomy would probably explain this fact by proposing that a sort of *punctum caecum* [i.e., a blind spot] is placed so as to mask the object that one does not wish to see."

7. The French editions have "Eivlys," which is "Sylvie" backward, but A. A. M. and R. M. are surely right to prefer this rendition. Sylvie was the name of Flammarion's first wife, but he did not marry her until 1874, so the use of the name here is presumably a coincidence.

8. Nestor, the king of Pylos, was the oldest of the kings supporting Agamemnon at the siege of Troy; he was noted for his wisdom and for a long lecture delivered to the assembled chiefs (recorded, of course, by Homer).

9. Antoine Lavoisier (1743–94) was one of the founders of modern chemistry and one of the prime movers behind the metric system of measurement. The writer and astronomer Jean-Sylvain Bailly (1736–93) became mayor of Paris after the storming of the Bastille but suffered a disastrous loss of popularity after declaring martial law to control the crowd gathered at Champ de Mars to call for the execution of Louis XVI. André Chenier (1762–94) was in the forefront of the revolution but made the mistake of objecting to the excesses of the Terror. Antoine-Nicolas de Condorcet (1743–94) was perhaps the most ironic victim of all, given that he was the principal architect and popularizer of the philosophy of progress.

10. The first French edition has a text break here, but it was eliminated in the revised edition, whose textual arrangement I have duplicated throughout.

11. The circular axes which astronomers superimpose on the sky in order to measure the relative positions of the stars were initially divided into twelve "hours" of sixty "minutes," each "minute" thus being equal to a degree of arc. It is because every minute is further separable into sixty "seconds" that the clock analogy continued in use until Flammarion's era, because astronomical measurements need to be made with sufficient accuracy to license the use of seconds, although the convenience of expressing such figures as degrees (further subdivided according to decimal convention) has now made the old system virtually redundant.

12. The figure of 76 is obtained by subtracting 180 (the number of degrees in half a circle) from 256; the figure of 46, by subtracting 44 from 90 (the number of degrees in a quarter of a circle).

13. The parallax of a star measures the extent to which its position relative to the stellar background changes when it is viewed from opposite extremes of the earth's orbit. As Flammarion goes on to observe, and document in his own footnote, there is a simple mathematical relationship between the distance that separates a star from our solar system and its parallax, the nearest stars demonstrating the greatest parallax. The astronomer who first measured the parallax of Capella was Friedrich Wilhelm Struve (1793–1864), who was "Russian" only in the sense that he was using the telescope at Dorpat, which was then in Russia (it is now in Estonia).

14. The version of Flammarion's footnote given in the 1897 translation is nonsensical because part of the equation has been accidentally omitted. Even Flammarion's version seems to me to be imperfect, and the imperfection survived the revision between versions, when he added the last sentence. The final version reads:

> Everyone knows that the farther away an object is the smaller it appears. An object that subtends an angle of one second is 202,265 times more distant than its own diameter, whatever that might be; because there are 1,296,000 seconds in a full circle, the ratio between the circumference of a circle and its diameter is 3.14159 [i.e., pi], and 1,296,00 divided by twice 3.14159 equals 206,265. Capella subtends an angle 22 times smaller than that of the radius [French, *demi-diametre*] of the earth's orbit; its distance is approximately 22 times greater. Capella is therefore at a distance

of 4,484,000 times the radius [French, *rayon*] of the terrestrial orbit. Future micrometrical measurements may modify these results concerning the parallax of this star, but they cannot change the principle upon which the conception of this work is grounded.

The second calculation is slightly fudged—I make it 4,397,065 if you divide 202,265 by 0.046, 4,449,830 if you multiply 202,265 by 22—but the arithmetical error is trivial in comparison with the inaptitude of the note's first sentence. The point to be made is that an object's apparent position shifts against a remote background when it is viewed from two different points, and the extent of the shift decreases with distance. Thus, if you hold your finger up in front of your face and view it first with the right eye and then with the left, its position seems to change. If you move the finger farther away, the extent of the positional change is reduced. In measurements of stellar parallax, the position of the earth at the two extremes of its orbit substitute for the two eyes, and the star for the finger. As Flammarion subsequently points out, however, even the nearest stars are so distant in comparison with the diameter of the earth's orbit that their apparent shifts of position relative to the stellar background—their parallax—is very small, measurable only in tiny fractions of a second of arc. The first published measurements of stellar parallax were those of 61 Cygni (in 1838), Alpha Centauri (in 1839), and Vega (1840).

15. The French lieue, corresponding to the English league, is four kilometers. The original text gives the second figure as "170 trillions 392 milliards de lieues"; but, in view of the fact that the word "trillion" is used differently in Europe and the United States and "milliard" is no longer used at all, I have set the number out in full. Unfortunately, Flammarion's estimation of Capella's distance from the sun differs considerably from more recent calculations based on more accurate measurements of its parallax.

16. The recent calculations to which the previous note refers place Capella's distance from the sun at approximately 45.6 light-years, so this figure is way off, but when one considers that measurements of stellar parallax were in their infancy and that mid-nineteenth-century telescopes and the photographic apparatus supporting their observations were much poorer than those available to twentieth-century astronomers, the error is not surprising. The principle underlying the thought-experiment is, of course, unaffected by the miscalculation.

17. François Arago (1786–1853) was elected to the Academy of Sciences

at the age of twenty-three. His studies in the physics of light included important work on the phenomena of polarization and refraction and explained the scintillation of starlight. He also worked in the field of electromagnetism. His politics were liberal, and he became a member of the revolutionary government of 1848, serving in the Ministry of War and the Ministry of Marine Affairs.

18. The mathematician Gaspard Monge (1746–1818) had been one of the founders of the École Polytechnique. Jacques-Philippe Binet (1786–1856) was a mathematician and astronomer; he never distinguished himself to the extent of his contemporary Arago.

19. Alexander Humboldt (1769–1859), German naturalist and writer, undertook several scientific expeditions throughout the world; his chief work was *Kosmos*.

20. "The Hundred Days" refers to the time that elapsed between 20 March 1815, when Napoleon re-entered Paris, and 22 June, the date of his second abdication. Following the battle of Waterloo, fought on 18 June 1815, the progress of the allies ranged against the French republican forces was swift and irresistible.

21. Elba was the site of Napoleon's first exile and St. Helena the site of his second.

22. The "three glorious days" of 27, 28, and 29 July 1830, when the Orleanist king Louis-Philippe replaced Charles X.

23. Philosopher Victor Cousin (1792–1867) became a professor at the Sorbonne in 1815; he held various government posts during Louis-Philippe's reign, his career as a statesman running parallel to that of the noted historian François Guizot (1787–1874).

24. The reference is to two famous generals, Louis de Lamorcière (1806–65) and Louis-Eugène Cavaignac (1802–57); the former led the bloody suppression of demonstrations mounted by the workmen of Paris in June 1848, while the latter was the unsuccessful rival candidate who competed with Louis-Napoleon for the presidency of the new republic in December of the same year.

25. The first edition has three years and eight months, while the 1897 translation, perhaps in response to an amendment of Flammarion's, does not mention Alpha Centauri at all, reading instead: "Upon neighbouring stars earthly events are not seen until four, six, ten years after their occurrence."

1. In the twenty-fourth canto of the *Purgatorio* Dante, Virgilius, and Statius reach the level of the Gluttonous—which is, of course, full of avid spirits whose appetites can never be satisfied.

2. Flammarion gives the position of the tract in question as "the 45th degree of north latitude and the 35th of longitude."

3. Modern calculations place Vega (Alpha Lyrae) about 26.4 light-years from the sun. Given that the crucial battles of the Crimean War took place in the autumn of 1854 and that Lumen is probably still referring back to his experiences in the autumn of 1864, Flammarion appears to be working on the assumption that Vega is 20 light-years away ($1864 - 1854 \times 2 = 20$). This is a slighter miscalculation than the one relating to Capella because Vega is nearer than Capella and its parallax is easier to measure.

4. Denis August Affre (1793–1848) was archbishop of Paris at the time of his death; he was mortally wounded while attempting to negotiate a truce.

5. The entry of Louis XVIII in 1815.

6. This hypothesis seems inadequate to explain why the events observed by Lumen seemed to be occurring in reverse order.

7. The idea that an infinite universe ought to contain an infinite number of worlds identical to the earth crops up periodically in speculative fiction, although it is nowadays usually affiliated with the notion of parallel worlds; a more elaborate argument sustaining the case can be found in J. B. S. Haldane's essay "Some Consequences of Materialism," in *The Inequality of Man and Other Essays* (1932).

8. "La théorie métaphysique des images" presumably refers to Plato's Theory of Forms, in which material objects and products of thought are held to be more or less imperfect reflections of the metaphysical Ideas that serve as their ultimate templates.

9. Although the idea of a "counter-Earth" in which certain familiar institutions are inverted is a commonplace of Utopian satire and science fiction, the analogy Flammarion uses to support the idea is obviously false. The example of mirror reversal might help us to imagine a world in which left and right were reversed but not one in which the order of historical events were reversed. (A left/right transformation would be more significant than it might seem, although Flammarion could not have been aware

of the significance of the fact that earthly life is made out of the laevo-rotatory isomers of organic molecules which might exist instead in a dextro-rotatory form—thus producing a seemingly similar but chemically alien world, as, for instance, in David Lake's *The Right Hand of Dextra* [1977]).

As with the previous hypothesis, this one surely would not have occurred to Lumen had he been able to observe that Louis XVIII's coach was racing across the Pont Neuf backward. Perhaps he was not able to—the subsequent account of the reversed battle of Waterloo suggests otherwise but cannot entirely clarify this issue. If not, the reader must presume that every time Lumen's attention was caught and held, it was captured by a single "still frame" within the unfolding sequence. Alternatively, the direction of his movement in space might have been spontaneously, unnoticeably, and momentarily reversed. (This last possibility is surely no less plausible than the questioner's earlier suggestion that Lumen must have described a tightly wound spiral course during his journey from Capella to Earth in order to avoid confusion by the rotation of the earth upon its axis and about the sun.)

10. The battle of the Pyramids occurred in 1798.

11. Lumen presumably elects to describe Jean-Jacques Rousseau (1712–78) as a botanist rather than a philosopher because he disapproved of Rousseau's opposition to the thesis that science and technology had improved the human condition.

12. The religious historian and celebrated orator Jacques-Bénigne Bossuet (1627–1704) was nicknamed "the Eagle of Meaux."

13. A diligence was a public stagecoach.

14. The first manned balloon flight launched by the Montgolfier brothers took place in 1783.

15. Flammarion's suggestion that the return to wilderness of the site of the luxurious Palace of Versailles "avait gagné un éclat incomparable" is, of course, the bitter sarcasm of a committed Republican.

16. Giulio Mazarini, alias Mazarin (1602–61), and Armand-Jean du Plessis, Cardinal de Richelieu (1585–1642), both served as ministers of Louis XIII, the son of Henry IV; Lumen presumably observed them at the Château de Saint-Germain-en-Laye.

17. The first Duc de Guise, Claude de Lorraine, and his brother Jean, a cardinal, founded an august dynasty during the reign of Francis I in the sixteenth century; the Guises were great rivals of the Bourbons.

18. "La Saint-Barthélemy" (the Night of St. Bartholomew) was a mas-

sacre of Protestants that took place on 23 August 1572, organized by the aforementioned Guises in collaboration with Catherine de Medici; it was a continuation of the campaign of terror begun at Vassy (see the following note).

19. Chaumont was the capital of the Haut-Marne (where Flammarion was born), a region notorious for sorcery trials; the Church of St.-Jean-Baptiste, which was built between the thirteenth and sixteenth centuries, must have seen many such scenes. Nostradamus was reputed to have lived for some time at the Château de Chaumont, where Catherine de Medici is reputed to have consulted him, but the story is probably apocryphal. The massacre of the Protestants carried out by François de Guise in 1562 at Vassy was one of the sparks that ignited the wars of religion.

20. This was the comet observed by Tycho Brahe (1546–1601), whose path convinced him and many others that the rigid crystal spheres proposed by Aristotle and accepted as doctrine by the Church could not exist, paving the way for acceptance of the heliocentric theory of the solar system.

21. Francis I and "Charles-Quint" (Charles V of Spain) were at odds, and frequently at war, with one another for thirty years.

22. The first edition has a supplementary clause here that is omitted from the revised edition and the 1897 translation, which translates as: "the little statuettes on his hat enabled me to recognize him." I have been unable to ascertain the significance of this comment, or to form a convincing hypothesis as to who "les deux sombres compères" of Louis XI (1423–83) might have been.

23. Jeanne d'Arc (1412–31) earned the soubriquet "vierge d'Orléans" (more usually, in France, "La Pucelle d'Orléans") when she assisted in lifting the siege of that city in 1429.

24. The French king Louis IX (1215–70) was canonized in 1297, having led the Seventh and Eighth Crusades (unsuccessfully). Frederick Barbarossa (i.e., Redbeard) (1123–90) was Holy Roman Emperor after 1152; his death in the Third Crusade—he drowned while crossing a river—was as futile and inglorious as Louis IX's, which is why Flammarion takes the trouble to mention him.

25. Peter the Hermit led one of the ridiculously disorganized "popular" crusades of 1095 before Godfrey de Bouillon gathered a real army in 1096, which eventually took Jerusalem in 1099—whereupon Godfrey became its king. They reminded Flammarion of the Italian poet Torquato Tasso (1544–95) because a translation of his epic poem about the First Crusade, *Geru-*

salemme liberata (1574) was a favorite work of nineteenth-century France; many schoolchildren were required to memorize passages from it.

26. Hugh Capet (938–96) became king of France in 987; the reference to his official cape is a weak pun on his name. The battle of Fontanet, fought on 25 June 841, was won by Charles le Chauve (i.e., the Bald) (823–77) and Louis le Germanique, who defeated their brother Lothaire; the subsequent Treaty of Verdun (1843) made Charles king of the West Frankish Kingdom (i.e., France). The Merovingian dynasty had previously ruled the region for three hundred years before the accession in 754 of Pepin the Short, father of Charlemagne (742–814) — whose coronation in Rome as effective leader of Christendom took place on Christmas Day 800. Charles Martel (688–741) halted the advance of the Moors into Europe; the reference to his "martelant les Sarrasins" is another weak pun (Martel means "the hammer"). Dagobert I (600–639) became king of France in 628 (the reference to Pope Alexander III is, of course, out of sequence, the building of Notre-Dame-de-Paris having commenced in 1163). This Brunhilde (*Brunehaut* in French) is Brunichildis (534–613), daughter of the Visigothic king Athanagilde; she was thought by some commentators (implausibly) to have been the historical model for the Brunhilde / Brynhild of Germanic and Norse legend who was betrothed to Siegfried / Sigurd; famed for her cruelty, Brunichildis was dragged to her death by a horse on the instruction of Clotaire II, the brother of her great rival Frédégonde (c. 545–97). Clovis (465–511) was the Merovingian king of the Salian (i.e., northern) Franks whose defeat of the Romanized Gauls ended their dominance of what is now France. He was a Christian convert and made Paris his capital.

27. Possession of Alsace-Lorraine, which lies west of the river Rhine, has long been disputed between France and Germany. Once part of Gaul, it was invaded by the Alemanni in the fourth century and remained part of the German Empire until the seventeenth century. Part of it was ceded to France in 1648; Louis XIV seized Strasbourg in 1681; and Napoleon reclaimed the rest. Flammarion was not to know, when he first wrote this paragraph, that Germany would take it back in the Franco-Prussian War of 1870–71. (It was returned to France in 1919 but temporarily lost yet again between 1940 and 1944.)

28. The Hôtel de Nesle was one of the most famous buildings of ancient Paris; the Abbey of Saint-Germain-des-Prés, whose church still stands, was founded in 558.

29. Nicolas Flamel (1330–1418) was a scholar of the University of Paris

credited by legend with a considerable (but probably unwarranted) reputation as an alchemist and sorcerer.

30. The final sentence of this paragraph is omitted from the 1897 translation, presumably by accident.

31. Heliogabalus, a Roman emperor of Syrian origin born in 204, reigned from 218 to 222. He was notorious for his madness, his cruelty, and his debauchery and was one of the key exemplars of "the Latin Decadence": an idea that had a powerful effect on writers contemporary with Flammarion who took delight in the proposition that late-nineteenth-century France had reached a phase in its history analogous to that of the late Roman Empire.

32. Vercingetorix, who was displayed in Julius Caesar's triumph of 46 B.C.E. and subsequently executed, was the chieftain who led the last revolt of the Gauls against Roman rule; the location of Alesia, the fort where he was captured, was a matter of some dispute, although the dominant opinion was that it was probably Alise-Sainte-Reine in the Côte d'Or.

33. This joke has an extra ironic twist, in that Napoleon was famous for his exceptionally short stature.

34. The Consuls were the chief magistrates of Rome after the expulsion of the last king in 510 B.C.E. The cities of Latium—the area surrounding Rome—had been bound into a league under Roman rule in 338 B.C.E., not long after the conquest of the Sabines to the north and the Samnites to the southeast. The "rape of the Sabine women" was a mythical attempt by Romulus to carry them off to populate the city he had founded. Flammarion's sarcastic reference to "moeurs antiques" (ancient manners) is echoed in the subtitle of Pierre Louÿs celebrated romance *Aphrodite* (1896), but it is unlikely that the influence was direct.

35. The Lydian king Candaules, also known as Myrsilus, was killed by his successor Gyges. According to legend, Candaules had allowed Gyges to see his wife's naked body, prompting her to conspire in his murder. In 1844 Théophile Gautier had published a novella based on the legend, "Le roi Candaule," in which the crucial display happens while the queen takes a bath.

36. Bailly, formerly mentioned by Flammarion as a regrettable victim of the French Revolution, formulated in his *Histoire de l'astronomie ancienne* [History of Ancient Astronomy] a theory of racial migrations based on consistent errors in astronomical tables brought back by missionaries from India. He concluded that the observations must actually have been made in central Asia; among many corollaries extrapolated from this thesis was the

proposition that Atlantis must have been the island of Spitzbergen in the Arctic Ocean—which, according to the protoevolutionist theory of natural epochs set out by the Comte du Buffon (1707–88), must have been comfortably warm before the earth cooled to its present state. Bailly disputed this matter with Voltaire in a long correspondence.

37. Although this brief digression is somewhat tongue in cheek, Flammarion is using the fancy of inverted time rather cleverly to address a controversial issue from a new perspective with the seriousness of a satirist.

38. Gebhard von Blücher (1742–1819) was the Prussian commander whose late arrival at Waterloo turned the battle decisively against Napoleon's forces.

39. Denis Raffet (1804–60) was famed for his lithographs depicting the conflicts of the period. I have been unable find any trace of a German poet called Sedlitz (or one active in the appropriate period with the far more likely surname of Seidlitz).

40. These two verses are left in French in the 1897 edition. That would be unreasonable if the lines really were a translation from the German, but not if they had actually been written in French. In the absence of any firm indication either way I have decided to translate them into English.

41. Eighteen Brumaire in the Revolutionary calendar (9 November 1799) was the day when Napoleon, having returned from Egypt in triumph, carried through his coup against the Directory.

42. It was a thought-experiment of exactly this type that persuaded Albert Einstein—who must have felt intuitively that the conclusion reached by Lumen, however safe it might seem to Flammarion, was wrong—to develop a theory of relativity that would allow the universe always to seem the same no matter how rapidly an observer was traveling relative to his point of origin.

43. Flammarion gives two figures here, both of which are miscalculated: 2,428,272,000,000 for the 365-day year, amended to 2,429,935,200,000 to take account of the divergence between the calendar year and the actual time taken by the earth to complete an orbit. I have followed the 1897 translation in giving only one figure—2,366,820,000,000—which seems very nearly correct to me.

44. Not having the modern notion of a galaxy available to him, Flammarion finds it convenient—if slightly paradoxical—to think of "other Milky Ways" as a series of "universes" contained within infinity; other astronomers preferred to refer to "sidereal systems."

45. Flammarion offers the figure of "less than five million years" as a (wildly inaccurate) result of this calculation; this time, for some unknown reason, the 1897 translation decides to follow his example, but I have substituted the correct answer. I have also amended the next paragraph but have been content to substitute "millions" for Flammarion's "five million."

46. Flammarion's "attraction" here refers to gravity rather than magnetism. The Einsteinian notion of gravity as a kind of curvature in space implies that a gravitational "field" does not need to be "transmitted" at all, although subatomic physicists continue to speak of "gravitons" by analogy with photons, retaining vestiges of the confusion that Lumen attempts to address in the remainder of this paragraph.

47. If this seems to make no sense it is because there is considerable confusion in Lumen's continual assertions that time does not exist outside the earth. His descriptions of historical events that he retraced are couched in durational terms and explained by reference to velocities measured in kilometers per second. If it make sense to speak of souls traveling at such velocities, how can duration be meaningless? His assertion that time and space are merely relative is a much better way of approaching this issue.

48. An alexandrine is a verse of twelve syllables, consisting of six iambic feet with the break after the third. It was the standard meter of French classical tragedy.

THE THIRD CONVERSATION

1. Flammarion is writing long before the discovery of X-rays by Wilhelm Röntgen (1845–1923) and the invention of wireless telegraphy by Guglielmo Marconi (1874–1937), both of which occurred in 1895. It is, therefore, not obvious that Lumen has good empirical grounds for the assertion that any electromagnetic waves can penetrate matter, even though it turned out to be true of some. The notion that light's wavelike properties necessitated the hypothesis of a "luminous ether" to serve as a medium for the propagation of light waves was virtually universal throughout the time when Flammarion produced the various editions of *Lumen*, but the theory involved no necessary assumption that "undulations in the ether" could not be blocked or stifled by material obstacles.

2. William Herschel (1738–1822) had begun studying the spectrum of light generated by the sun in 1800. In 1814 Joseph von Fraunhofer

(1787–1826) began passing sunlight through a narrow slit before dispersing its spectrum through a prism, thus producing the array of "Fraunhofer lines" that formed the basis of spectroscopic astronomy. More sophisticated equipment enabled the science of spectral analysis to make rapid progress after 1859, most notably in the work of Robert Bunsen (1811–89) and Gustav Kirchhoff (1824–87). In 1861 Bunsen began to identify new elements (caesium and rubidium) by means of spectral analysis.

The original version of *Lumen* was written before the first cosmic Doppler shift—Christian Doppler (1803–53) having proposed the effect in 1842—was detected by the British astronomer William Huggins (1824–1910) in 1868. Huggins showed that the star Sirius was moving away from our solar system at a speed of fifty kilometers a second, but Flammarion evidently did not think it worth incorporating that observation into later editions of the book. It is interesting to wonder what flights of fancy he might have built upon it had he realized its significance, but he could not have extrapolated therefrom to the idea of an expanding universe. Attempts to measure the Doppler shifts of nebulas had to wait until the development of dry photographic plates and the longer exposure times they permitted made the techniques of measurement far more exact.

3. This kind of rhetoric has come increasingly to the fore as the progress of science has rendered its discoveries more esoteric. What the argument amounts to, in sum, is that the fulfillment of one improbability licenses faith in the fulfillment of others quite unrelated to it, and that anyone who lacks understanding of the theory underlying one fact has no right to challenge the assertion of another, however unlikely or unsupported by evidence it may be. It is a horribly bad argument, utterly unworthy of Flammarion or his spokesperson, and quite unnecessary to support the case that Lumen goes on to make regarding the incompleteness of sensory information. This is, however, the second time that Flammarion has begun a supplementary dialogue in a very defensive mood, and one is bound to suspect that he is reacting with a measure of desperation to criticism of his earlier endeavors.

4. The 1897 translation substitutes "billions" for Flammarion's "trillions" here (but not, oddly enough, in the paragraph above); this might be reckoned correct, in that the two terms are ambiguous, but it seems more sensible to retain the current American usage in this translation; Flammarion's subsequent expansion of the first figure makes it clear that he is speaking of millions of millions.

5. This conflation of the frequencies of light and sound into a single scale is slightly peculiar; it forms the basis of an odd French science fiction novel, *L'Homme, cette maladie* (1954; translated into English in 1956 as *The Trembling Tower*) by Claude Yelnick, although the idea may not have been taken directly from Flammarion.

6. Nowadays called infrared radiation; Flammarion calls the rays "caloric" because of their association with radiant heat.

7. Nowadays called ultraviolet radiation; Flammarion calls the rays "chemical" because their properties were studied by pioneers of photography exploring the range of the chemical effects of light.

8. This kind of statement is difficult to justify, although modern physicists have made considerable strides in devising instrumentation to detect, measure, and analyze "vibrations" (i.e., waves) or "movements" (i.e., particles) that make no impact on our own sensory apparatus. Pseudoscientific occultists have always been excessively fond of deploying the argument that the world is full of "vibrations" inaccessible to our ordinary senses — though not, perhaps, to an extraordinary "sixth sense" possessed by a favored few — but few of them have been able to keep up with developments in physics well enough to modernize their jargon.

9. This is a key element in the attempt to understand the notion of alien existence; subsequent developments in physics permitted Flammarion's idea to be explored very cleverly by such hard science fiction writers as Hal Clement, whose story "Proof" (1942) is one of the finest examples of this kind of hypothetical extrapolation.

10. Although the use of the word "forms" is suggestive of Platonic idealism, this argument is better regarded as a version of the crucial distinction made by Immanuel Kant between "things in themselves" (noumena) and "things as they appear to the senses" (phenomena).

11. This comment warrants special attention because Flammarion modified it to form the title of this section (which I have left in Latin because it is difficult to find an English equivalent that creates the right impression). "Homunculus" means "little man," so the implication might conceivably be akin to stating that a human being is a mere pygmy among hypothetical giants, but in the days when embryology was not well understood, the supposed seed from which a new human being was generated was also referred to as a "homunculus," so Flammarion probably means to imply that the human race has much development yet ahead of it, in an evolutionary

sense. The latter notion has been deployed to some symbolic effect by Arthur C. Clarke, particularly in the final scene of the movie *2001: A Space Odyssey* (1968).

12. The notion of a dark star covered in natural photographic pigments accumulating images of earthly events as it turns is bound to seem utterly bizarre to modern readers, but it is worth noting that it was written long before the invention of the cinematographic technique of accumulating a series of images on a roll of film.

13. This cylindrical object is even more difficult to credit than the photographically sensitive sphere, but it is worth observing its anticipation of the method by which information was aggregated on Thomas Edison's early phonograph cylinders.

14. As a citizen of a Catholic country, Flammarion would have grown up with the idea of purgatory, so this particular embellishment of his scheme of spiritual evolution is perhaps only natural. Flammarion was by no means the last writer to bring the speculative ingenuity of a mathematician and natural scientist to the design of a hypothetical scheme of divine judgment. The English mathematician Charles Howard Hinton (1853–1907) was similarly fond of employing ingenious geometrical arguments to facilitate the permanent exposure of all vices and virtue to judgmental examination and recompense; his two series of *Scientific Romances* (1884–85; 1902) mingle essays and *contes philosphiques* in a distinctly Flammarionesque manner. The essays on the fourth dimension collected in the first series almost certainly inspired the introductory discourse by which H. G. Wells sought to increase the plausibility of *The Time Machine*.

15. Or, in modern parlance, "let's not go there." It is easy enough to understand why Flammarion felt it diplomatic to drawn a veil across this line of speculation, but just as easy to understand why more recent science fiction writers, like Gardner Hunting in *The Vicarion* (1926), T. L. Sherred in "E for Effort" (1947), Bob Shaw in *Other Days, Other Eyes* (1972) and Stephen Baxter and Arthur C. Clarke in *Light of Other Days* (2000) have been progressively more fascinated with the idea of an eventual annihilation of privacy and deception. It is difficult to imagine that any marriage or larger-scale political entity could survive the kind of interrogation of honesty that Lumen's questioner proposes—in which case, Napoleon's clinically calculated and straightforwardly instituted purgatory might be one of the simpler varieties to be found within this scheme.

On the other hand, Lumen's insistence on the imperishability of light-transmitted evidence does leave some important questions unasked and unanswered. Are actions taking place at night as easily visible to the soul's sight as those carried out in daylight? Are those carried out at noon, when rays of light traveling directly upward would fly straight into the sun, as easily visible as those taking place at four o'clock? It is, of course, necessary for Flammarion to ignore the effect of the atmosphere in scattering the rays of light reflected from the earth's surface, and he never quite makes up his mind how to deal with the obscuring effect of clouds, but modern readers may think it odd that neither he nor his interrogator raises the question of whether night is an adequate cloak for secret activities.

16. At the time when *Lumen* was written there was no worldwide system of time zones, and individual towns were free to make their own estimates of local time, relative to the sun's zenith. Paris and Brest (on the coast of Brittany) are nowadays in the same time zone despite the difference in their longitudes, but we are all familiar with the distortions of time that occur when we take long-distance flights.

17. Georges Cuvier (1769–1832) was the founder of the sciences of paleontology and comparative anatomy. His establishment of the homologous nature of the relationship between skeletal structures modified to perform different functions (as, for instance, between wings adapted for flying, legs for walking, and flippers for swimming) was a key element in the idea of a unified nature that was central to the evolutionary theories of Lamarck and Darwin.

THE FOURTH CONVERSATION

1. At this point Flammarion's text and the 1897 translation launch into a long recap intended to refresh the memories of readers following the series of conversations in its serial version. I have let briefer recapping passages stand, on the assumption that they might be helpful to the reader, but this one—although it must have been necessary when the serial version resumed after a two-year suspension—seems quite redundant in the context of the collection, so I have taken the liberty of displacing it from the text to these notes. It runs as follows:

I know that light, whatever it may be, is the agent by which objects are rendered visible to our eyes, that it is not transmitted instantaneously from one point to another, but gradually, like all motion. I know that it flies at the rate of 75,000 leagues a second, that it runs 750,000 leagues in ten seconds and 4,500,000 every minute. I know that it takes more than eight minutes to cross the distance of 37,000,000 leagues that separates us from the sun. Modern astronomy has made these facts familiar.

Do you fully realize the implications of its undulatory movement?

I think so. I compare it to that of sound, although it is accomplished on a much vaster scale. By undulation following undulation, sound is diffused in the air; when the bells peal forth, their sonorous voice is heard by those living around the church at the moment when the clapper strikes the bell, but is not heard until a second later by those living at a distance of three and a half hectometers, two seconds later by those about seven hectometers away, and three seconds later by those about a kilometer distant from the church. Thus sound reaches one village after another by degrees, as far as it can go. [The 1897 text gives the three figures as "492 yards, 765 yards, and 1,093 yards," demonstrating a remarkable lack of arithmetical acumen.]

In the same way, light passes successively from one region in space to another at a greater distance, and travels without being extinguished into the farthest realms of Infinity. If we could see from the earth an event that is taking place on the moon—for instance, if we had telescopes powerful enough to perceive a fruit falling from a tree on the moon's surface—we would not see the fall at the moment of its occurrence but about one and a quarter seconds afterward, because light requires that time to travel from the moon to the earth. Similarly, if we could see an event taking place upon a world at a distance ten times greater than the moon's, we would not witness it until thirteen seconds after it had actually happened. If that world were a hundred times further off than the moon, we could not see an event until 130 seconds had elapsed, if a thousand times, after 1,300 seconds, or 21 minutes 40 seconds—and so on, according to the distance.

Exactly; and you are aware that the luminous ray sent to the earth by the star Capella takes seventy-two years in reaching it. It follows, therefore, that if we only receive the luminous ray today, which left its surface seventy-two years ago, the denizens of Capella see only that which happened on the earth seventy-two years ago. The earth reflects into space the light that it gets from the sun, and from a distance it appears as brilliant as Venus, Jupiter, and the other planets lit by the same sun appear to you. The luminous aspect of the earth, its photograph, travels through space at the rate of 75,000 leagues per second and reaches Capella only after seventy-two years of incessant travel. I recall these elementary principles in order that you may have them thoroughly fixed in your memory; you will then be able to comprehend without difficulty the discoveries I have made in the course of my ultraterrestrial life since our last conversation.

These principles of optics are, to my mind, clearly established. The day after your death in October 1864—when, as you have confided to me, you found yourself rapidly transported to Capella, you were astonished to arrive there at the moment when the philosophical astronomers of the region were observing the earth in the year 1793 and witnessing one of the most significant incidents of the French Revolution. You were not less surprised to see yourself again as a child, running about in the streets of Paris. Then, leaving Capella and coming nearer to the earth, you arrived at the zone where that part of the terrestrial photography passed before your eyes that showed you your infancy, and you saw yourself at six years of age—not in memory, but in reality. Out of all your previous revelations, this is the one I had the most difficulty believing—that is, in grasping its meaning.

That which I now wish to make you understand is stranger still. But it was necessary for you to admit the first point in order to understand this one. On leaving Capella and approaching the earth, I saw again my seventy-two years of earthly existence; my entire life, such as it had been, passed before me, for in approaching the earth I passed through successive zones of earthly scenes, where I saw, spread out as if on a scroll, the visible history of our planet. This was because, in going back toward the earth, I was continually meeting the various zones that carried the visible history of our planet—that of Paris as well as my own—through space. Having thus taken, in one day, a retrospective survey of the road that it had taken light seventy-two years to traverse, I had reviewed my whole life in that one day, even perceiving my own interment.

It is as if, on returning from Capella to the earth, you had seen in a mirror the seventy-two years of your life, photographed year by year. The one the furthest from the earth, which had started first and was the oldest, showed events as they were in 1793; the second, which left the earth a year later and had not yet reached Capella, contained those of 1794; the tenth, those of 1893; the thirty-sixth, having reached the midway point, gave those of 1829; the seventy-first, those of 1864.

It is impossible to have a firmer grasp of these facts, which seem so mysterious and incomprehensible at first sight. Now I can recount to you that which happened to me on Capella, after having thus witnessed again my existence on the earth.

2. Lest anyone should be in doubt, Flammarion is being sarcastic. He is mocking the racial theorists of his day, who disputed in deadly earnest as to where the earthly "races" ought to be placed on a scale of moral and intellectual advancement, usually reaching the conclusion that the most advanced race was the theorist's own and the most primitive the one which—for whatever whimsical reason—he most disliked.

3. "Protozoic era" was a now-obsolete term used in the nineteenth century to refer to the earliest evolutionary phase of earthly life. The notion of a society in which no sexual differentiation exists between human beings was not original to Flammarion; Gabriel de Foigny's *La Terre australe connu: c'est à dire, la description de ce pays inconnu jusqu'ici* (1676; trans. as *A New Discovery of Terra Incognita Australis, or the Southern World, by James Sadeur, a Frenchman*, 1693) had already suggested that androgyny might be a necessary condition of true social equality.

4. The Christian saint Francis of Assisi (1182–1226) and the Pythagorean philosopher and reputed miracleworker Apollonius of Tyana (c. 4 B.C.E.–c. 97 C.E.) were both credited by legend with this improbable ability.

5. The Brocken is the highest peak in the Hartz Mountains in Germany. Its summit is sometimes enveloped in a thick mist, which can serve as a magnifying lens at sunset, the resultant refracted image being a vague but potentially terrifying "specter." The other two peaks cited are in Switzerland.

6. Most modern speculators would, of course, derive a diametrically opposite result from this thought-experiment—a result that doubtless seems as obvious and unchallengeable to them as Flammarion's does to him.

7. The first edition has "Plusieurs Pères de l'Église" (Many Church Fathers) instead of "Les anciens" and "D'autres" (Others) instead of "Les modernes."

8. This paragraph and the preceding interjection are absent from the first edition.

9. Palingenesis, in this context, is the doctrine of continual rebirth, also known as metempsychosis.

10. "Carbolic acid gas" refers to phenol, easily obtainable in vaporous form by the distilling of wood or coal.

11. The term "infusoria" is nowadays applied to a group of ciliate pro-

tozoans, but microscopic images were still plagued by chromatic aberration in Flammarion's day, and the word was then used to refer to a heterogeneous set of organisms found in decaying tissue.

12. When *Lumen* was written, organic chemistry was in its infancy. Chemical stains were not yet used to render tissues and their component cells more easily visible under the microscope, so Flammarion's notion of the metabolic processes by which the body's cells were made and renewed is understandably primitive. His contention that there might be alien ecologies in which all the nutritional requirements of complex organisms could be supplied by a process combining respiration and alimentation retains a certain plausibility nevertheless; some sea creatures that obtain both oxygen and foodstuffs from the water that surrounds them employ a common "pumping system" to supply their gills and digestive systems.

13. In the first edition all but the first and last sentences of this passage are credited to Lumen, and there is an additional (but entirely superfluous) passage in the first part of Lumen's next speech.

14. Basileus, or Basile, is a character in *The Barber of Seville* and *The Marriage of Figaro* by the playwright Pierre Beaumarchais (1732–99); his name became synonymous with "slanderer" in French parlance. The scathing satire of this passage is atypical of Flammarion's method, but there is no doubting the depth of his feeling.

15. The primitive state of microscopy in the mid-nineteenth century meant that Flammarion had no inkling of the richness of those life-forms that are invisible to the naked eye. The crucial distinction made between plants and animals nowadays relates to photosynthesis, but that process had yet to be analyzed and defined, so Flammarion inevitably thinks of the key difference as locomotion.

16. Lumen is here equating "soul" (*âme*) with what he defined in an earlier conversation as "vital energy." This is confusing, because the earlier passage was careful to draw a distinction between the vital energy orchestrating a living system and the intelligence capable of survival after death.

17. The term "monad" (*monade*) is used here to embrace both simple inorganic molecules and what we would nowadays call cells. Because of the primitive nature of mid-nineteenth-century microscopes, the fine structure of organic matter and the origins of embryos were still mysterious, so Flammarion is limited in the imaginative resources he can bring to bear on the question of how organic individuality is determined. The thesis he goes on to develop is that the basic constituents of living tissue are complex mole-

cules—as, indeed, they are—but he has not the means to make a category distinction between molecules and cells.

18. The French translation of the *Arabian Nights* made by Antoine Galland (1646–1715) left a deep and enduring impression on French culture, but the questioner's reference to it at this point seems a trifle odd.

THE FIFTH CONVERSATION

1. What was originally Part IV of the fourth dialogue is separated out in the revised text as a fifth conversation. The opening paragraph is abbreviated somewhat, but the text then proceeds much as it had in the first edition, except that the first few references to Lumen's memory of having actually been the alien entity he observes, 2,400 years before, are removed.

2. *Cereus giganteus* is the Saguaro, an arborescent cactus that grows in the deserts of Mexico and the southwestern United States.

3. The "ampullae" (*ampoules*) to which Flammarion is referring are those used for attachment by echinoderms such as starfishes, not "certain plants" (*certaines plantes*).

4. Jean-Baptiste Molière (1622–73) and Rabelais are cited here as exemplary farceurs.

5. *Lumbricus* (which the 1897 translation renders, nonsensically, as "lombric") is a genus of earthworms. The example is not a good one; although the body of an earthworm is segmentally organized, the capability of each segment to live independently, if severed from the whole, is very limited. The example that follows it, of the tapeworm, is far better; although the embedded head generates the other segments in the manner observed by Flammarion, each segment is, in effect, a complete individual. Leeches, on the other hand, are not segmentally organized at all, although their powers of regeneration—like those of other flatworms, especially planarians—are nevertheless considerable.

6. The modern equivalent of this quaintly formulated notion is the distinction drawn between the central and autonomic nervous systems.

7. Hippolyte Rivail (1804–69), alias Allan Kardec, was the leading advocate of spiritualism in France; he published *Le Livre des esprits* [The Book of Spirits] in 1856 and *Le Livre des mediums* [The Book of Mediums] in 1864. Flammarion, who joined Kardec's psychical research society in the early

1860s, delivered a eulogy at his funeral in March 1869; this passage must have been written soon afterward.

8. This contradicts an earlier passage, which asserted that clouds could not obscure spiritual sight—and that even solid matter might, in principle, be no barrier to it. The means by which the spiritual eye defies the principle of perspective remains, in any case, stubbornly unclear.

9. The text following this text break is considerably rearranged in the revised version, partly because the first edition introduces a reference to the impending dawn long before the conversation actually concludes. It makes good editorial sense to move that passage closer to the end, although the introduction of several text breaks in rapid succession (all of which are ignored in the 1897 translation, although I have kept them) may seem a trifle eccentric to some readers.

10. The 1897 translation offers the obviously incorrect "loadstone" rather than "asbestos" as a translation of "l'amiante," apparently having confused the word with "aimant" several paragraphs earlier—which the 1897 translation also gives as "loadstone" although I have preferred "magnet."

11. The following two paragraphs were added to the 1897 edition for the first time; it is interesting to observe that Flammarion neglects the simplest means of producing perpetual daylight, making no reference to a hypothetical planet that presents the same face perpetually to its primary, as the moon does to the earth.

12. "Barytes" here refers to salts of barium.

13. The paragraphs between this point and the next text break are slightly rearranged and considerably augmented in the 1897 translation, presumably according to Flammarion's instruction.

14. The next three paragraphs are original to the 1897 translation.

15. The 1897 translation has "tenths," which is nonsensical, although it is an accurate translation of Flammarion's "dixièmes"—which occurs in both the first and revised editions, although the situation of this block of text is different.

16. This notion was by no means original to Swedenborg, having previously been part of various mystical cosmologies. Echoes of it can be traced back to a number of creation myths, including the Norse myth in which the earth and heavens are formed from various parts of the body of Ymir, progenitor of the frost giants, and a Hindu myth contained in the *Rg Veda* in which creation consists of the dismemberment of Purusa, the primeval man.

17. This paragraph is original to the 1897 translation; even so, Flammarion was writing at the very infancy of slow-motion and time-lapse cinematography.

18. Urania, the muse of astronomy (*Uranie* in French) was to play Lumen's role in Flammarion's next popularization of these same ideas, *Uranie* (1889).

19. The reference is to the famous allegory of the cave in the *Republic*.

20. The 1897 translation renders "l'immensité," incorrectly, as "speed."

BIBLIOGRAPHY

WORKS BY CAMILLE FLAMMARION

L'Astronomie et ses fondateurs: Copernic et la découverte du système du monde. Paris: Marpon et Flammarion, 1891.

Astronomie populaire: description générale de ciel. Paris: Marpon et Flammarion, 1880. (Trans. by J. Ellard Gore as *Popular Astronomy: A General Description of the Heavens*. New York: Appleton, n.d.; London: Chatto & Windus, 1894.)

L'Atmosphère: description des grands phénomènes de la nature. Paris: Hachette, 1871. (Trans. by C. B. Pitman [ed. by James Glaisher] as *The Atmosphere*. London: Sampson Low, Marston, Low & Searle, 1873.)

Clairs de lune. Paris: Flammarion, 1894.

Contemplations scientifiques. Paris: Hachette, first series, 1869; second series, 1887.

Contes philosophiques. Paris: La Revue, 1911.

Dans le ciel et sur la terre: tableaux et harmonies. Paris: Marpon et Flammarion, 1886.

[Translator] *Les Derniers jours d'un Philosophe; Entretiens sur la Nature et sur les Sciences, de sir Humphry Davy*. Paris, Didier et cie, 1869.

Dieu dans la nature; ou le Spiritualisme et le Matérialisme devant la science moderne. Paris: Didier et cie, 1867.

L'Éruptions volcanique et et les tremblements de terre: Krakatoa — La Martinque — Espagne et Italie. Paris: Flamarion, 1902.

Les Étoiles et les curiosités du ciel: description complète du ciel visible à l'oeil nu et de tous les objets célestes faciles à observer; supplement de l'astronomie populaire. Paris: Marpon et Flammarion, 1882.

La Fin du monde. Paris: Flammarion, 1894. (Trans. by J. B. Walker as *Omega: The Last Days of the World*, New York: Cosmopolitan, 1894.)

Des Forces naturelles inconnues à propos des phénomènes produits par les frères Davenport et les mediums en générale: étude critique. Author given as Hermès. Paris: Didier et cie, 1865. (Reprint. Author given as Camille Flamarion. Paris: Flammarion, 1907. Trans. as *Mysterious Psychic Forces:*

An Account of the Author's Investigations in Psychical Research, together with those of other European savants. Boston: Small & Maynard, 1907.)

Les Habitantes de l'autre monde; révélations d'outre-tombe. 2 vols. Paris: Ledoyen, 1862–63.

Histoire du ciel et des différents systèmes imaginés sur l'univers. Paris: Bibliothèque d'éducation et récréation, 1872. (Trans. [edited by J. F. Blake] as *Astronomical Myths, Based on Flammarion's "History of the Heavens."* London: Macmillan, 1877.)

L'Inconnu et les problèmes psychiques. Paris: Flammarion, 1900. (Trans. as *L'Inconnu, the Unknown*. London and New York: Harper, 1900.)

Lumen. Paris: Marpon et Flammarion, 1887; expanded edition, 1906.

Les maisons hantées, en marge de la mort et son mystère. Paris: Flammarion, 1923. (Trans. as *Haunted Houses*. London: Unwin, 1924; New York: Appleton, 1924.)

Memoires biographiques et philosophiques d'un astronome. Paris: Flammarion, 1912.

Les Merveilles célestes; lectures du soir. Paris: Hachette, 1865. (Trans. by Mrs. Norman Lockyer as *The Wonders of the Heavens*. New York: Scribners, 1871, and as *The Marvels of the Heavens*. London: Bentley, 1872.)

Le Monde avant le création de l'homme; origines de la terre, origines de la vie, origines de l'humanité. Paris: Marpon et Flammarion, 1885.

Les Mondes imaginaires et les mondes réels: voyage pittoresque dans le ciel et revue critique des théories humaines, scientifiques et romanesques, anciennes et modernes sur les habitants des astres. Paris: Didier et cie, 1864; expanded edition, Paris: Marpon et Flammarion, 1892.

La mort et son mystère. 2 vols. Paris: Flammarion, 1920–22. (Trans. by Latrobe Carroll and E. S. Brooks as *Death and Its Mystery*. 3 vols. New York: Century, 1921–23.

La Planète Mars et ses conditions d'habitabilité. Paris: Gauthier-Villars, 1892; expanded edition 1909.

La Planète Venus, discussion générale des observations. Paris: Gauthier-Villars, 1897.

La Pluralité des mondes habitées: étude où l'on expose les conditions d'habitabilité des terres célestes, discutées au point de vue de l'astronomie, de la physiologie et de la philosophie naturelle. Paris: Didier, 1862.

Récits de l'infini: Lumen; Histoire d'une comète; Dans l'infini. Paris: Didier et cie, 1872. (Trans. by S. R. Crocker as *Stories of Infinity: Lumen; The History of a Comet; In Infinity*. Boston: Roberts Bros., 1873. Expanded edition as

Récits de l'infini: Lumen, histoire d'une âme; Histoire d'une comète; La Vie universelle et eternelle. Paris: Marpon et Flammarion, 1892.)

Rêves étoilés. Paris: Flammarion, 1914. (Trans. by E. E. Fournier d'Albe as *Dreams of an Astronomer*. London: T. Fisher Unwin, 1923.)

Stella. Paris: Flammarion, 1897.

Les Terres du ciel: description astronomique, physique, climatologique, géographique des planètes qui gravitent avec la terre autour du soleil et l'état probable de la vie à leur surface. Paris: Didier, 1877.

Uranie. Paris: Marpon et Flammarion, 1889. (Trans. by Mary J. Serrano as *Uranie*. New York: Cassell, 1890 Trans. by Augusta Rice Stetson as *Urania*. Boston: Estes & Laurist, 1890; London: Chatto & Windus, 1891. Trans. by E. P. Robins as *Urania*. Chicago: Donohue, Henneberry & Co., 1892.)

Voyages aériens: impressions et études. Paris: Marpon et Flammarion, 1881.

SECONDARY SOURCES RELATING TO CAMILLE FLAMMARION AND *LUMEN*

Bleiler, Everett F. *Science Fiction: The Early Years*. Kent, Ohio: Kent State University Press, 1990, pp. 248–50.

Fodor, Nandor. *Encyclopaedia of Psychic Science*. N.p.: University Books, 1966, pp. 140–41.

Gillispie, Charles Coulston, ed. *Dictionary of Scientific Biography*. New York: Scribner's, 1972, vol. 5, pp. 21–22.

Lofficier, Jean-Marc, and Randy Lofficier. *French Science Fiction, Fantasy, Horror and Pulp Fiction*. Jefferson, N.C.: McFarland, 2000, p. 565.

Stableford, Brian. "Comic Perspectives in 19th Century Literature." *Métaphores* 15/16 (1988): 51–60.

———. "Lumen." In *Survey of Science Fiction Literature*, ed. F. Magill. Englewood Cliffs, N.J.: Salem Press, 1979, pp. 1294–98; abridged in the same publisher's *Magill's Guide to Science Fiction and Fantasy Literature*, 1996, pp. 572–73.

———. "Far Futures." In *Earth Is but a Star: Excursions through Science Fiction to the Far Future*, ed. Damien Broderick, Crawley, W.A.: University of Western Australia Press, 2001, pp. 47–76.

Versins, Pierre. *Encyclopédie de l'Utopie, des voyages extraordinaires et de la science fiction*. Lausanne: L'Age d'Homme, 1972, pp. 336–38.

www.culture.fr / culture / flammarion /
www.iap.fr / saf / flammarion.htm

OTHER WORKS

Amis, Martin. *Time's Arrow*. London: Jonathan Cape, 1991.

[Béthune, Chevalier de]. *Relation du monde de Mercure*. 2 vols., Geneva: Barillot, 1750.

Baxter, Stephen, and Arthur C. Clarke. *Light of Other Days*. New York: Tor, 2000.

Borel, Pierre. *Discours nouveau prouvant la pluralité des mondes; que les astres sont des terres habités, et la terre un estoile, etc*. Geneva, 1657.

[Clarke, Arthur C., screenwriter]. *2001: A Space Odyssey*. Film directed by Stanley Kubrick, 1968.

Clement, Hal. "Proof." In *Astounding Science Fiction*, June 1942, pp. 101–9.

Cyrano de Bergerac, Savinien. *Fragment d'histoire comique contenant les états et empires du soleil*. Paris: Charles de Sercy, 1662 (Trans. as below).

———. *Histoire comique contenant les états et empires de la lune*. Paris: Charles de Sercy, 1657. (Trans. by Richard Aldington in *Voyages to the Moon and Sun*. London: Routledge, 1923; New York: Dutton, 1923. Trans. by Geoffrey Strachan in *Other Worlds: The Comic History of the States and Empires of the Moon and Sun*. London: Oxford University Press, 1963.)

Daniel, Gabriel, *Voyage du monde de Descartes*. Paris: S. Bernard, 1691. (Trans. as *A Voyage to the World of Cartesius*. London: T. Bennet, 1694.)

Davy, Humphry. *Consolations in Travel: The Last Days of a Philosopher*. London: John Murray, 1830. Reprint. London: Cassell [National Library series], 1889.

Dick, Philip K. *Counter-Clock World*. New York: Berkley, 1967.

Foigny, Gabriel de. *La Terre australe connu: c'est à dire, la description de ce pays inconnu jusqu'ici*. Geneva: 1676. (Trans. as *A New Discovery of Terra Incognita Australis, or the Southern World, by James Sadeur, a French-man*. London: J. Dunton, 1693.)

Fontenelle, Bernard le Bovier de. *Entretiens sur la pluralité des mondes*. Paris: C. Blageart, 1686. (Trans. by Sir W. D. Knight as *A Discourse of the Plurality of Worlds*. Dublin: William Norman, 1687. Trans. by Mrs. A[phra] Behn as *A Discovery of New Worlds*. London: William Ganning, 1688. Trans. by Mr. Glanvill as *A Plurality of Worlds*. London: Bentley &

Magnes, 1688. Trans. by H. A. Hargreaves as *Conversations on the Plurality of Worlds*. Berkley and Los Angeles: University of California Press, 1990.)

Gautier, Théophile. "Le roi Candaule" (1844). In *Nouvelles*. Paris: Charpentier, 1845.

[Godwin, Francis]. *The Man in the Moone or a Discourse of a Voyage Thither* by Domingo Gonsales, the Speedy Messenger. London: Kirton & Warre, 1638.

Haldane, J. B. S. *The Inequality of Man and Other Essays*. London: Chatto & Windus, 1932.

Hilliard, A. Rowley. "Death from the Stars." In *Wonder Stories*, October 1931, pp. 612–23.

Hinton, C. H. *Scientific Romances*. 2 vols. London: Swan Sonnenschein, 1884–85.

——. *Scientific Romances. Second Series*. London: Swan Sonnenschein, 1902.

Hodgson, William Hope. *The House on the Borderland*. London: Chapman & Hall, 1908.

[Holberg, Ludvig]. *Nicolai Klimii iter subterraneum*. Leipzig: J. Preussii, 1741. (Trans. as *A Journey to the World Under-Ground by Nicholas Klimius*. London: Astley & Collins, 1742.)

Hunting, Gardner. *The Vicarion*. Kansas City, Mo.: Unity School of Christianity, 1926.

Huygens, Christian. *Cosmotheoros, sive de Terris coelestibus earumque ornatu conjecturae*. Hagae-Comitum: A. Moetjens, 1698. (Trans. as *The Celestial World discover'd, or Conjectures concerning the inhabitants, plants and products of the worlds in the planets*. London: T. Childe, 1698.)

Joncquel, Octave, and Théo Varlet. *L'Agonie de la terre*. Amiens: E. Malfère, 1922.

——. *Les Titans du ciel*. Amiens: E. Malfère, 1921.

Kant, Immanuel. *Allgemeine Naturgeschichte und Theorie des Himmels*. Königsberg and Leipzig: J. F. Petersen, 1755.

Kepler, Johannes. *Joh. Keppler Mathematici Olim Imperatorii. Somnium se opus posthumus de astronomia lunare*. Frankfurt, 1634. (Trans. by Everett F. Bleiler as "Somnium: or the Astronomy of the Moon, An Allegory of Science by Johannes Kepler." In *Beyond Time and Space*, ed. August Derleth. New York: Pelegri & Cudahy, 1950. Trans. and annotated by Edward Rosen as *Kepler's Somnium. The Dream, or*

Posthumous Work on Lunar Astronomy. Madison, Wisc.: University of Wisconsin Press, 1967.)

Kircher, Athanasius. *Itinerarium Exstaticum quo mundi opificium, etc*. Rome: V. Mascardi, 1656.

Lake, David. *The Right Hand of Dextra*. New York: DAW, 1977.

Lamarck, Jean-Baptiste, Chevalier de. *Philosophie Zoologique, ou Exposition des considérations relatives à l'histoire naturelle des animaux*. 2 vols. Paris: Dentu, 1809.

[Macpherson, James]. *Fingal, an ancient epic poem in six books*. London: T. Becket & P. A. de Hondt, 1762.

———. *Temora, an ancient epic poem in eight books*. London: T. Becket & P. A. de Hondt, 1763.

Nau, John-Antoine. *Force ennemie*. Paris: Éditions de la Plume, 1903.

Poe, Edgar Allan. "The Conversation of Eiros and Charmion." *Burton's Gentleman's Magazine*, December 1839. Reprinted in *Tales of the Grotesque and Arabesque*. 2 vols. Philadelphia: Lea & Blanchard, 1840.

———. *Eureka, a prose poem*. New York: G. P. Putnam, 1848. Reprinted as *Eureka—An Essay on the Material and Spiritual Universe*. In *Complete Works of Edgar Allan Poe in 10 Volumes*, vol. 10. New York: Fred de Fau & Co., 1902. (French trans. by Charles Baudelaire as *Eureka*. Paris: Michel-Lévy frères, 1864.)

———. "'Hans Phaal." *Southern Literary Messenger*, June 1835. Reprinted in *Tales of the Grotesque and Arabesque*. 2 vols. Philadelphia: Lea & Blanchard, 1840. (Most reprints retitled "The Unparalleled Adventure of One Hans Pfaall.")

Restif de la Bretonne, Nicolas-Edme. *La Découverte Australe par un homme volant ou la Dédale français*. 4 vols. Paris: Veuve Duschensné, 1781.

———. *Les Posthumes, lettres réçues après la mort du mari par sa femme, qui le croit en Florence*. Paris: Duchêne, 1802

Robida, Albert. *L'Horloge des siècles*. Paris: F. Juven, 1902.

Rosny, J. H., aîné. *La Mort de la terre*. Paris: Plon, 1910.

———. *Les Navigateurs de l'infini*. Paris: Oeuvres Libres, 1925.

———. *Les Xipéhuz*. Paris: Savine, 1887. (Trans. [with *La Morte de la terre*] by George Edgar Slusser in *"The Xipéhuz" and "The Death of the Earth."* New York: Arno, 1978.)

Roumier, Marie-Anne de (Mme Robert). *Les Ondins, conte moral*. Paris: Delalain, 1768.

———. *Voyages de Mylord Céton dans les sept planètes, ou le nouveau mentor*. 5 vols. Paris: La Haye, 1765–66.

Shaw, Bob. *Other Days, Other Eyes*. London: Gollancz, 1972.

Sherred, T. L. "E for Effort." *Astounding Science Fiction*, May 1947, pp. 119–62.

Stapledon, Olaf. *Star Maker*. London: Methuen, 1937.

Swedenborg, Emanuel. *Arcana coelestia quae in Scriptura sacra seu verbo Domini sunt detecta, etc.* (Written 1749–56.) 13 vols. Tübingen, 1833–42.

Swift, Jonathan. *Travels into Several Remote Nations of the World in Four Parts by Lemuel Gulliver, first a Surgeon, and then a Captain of Several Ships*. 2 vols. London: Bejamin Motte, 1726. (Often reprinted as *Gulliver's Travels*.)

Varlet, Théo. *La Grande panne*. Paris: Portique, 1930.

Voltaire. *Le Micromégas de mr. de Voltaire*. London [so advertised, but probably Berlin], 1752. (Trans. as *Micromegas, A Comic Romance. Being a Severe Satire upon the Philosophy, Ignorance, and Self-Conceit of Mankind*. London: Wilson & Durham, 1753.)

Wells, H. G. *The Time Machine*. London: Heinemann, 1895.

———. *The War of the Worlds*. London: Heinemann, 1898.

[Wilkins, John]. *The Discovery of a World in the moone, or a discourse tending to prove that 'tis probable there may be another habitable world in that planet*. London: M. Sparks & E. Forrest, 1638; Book II published as *A Discourse Concerning a New World and Another Planet*. London: John Maynard, 1640.

Yelnick, Claude. *L'Homme, cette maladie*. Paris: Éditions Métal, 1954. (Trans. as *The Trembling Tower*. London: Museum Press, 1956.)

About the Author

Camille Flammarion (1842–1925) was a well-known French astronomer and writer and a highly successful popularizer of science during the late nineteenth century.

About the Translator

Brian Stableford is a Lecturer in Creative Writing at the School of Cultural Studies, King Alfred's College, Winchester. He is the author of more than eighty books (his pseudonyms include Brian Craig and Francis Amery), both fiction and nonfiction, including *The Empire of Fear* (1988), *Werewolves of London* (1990), *The Cassandra Complex* (2001), *Scientific Romance in Britain, 1890–1950* (1985), and *Glorious Perversity: The Decline and Fall of Literary Decadence* (1998). His translations from French include *The Angels of Perversity* by Remy de Gourmont (1992), *Vampire City* by Paul Féval (1999), and *Nightmares of an Ether-Drinker* by Jean Lorraine (forthcoming in 2002).

THE WESLEYAN
EARLY CLASSICS OF
SCIENCE FICTION
SERIES

GENERAL EDITOR,
ARTHUR B. EVANS

Invasion of the Sea *Jules Verne*

The Mysterious Island *Jules Verne*